Gabriel Hawke Novels

Murder of Ravens

Mouse Trail Ends

Rattlesnake Brother

Chattering Blue Jay

Fox Goes Hunting

Turkey's Fiery Demise

D1545795

Stolen Butterfly
A Gabriel Hawke Novel
Book 7

Paty Jager

Windtree Press
Hillsboro, OR

This is a work of fiction, Names, characters, places, and incidents either are the product of the author's imagination or are used fictitiously, and any resemblance to actual persons living or dead, business establishments, events, or locales, is entirely coincidental.

STOLEN BUTTERFLY

Contact Information: info@windtreepress.com

Windtree Press
Hillsboro, Oregon
http://windtreepress.com

Cover Art by Christina Keerins
CoveredbyCLKeerins

PUBLISHING HISTORY
Published in the United States of America

ISBN 978-1-952447-77-8

The proceeds from the sale of this book will go to the non-profit Enough Iz Enough. This is a community outreach organization that advocates for MMIW on the Confederated Tribes of the Umatilla Reservation.

I have **special thanks** to Kola Shippentower-Thompson, who gave me personal knowledge about losing family members and never having answers. And for her help in filling in the blanks I didn't know about the reservation and the casino business. Also, for this lovely review of the book:

The story was captivating, I couldn't put it down. So many memories were brought to surface, so many emotions, like this has been lived before, because it has, this is a glimpse into our reality in the Reservation. Thank you for seeing us & helping tell part of the story. Kola Shippentower-Thompson Enough Iz Enough, Co-Founder & Director

Other people I would like to thank for their knowledge and input on the book are:

Carmen Peone

Franklin Hunting

Louis Brewer

Patrick Williams

Chapter One

"Gabriel, you need to come to the rez. Sherry Dale is missing and no one will listen to me."

Hawke had answered the phone half asleep out of habit. But hearing his mom's worried voice brought him awake in a flash. Rubbing his face and peering at the red six and two zeroes on his clock, he groaned. He'd had a late night helping with an accident. He'd been the only Oregon State Trooper available to go out north. Everyone else on duty was either floating the Snake River to catch fishing infractions or along the Wallowa River. "Are you sure she's missing? If you called her and she didn't answer, she's probably still asleep."

"Gabriel, I didn't try to call her this morning. She never showed up last night after work to pick up Trey."

Now he sat up, swinging his legs over the edge of the bed. "Has she ever missed picking up her boy?"

"No. If she's running late, she always calls. But

that tribal said she was either partying or found a boyfriend when I called the tribal station last night about ten. She doesn't have a boyfriend and she doesn't party. She's a good girl."

"Did he tell you to wait seventy-two hours?"

"Yes. He said she'll get a hold of me in the morning and I'll see she was just having fun. When I tried to argue, he also said that if she was at work, then I should call the Pendleton police. I called them as soon as I hung up from the tribal. Pendleton said the same thing. Wait seventy-two hours. She could have had a car accident and be laying somewhere hurt."

"What about her family?" He remembered meeting the young woman a couple times when he'd visited his mom and the woman had come by to pick up her boy. She seemed like someone who wouldn't leave her son.

"She doesn't have anything but an old drunk uncle who wouldn't even know when he last saw her and the boy." She sighed. "I haven't slept all night worrying. Can you come over and look for her? I don't know who else to call."

"The good news, it's July. The weather is good. A bit hot, but good. If she's had an accident she won't freeze to death. I should be able to get some time off." He stood as Dog whined at the door of his one room apartment over the Trembley's indoor horse arena.

He opened the door and the animal bounded down the stairs. His horses and mule nickered and whinny-hawed. "I'll be there this morning. Today and tomorrow are my days off. I can look for two days and if I need more, I'll call Sergeant Spruel and see what I can do."

"Thank you, Gabriel. I don't know what to tell

Trey. He'll be staying with me until we can find Sherry."

"I'll see you in three hours." He ended the call, dressed, and hurried down to feed his animals and let Herb and Darlene, his landlords, know he and Dog would be gone for a couple or more days. The epidemic of Indigenous women, children, and even men, going missing or found murdered on and off reservations, needed to be addressed. He wanted to keep a positive outlook for his mom's sake, but there was no telling what could have happened to Sherry. The one thing he did know, both his mom and Trey deserved answers. Not the years many had of never knowing what happened to their loved ones.

After feeding, he walked to the back door of the Trembley house and knocked.

Darlene opened the door. The smell of coffee and something sweet wafted out the door. "Hawke, you're up early." She opened the door wide, inviting him in.

He stepped through, his stomach growling.

"Sit down. Darlene just pulled sweet rolls out of the oven," Herb said, sitting at the table, a piece of bacon in one hand and a coffee cup in the other.

"If you don't mind my eating and running." Hawke sat at the table next to Herb.

Darlene handed him a plate and fork. "Help yourself."

"You headed back to work so soon after coming in late last night?" Herb asked.

While his landlords were always helpful knowing the gossip and affairs of others in the county, which had helped him solve several murders, he didn't like that they had such an interest in his life.

"No. Mom called. A mother of one of the kids she watches never showed up last night. The tribal police are giving her the run-around. I have two days off. Told her I'd come see what I can find out."

Darlene shook her head. "I've read stories about how many Native American women go missing and their bodies are found months or even years later. Doesn't anyone care to look for them?"

"There's a lot of reasons. One being most law enforcement, on and off reservations, aren't tribal members. They tell the families the women went off with a boyfriend or were partying. With no one really looking, we don't know what happens to them. Those families never get any answers. I hope I can find her in a stalled car on a stretch of road where there's no cell service. That would be the ideal. We'll see." He ate a roll, some bacon, an egg, and drank coffee, before standing. "Thank you for this. It saved me grabbing something on the road. Could you keep an eye on my crew? I'll let you know how long Dog and I will be gone. Hopefully, just the two days, but if I can't find her by then, I'm going to take vacation days. Mom won't rest until she knows."

"Don't worry about your animals. We'll take care of them." Darlene slipped two of the rolls into a plastic bag. "For the road."

"Thanks!" He stepped out the back door and nearly tripped over Dog. "Hey, if you hadn't been chasing a cat, you could have come in."

He patted the dog on the head and strode across to the arena. He'd pack and hit the road. He'd call

Sergeant Spruel as he drove. Save time that way.

<>><<>><<>>

Rather than go to his mom's and backtrack, he went straight to Pendleton and drove Mission Road out to his mom's searching for any vehicles that looked in distress or abandoned. He didn't find any stranded vehicles. There were a couple of stretches of open space, but enough houses set along the road that someone would have noticed a car sitting on the side and investigated. Especially one that they would see every day as Sherry went to and from work.

He drove by Mission Market and on down to the group of older houses in the neighborhood where he'd grown up. He parked his pickup, remembering good times and bad.

Mom met him at the door. "I'm so glad you could come help." She hugged him tight before pulling him into the small three-bedroom house he'd lived in after his father dropped he and his mom off at her parent's, here, on the Umatilla Reservation. His father never contacted them after that. He'd liked the ladies. When Mom gave him an ultimatum of his family or his women friends, he'd chosen the women.

His father's love of multiple women was one of the reasons Hawke hated having his name linked to any woman romantically. He was a one-woman man and he didn't want the woman he was interested in, namely Dani Singer, to ever think he was fooling around with someone else. He'd remained loyal to his wife until she'd divorced him for arresting her brother on drug charges twenty years ago.

"I drove Mission Road to see if she might have

11

broken down on her way home. I didn't see any sign of her car."

"Where's momma?" Trey, the boy Hawke remembered, walked down the hall from a back bedroom. He was dressed, but his rumpled clothes and rubbing his eyes said he'd been sleeping.

"She was held up at work," Mom said, putting an arm around Trey and giving Hawke her mama bear glare.

"Hey Trey, why don't you tell me all the things you know about your momma. It will be a fun game to help you not miss her so much." Hawke led the boy into the kitchen. "Got any cookies and milk?" he asked his mom.

She quickly put a plate of cookies on the table and a tall and short glass of milk in front of them.

"Do you know the names of your momma's friends?" Hawke pulled out a notepad and pen.

"Why you writin' it down?" Trey asked, dipping a cookie in his glass of milk.

"Because I have a bad memory."

"You are kinda old. Not as old as Mimi, but old and she doesn't have to write things down to remember them."

Hawke picked up a cookie and dunked it in the milk like the boy. He might be fifty-three, but he still loved his cookies and milk.

"Hey!" Trey grinned. "You like to make your cookies soggy, too?"

"Yeah," Hawke smiled back at the boy. "Can you think of any of your momma's friends?" He persisted.

"Morning." The boy shoved the cookie in his

mouth.

"Yes, it's still morning." Hawke said. "What does that have to do with your mom's friends?" After having spent time with Kitree, a girl he saved and who later was adopted by friends, he knew kids could get off track easily when being asked questions.

The boy shook his head and swallowed the cookie. "Momma's friend name is Morning."

Hawke glanced at his mother.

She nodded. "Morning Farrow. She and Sherry went to school together. I'll give her a call."

"Ask her to come over." Hawke flicked his gaze toward the boy. "Maybe you and Trey can find something to do while she's here?"

His mom nodded and went over to the phone hanging on the kitchen wall.

Hawke dunked his cookie and asked Trey, "Does your mom have any men friends who come over?"

Trey shook his head. "She doesn't want me to learn bad habits. That's what she says."

"She's never had any man come to where you live?" Hawke persisted.

"Grandfather Thunder. Momma pays him to live behind his house."

Hawke glanced up at his mom as she hung up the phone. "They live at Silas Thunder's place?"

"Yes. The small trailer behind his. The one his son lived in before he died." His mother tipped her head back and whispered a prayer.

He wasn't sure if it was for Silas, his son, or Sherry.

Chapter Two

Hawke had all the information he could get from his mom and Trey when there was a knock on the door.

"You answer that while I take Trey out back," Mom said, picking up a box of toys and heading for the door. "Come with me, Trey."

The boy followed her, and Hawke headed to the front door.

Another frantic knock resounded as he grabbed the knob and pulled.

"Oh!" The young woman's hand still remained in a position to knock.

"You must be Morning. I'm State Trooper Hawke, Mimi's son. Come in." He held the door open and waved the woman dressed in sweats, a t-shirt, and running shoes into the house. It was Wednesday. He wondered that she could come over on a work day.

"Yes, I can't believe that Sherry is missing." She dropped onto the couch and stared at him. "What happened?"

"That's what I want to know. Did she go to work yesterday?" He studied her as he pulled out his small notebook.

"Yeah, I talked to her during her lunch break. We were making plans for a friend's baby shower. Oh God! It's this weekend." The woman's eyes widened and her hand covered her mouth. "Will you find her before then?"

"I hope so, for Trey and my mom's sakes. What can you tell me about any boyfriends?"

She shook her head, loosening the shaggy bun on her head, making it tip a bit to the side. "None. She's sworn off men and dating until Trey is grown. That piece of shit that knocked her up and fled soured her on men. He told her no matter what he'd take care of her and Trey, then as soon as the baby arrived, he was gone." Her forehead wrinkled in a frown.

"Does she go to bars or drink?" Hawke had a feeling he already knew the answer given what the woman had just said.

"No. Not bars. Once in a while we open a bottle of wine and have a pity party but never get drunk to where we don't know what we're doing. That's what doesn't make sense. She wouldn't have been anywhere to get into trouble." She stopped and tapped her painted nails on the shoulder bag sitting in her lap. "She does go to the casino once a month, but that's because Grandfather Thunder begs a ride off her."

"Could he have asked her to take him last night? Before she came here to get Trey?"

"No. He only goes on weekends when there are

more people there to watch." She grinned. "He's a people watcher. Don't get me wrong, he plays the slots, but he also watches people."

Hawke remembered that about the old man who hadn't been that old when Hawke was a boy living on the reservation. Back then Silas Thunder, now called Grandfather Thunder to the younger generation, had a family; a wife, son, and daughter. Hawke had played ball with the son. The man had lost them all and taken in everyone else on the reservation as his family.

"You can't think of anyone Sherry said was being pushy or nosey?"

"You mean a guy?" She wrinkled her nose. "She did say there was a guy at the casino the last time she was there who kept following her around and tried to start up a conversation."

"Indian?"

"No. White. She said he gave her the creeps. And before you ask, she didn't get his name because she didn't care for him to think she was interested." She tapped her fingers some more. "Oh, and there was someone at work that keeps asking her out. Wade something. But she always turns him down."

"Thank you. We haven't told Trey his mom is missing, so don't say anything to him. But he might like to see another friendly face." Hawke shoved the notebook in his pocket and headed to the door, picking up his Stetson. "Tell Mimi I'm going to ask more people questions. Not sure when I'll be back."

"I will. I hope you find her soon. And not just because of the baby shower. Too many women who go missing here are never found."

Hawke nodded and whistled for Dog. His canine companion ran into the living room. "Let's go."

His first stop would be the bank. Best to get all the information about when Sherry left the day before, who she might have been with, and to question the man who repeatedly asked her out.

Backtracking how he'd arrived at his mother's place, taking Mission back into Pendleton, he found the bank where the missing woman worked. While he wasn't in uniform, he had his badge and he used it to get in to see the manager, Ms. Terrel Stern.

"Trooper Hawke, I'm glad to see you. We've been worried about Sherry Dale. She hasn't shown up for work and she isn't answering her phone."

"That's why I'm here. She never picked her boy up from the sitter last night."

"Oh no! Do you think something happened to her?" The woman appeared to be genuinely upset.

"That's what I'm here to find out. What time did she leave?"

"Her usual time, five-thirty. I was still here. She said good night to me and Wade Benson, the business loan officer."

"How long was Mr. Benson here after Ms. Dale left?" Hawke wondered if this was the Wade who had repeatedly asked the missing woman out.

"We were both here until six discussing a loan he didn't think had enough security." She picked up her phone. "Who would you like to speak to?"

"Mr. Benson and anyone else who works here that she is friends with." Hawke waited as the woman asked for a man and a woman to be sent in. Then she called another line and asked Mr. Benson to come to her office.

A knock and the door opened. Two men and a woman walked in.

"Phil, Shirley, Wade, this is State Trooper Hawke. He has some questions for you about Sherry."

"What about Sherry?" The man in the suit and tie asked.

"Can I get your full names first?" Hawke asked.

The suit and tie said, "Wade Benson."

The man in the sweater vest and tie said, "Phil Little."

The woman said, "Shirley Hardy."

"Thank you. Did any of you speak with Sherry yesterday?"

"Why? What's happened to her?" Benson asked.

"She never picked up her son from the sitter's last night. No one has seen her. I'm trying to piece together any information I can get to figure out where she might be."

The woman gasped. "She'd never not pick up Trey. She loves that little boy. We had lunch together. She was talking on the phone with a friend, planning a baby shower for someone. She said she had to pick up a couple of things from the store before she went home, but that was it."

"Do any of you know anything about a boyfriend? Or if she liked to go anywhere after work?"

"As far as I know she doesn't have one," Shirley said.

Hawke peered at Benson. "You ever hear of one?"

"I asked her out several times but she always

refused me."

"That make you mad?" Hawke asked.

The man took off his glasses and wiped them with a handkerchief he'd pulled from a pocket. "No. It made me sad that she wouldn't even give me a chance."

Hawke shifted his attention to the other man. "Were you friends or a boyfriend?"

The man laughed. "Friends. I wouldn't have turned Wade down for a date."

Seeing that this man wouldn't have any love interest in Sherry, he asked, "What did she tell you about her life? Anything that might shed a light on where she could be?"

"She talked a lot about Trey. And Grandfather Thunder. I thought it was some kind of Native American religious thing until she, her son, and this old man showed up at my house for a barbecue one Saturday. Turns out he's an ancient man she rents from on the reservation."

"They come over to your place often?" Hawke asked.

"No. Just the one time. It was my birthday." Little smiled. "I only invited special people who don't treat me any different." His gaze flicked to Benson.

"None of you have any idea where she could have gone?" He glanced at his notes. "You said she was going to the store. Any idea which store?"

Shirley shook her head. "It could have been any of them. We never talked about shopping for groceries."

"Thank you. If you think of anything, here's my card." He handed everyone in the room one of his cards.

"Are you investigating this because it's a person from the reservation?" Benson asked.

"No. Tribal Police and the City Police told my mother, the woman who watches Trey, that they wouldn't do anything until Sherry is missing seventy-two hours. She called me knowing how crucial it is to get right on a missing person investigation. Thank you for your time." Hawke stood, put his hat on his head, and walked out of the bank.

On the street, he decided to see if he could light a fire under the City Police to check with the grocery stores to see which one Sherry went to and if there were any cameras to see who she might have encountered.

Chapter Three

"We told the woman who called in, we have to wait seventy-two hours. These reservation women get liquored up and forget they have kids at home or decide they've had enough and walk out."

Hawke stared at the bald-headed detective in his fifties that he'd been referred to when he explained why he was there. "Detective Lockland. You are stereotyping the reservation women. Most have strong motherly instincts and wouldn't go on a drunk or walk away from their families. This woman happens to be one of those. She works at the bank in town, never misses picking her son up from the sitter, and doesn't go out partying and drinking."

"How do you know that? Her family could be lying to you." The man wasn't about to back down from his stand on what he thought to be the truth.

Ignorance about his people was something Hawke had fought all his life. "I know because I've been interviewing the people she works with and the people she spends time with. Something that might help us find her faster if you had done the same last night when my mother called you."

The man leaned back in his chair and smiled. "Now I see. You're one of them. Does your superior know you're here poking around in someone else's case?"

"Then you are going to investigate? If this is your case?" Hawke held back the disdain he felt for the man as the detective stuttered and tried to say it wasn't a case until seventy-two hours had passed.

"I can't talk to people on the reservation and canvas all the grocery stores in town at the same time. Could you at least send an officer to the stores with a photo and see if anyone remembers seeing her last night and if they saw anything unusual?" Hawke pulled the photo his mom had given him of Sherry and Trey taken at Christmas. He handed it to the detective. "This is the woman you say is sleeping off a drunk or running from her child."

Lockland looked at it and grinned. "She's not bad to look at. You sure she doesn't have a boyfriend she shacked up with for the night?"

"Yes. Everyone I've talked to, my mother, Sherry's best friend, and her co-workers say there is no man in her life. Only her son." Hawke stood. "I'll call you tonight to see if you've heard anything." He walked out of the man's office without waiting for a reply.

On the drive back to Mission, a community on the reservation, he called Sergeant Spruel.

"Hawke, what are you doing calling me on your

day off?"

"My mom called this morning—"

"Did something happen?" Spruel cut him off.

"Not to her, but the mother of a boy she watches never showed up last night. She couldn't get the Tribal Police or the Pendleton City cops to do anything, so she called me. I'm not liking what I've dug up so far. I'm requesting a week's vacation starting Friday."

"You sure this woman didn't just get tired of being a mother and take off?"

"Not you too!" Hawke blew out a breath.

"Hey, I'm just saying what is the usual thing when a mother takes off. No matter what race they are."

"This mother didn't leave her son. According to my mom and the people she works for, her son is her world. She doesn't date, doesn't party, and is always on time and punctual. Something is wrong. Too many Indigenous women are never looked for because of the same statement you just made. I'm going to find her." He'd made up his mind as he'd talked with Sherry's best friend, that foul play had caused the woman to not pick up her son. He planned to find out what kind.

"I trust your instincts. I'll put you down for a week of vacation, but do you really think you can find her in that short of a time? You do have a lot of days built up, but you can't leave us one man short for too long."

"If I haven't found her or what happened to her in a week, I'll come home. It will mean we'll never know." A lump of dread settled in his gut. He didn't like leaving anything undone. It meant he hadn't tried hard enough.

"Ok. I'll adjust the work schedule accordingly.

And Hawke, you know you can count on the State Police if you need help."

"Yeah. I know." Hawke ended the call as he pulled up to the Tribal Police station. The building sat at the edge of a field with the Confederated Tribes government building across the street to the north.

He walked into the building and up to the tinted window. Hawke spoke into the round, grill-looking speaker in the window and asked for a detective after stating his name and flashing his trooper badge. The voice behind the window said, "Detective Jones will be right out."

Hawke thanked the person and strode over to the front window to look out. He knew a couple of the tribal officers. They'd helped him keep watch on his mom's place when he had hid Kitree on the reservation.

A tall, thin, Caucasian man in his forties entered the lobby. He held out a hand. "Detective Jones, you must be Trooper Hawke? I was expecting someone in uniform."

Hawke stood, shook hands, and said, "My mom, Mimi Shumack, called here last night about a missing woman. She was told to wait seventy-two hours because the woman was probably out partying. I'm here to look into the missing woman, officially."

"Oh, yeah, I remember seeing that call when I came in this morning. Yeah, these women tend to take off with a boyfriend or party and not come home for a day or two. She'll be back."

"No, she won't. Not unless we look for her. Sherry Dale, from what I've learned from her co-workers, best friend, and my mom, doesn't have a boyfriend and doesn't drink." He was getting tired of repeating himself. Especially to law enforcement members who are sworn to protect the public.

"She had to have come to foul play. I'd like your officers to do a thorough search of the reservation." He stared the man in the eye.

"Like hell you can come in here and tell me what I need to do. We wait seventy-two hours. Then we'll either see the woman has come crawling back home or we look for her."

"Where's the Chief of Police?" Hawke was going to take this higher.

"He's at a conference in Portland. I'm in charge." The gleam in the man's eyes said he wasn't about to help Hawke out.

"When this woman's body is found, her death is on you." He slammed his hat on his head and stormed out of the building. What was wrong with all these arrogant sons of bitches! A woman's life could be in peril, and they all sit back looking down their noses at any attempt to find her.

His phone rang. Mom. "Hawke," he answered the same as he did for anyone.

"Have you learned anything?" she asked.

"That the police around here are arrogant bastards."

"I could have told you that."

He chuckled. "I'm going to talk to Silas Thunder and take a look around in Sherry's trailer. Are you and Trey doing okay?"

"Yes. I'm gathering some help."

"What kind of help?"

"I've called on some friends to help us get the word out about Sherry being missing. Gotta go."

The line went silent. He stared at his phone, wondering what his mom was up to.

Driving out to Silas Thunder's place, Hawke had a million scenarios running through his head of what could have happened to Sherry. Anyone could have pretended to be in distress, the woman could have stopped, and the assailant tried to rob or rape her, something could have gone wrong, she was killed and her car and body dumped. He didn't like those scenarios and it didn't make sense that no one had seen anything. Everyone in a small community were nosey. He knew for a fact the rez had a gossip line like everywhere else. There had been more than once, he'd get home from school or hanging out with friends and his mom would know what he'd been up to before he'd told her.

He just needed the right people to ask the right questions. Maybe that was what his mom was doing. Gathering the people others on the rez would talk to.

Grandfather Thunder as everyone called him these days, had a nice place along the Umatilla River. Hawke remembered he'd had a small trailer put in years ago for his mother and later his son lived in it until his death. That must be the place where Sherry and Trey lived.

He parked in front of the house. It was a bit run down but nothing a few cans of paint and youth couldn't remedy. One old rusted pickup sat to the side of the yard. Tall grass grew up around the wheels, but it had flowers planted inside the open hood and on the seat, which could be seen from the open driver's door.

A dog barked. Hawke scanned the area and found the fat black dog smacking its tail on the porch in welcome. "Looks like you can get out," Hawke said to Dog, stepping out and letting the animal leap to the ground and start sniffing.

"Interesting dog you got there."

Hawke focused on the area the voice had come from. In the shadow of the house, behind the screen door, stood the silhouette of a man.

"Silas Thunder?" Hawke asked.

"Yeah, and you are?" The man didn't step out on the porch.

"Gabriel Hawke. Mimi Shumack's son. I'm with the Oregon State Police." He walked toward the house, pulling on the chain around his neck to draw his badge out from under his shirt for the man to see.

"Mimi's boy? You're a man. Getting to be an old man." He opened the screen door, inviting Hawke in, and walked over to a recliner that had to have been one of the first models.

Hawke followed after telling Dog to stay. He removed his hat and sat on the edge of another recliner that looked just as old as the one the man sat in.

"What are you doing coming to see me? Is it something to do with Sherry?" The man leaned forward. Concern etched even more lines on his weathered face.

"Why do you ask?"

"She and the boy didn't come home last night. They are always here no later than six-thirty. And their lights come on about seven every morning. They load up into the car about eight and come home at six-thirty. Just like clockwork. Except on weekends and holidays. Then they come see me and go visiting her friend." His eyes teared up. "Somethin' happened didn't it?"

"That's what I'm trying to find out. Mimi called me early this morning." He went on to tell the man about his and his mom's try at getting the police involved. "I've decided to take a week's vacation and look into it myself. Can you tell me if there has been anyone unusual hanging around the area?"

The man shook his head. "Not that I've seen. Me and Three Foot go for a walk about midday every day unless the weather's bad."

He pointed to the east of his place. "You might ask Debra next door. She's retired now and spends more time at home. She might have seen something. She's the one who plants the flowers in my truck. She said that would make it less of an eye sore." He chuckled. "That woman is always coming up with something."

"Sherry's friend, Morning, said that Sherry takes you to the casino once a month. Have you noticed anyone there taking an interest in her?" He remembered the friend's comment that the man liked to watch people.

"She's a pretty girl. Men are always lookin' her way. Not that she'd give them a look."

"Has there been anyone in particular that pushed himself on her?" Hawke asked.

The man tapped a crooked finger on the arm of the chair. "There was one, last month that followed her. But I didn't see him around this month. Probably someone passing through. You know the casino is just off the freeway. That's why they put it there. To draw in more people and make it convenient for locals."

"When did you go to the casino last month? The date?" Hawke thought he'd take a drive over to the Spotted Pony Casino and see if he could get a look at the surveillance tape for that night. Maybe the man hadn't really taken no for an answer.

"We always go the last weekend of the month. That's when the machines are the loosest." The man grinned. "I can always make enough to get groceries to last me until my check comes in."

Hawke smiled. He could tell the trip to the casino was more of a social thing than making money. "I'd like to take a look in Sherry's trailer. Do you have the key?"

"Just walk out and open the door. There is only a deadbolt on the inside." The man's cheeks grew darker. "I keep saying I'll get a knob that locks on it, but always forget when I'm in town."

"Thank you. If you think of anything else, give me a call." Hawke handed the man his card and walked out the front door. He and Dog walked around the house to the trailer sitting behind and to the side.

He climbed the three steps to the small wood porch and turned the knob. Just like Silas said, it opened.

Chapter Four

The missing woman had a thing about order. Everything was in its place. Even the small bedroom where Trey slept. The toys were in a box or lined up on top of a small dresser. His bed was neatly made and his pajamas folded on the pillow. Hawke didn't remember his mom ever folding his pajamas. And it had been up to him to make his bed. She had worked two jobs and didn't have time.

Sherry's room was as neat and tidy as the rest of the house. The only photos were one of a couple in their forties and two of Trey. One as a baby and one as a toddler. He didn't find any letters, cards, or photos stashed anywhere.

The living room had one large photo of Trey and Sherry smiling at the camera. The magazines were of home decorating. The kitchen was spotless. No food left out to attract ants or mice.

Her home told him nothing about where she might

be. He checked all the cupboards and the refrigerator. There wasn't a drop of alcohol in the place. That kind of blew a hole in the theory of the tribal and city detectives.

He took photos to show proof this woman wasn't as they had stereotyped her.

Before leaving the trailer, he gathered some clothes for Trey in a bag he found hanging in Sherry's closet. Descending the three steps, he glanced at the house next door. Couldn't hurt to talk to the neighbor.

He dropped the bag off in his pickup before heading to the neighbor's. Dog ran ahead of him as they walked the length of the fence between the properties and then walked to the rock path that led up to the door of the small home.

"Can I help you?" A petite woman, he judged to be in her sixties, stood from beside a flower bed.

"Silas said I might want to come over and have a word with you." Hawke drew out his badge, holding it in front of him as he walked toward her.

Dog ran up to the woman, sniffed her, and wagged his tail. Dog was a good judge of character. After hearing how the woman planted flowers in her neighbor's pickup, Hawke had a pretty good idea the woman would be of good character.

"I'm Oregon State Trooper Hawke. My mom is Mimi Shumack."

"Oh, I'm pleased to meet you." She held out a gloved hand, shrugged, pulled her hand back, and drew the glove off, before stretching out her hand to shake, again. "The kids she watches love her."

He shook hands. "Thank you. She loves the kids.

Can I get your name?"

"Sure, I'm Debra Bolden. I taught school here on the reservation for over thirty years. I still substitute when they need me." She pulled off the other glove and waved them toward the house. "Come around back. I have iced tea I made this morning chilling in the fridge."

Hawke followed the woman around to the backyard. A small inviting deck had an awning over it.

"Have a seat. I'll bring the drinks out and you can tell me why you are asking Silas and me questions." She disappeared into the house.

Dog plopped his butt down beside Hawke's chair.

"Good boy." Hawke petted the dog's head while he waited for the woman to return. It was peaceful sitting here, admiring the woman's garden, and hearing the rush of the Umatilla River in the background. This would be a pleasant visit if he wasn't searching for a missing woman.

"I didn't know if you preferred your tea sweetened, so I brought out the sugar bowl." She set a tray with a pitcher of tea, two glasses, two long spoons, and a bowl of sugar on the table between the two chairs.

Mrs. Bolden poured tea into the glasses and handed one to Hawke. "Why are you here?"

"Your neighbor is missing."

"You said you talked to Silas." Then it dawned on her. "Sherry or Trey?"

"Sherry. My mom—"

"Watches Trey. How is he doing? Those two are inseparable when she's not at work." Worry added to the crow's feet around the woman's eyes. When he first walked up to her, he'd noticed she wasn't Indian. If she was, there was very little in her DNA. Her pale blonde hair had streaks of gray and her skin was as pale as a plucked chicken.

"Trey is fine. He's staying with Mimi. I'm worried about Sherry. Her co-workers said she left work as usual last night, but she never arrived at my mom's to pick up Trey. Her car hasn't been found. There seems to be no trace of her. Have you seen anyone suspicious hanging around?" That's when it hit him, he hadn't asked about Trey's father. Morning had said he walked out. Could he have come back and for some reason wanted to get rid of Sherry so he could have his boy?

Mrs. Bolden shook her head. "I've been spending lots of hours in my yard. It's coming on the hottest part of the summer and I need to make sure the flowers are well watered or they'll die. I haven't seen any unfamiliar vehicles. And none that seem to be hanging around." She sipped her tea and then set the glass down and peered at him.

"There was one night several weeks ago that I was sitting out here and I heard Sherry talking on the phone to someone."

"How do you know she was talking on the phone?" He raised the glass to his lips.

"It was a one-sided conversation, and I could hear her voice, going back and forth, like she was pacing. She was trying to convince someone to stop asking and to leave her alone. About the time I thought to walk over and tell her to just hang up, she did."

Hawke pulled out his notepad. "Can you narrow down the date any?" He made a note to get a warrant for the woman's phone log.

Mrs. Bolden shook her head. "I just know it was several weeks ago…"

"Mom! Are you in the house?" called a female voice.

"Out back!" Mrs. Bolden replied.

The back screen door opened and a woman close to forty, with dark blonde hair pulled up in a ponytail, wearing a faded Army t-shirt and knee length shorts, stepped out onto the deck. She wore running sneakers. A prosthetic leg stuck out of her right shoe. The woman stopped, studied him, and walked over to another chair next to the house. She picked it up and carried it over to the table, a bit of a limp to her gait.

"Who are you?" she asked, sitting down. Her gaze hadn't left him since her first glance.

"State Trooper Hawke. You are…"

She held out a hand. "Dela Alvaro, her daughter."

Her grip was firm. She had a wary, no-nonsense attitude.

"Pleased to meet you. Were you out running?" Hawke asked, raising his iced tea to his lips.

She frowned. "Do you think I can't run?"

He shook his head. "No. You've been sweating, you have on running shoes, and you weren't here when I arrived, but there are two cars sitting in the driveway."

Mrs. Bolden stood. "I'll get you a glass so you can have some iced tea."

When the older woman left, Ms. Alvaro asked, "What are you doing here? Why are you talking to my mom?"

"Sherry, her next-door neighbor is missing."

Hawke watched the concern and then the anger cross the woman's face.

"What do you mean by missing?" She leaned forward, her arms crossed on the table, peering into his eyes.

"Just that. She didn't pick up Trey last night." He took a sip of the iced tea.

The woman slammed a fist on the table and stood, nearly knocking the chair she'd been sitting on backwards. "Shit! Not again!"

That piqued Hawke's attention. "What do you mean not again? Has someone else gone missing?"

She swiped at the one tear trickling down her face. "Six months ago." She turned angry eyes on him. "Indigenous women are killed or missing at a greater rate than women of other ethnicities."

Mrs. Bolden returned, glanced at her daughter, and put an arm around her shoulders. "I'd hoped you wouldn't hear this from anyone else."

"Were you and Sherry close?" Hawke asked, wondering if the missing woman had a girlfriend rather than a boyfriend.

"No. Just talked a bit when she'd come to the casino with Silas. But she's the second person I've known personally who has gone missing." Ms. Alvaro settled back down in her chair and sipped the iced tea her mom placed in front of her. "In high school, my senior year, my best friend was raped and left." Her bottom lipped quivered. "We'd gone into Pendleton. I had to get home to get ready for a basketball game. She didn't want to leave. Said she'd find a ride home." Ms. Alvaro's eyes held more sorrow than he'd ever seen in a person's eyes before. "When I called the next morning, her mom said she hadn't returned home. Thought she'd spent the night with me." She swiped at the tears trickling down her cheeks. "Her family, mom, and I all went out looking. We walked on both sides of Mission Road looking for her. Two days later, State Police found her body alongside the freeway. She'd been raped, beaten, and dumped." She picked up the drink and swallowed it down as if it would fortify her.

"I'm sorry to hear you had to go through that." Hawke studied her. "You mentioned you spoke to Sherry at the casino. Do you frequent the Spotted Pony?"

She put the glass down. "I'm security at the casino."

This was a perfect coincidence. "I would like to look at surveillance at the casino from a month ago when Silas and Sherry were there. Can you arrange that?"

"If you think it will help find Sherry, I can make it happen. I go in to work around ten usually, tonight the head of security has to leave early, so I'll be there at eight. I'm the night security manager. Do you want to come by tonight?"

Hawke did, but he'd have to swing by and fill his mom in on what he knew so far. "I'll be there at eight." He held out his card. "Hang on to this in case you think of anything or I need to come to the casino sooner. I'm going to head home and let my mom know what I've found out so far."

"Don't you have to report to your superior?" Ms. Alvaro studied him. "You aren't some vindictive relative seeking revenge, are you?" She put her hand to her hip as if she were going for a weapon. She'd been trained military or law enforcement.

"My superior knows I am here and what I'm doing. However, the Pendleton City Police and Tribals blew my mom off when she reported Sherry missing. They told her to wait—"

"Seventy-two hours. Damn, I hate that number!" Ms. Alvaro said with a ferocity he figured meant she'd lost more than her high school friend on this reservation. "Who did you talk to at the Tribal Police?"

"Detective Jones."

She snorted. "He wouldn't turn over a rock if his mother was under it. Talk to Jacob Red Bear. He's just an officer, but he'd use his time on duty and off looking for the vehicle." She recited a phone number. "His sister was the friend I lost. He works overtime if there is someone missing. I'd be surprised if he wasn't already out there driving the dirt roads looking for her and the vehicle."

"Thanks. I'll call him as soon as I get in my truck. And I'll see you at the casino later."

"Copy."

Hawke whistled for Dog who had wandered off to smell the flowers and sprinkle them with his scent. He was glad Mrs. Bolden wasn't facing the yard or she would have seen Dog lift his leg several times on her colorful flowers.

In his vehicle, he dialed the number Dela gave him. It went straight to voicemail.

"Officer Red Bear, I'm Trooper Hawke of the State Police. I'd like to connect with you about Sherry Dale, who is missing." He left his number and started his truck as his stomach grumbled. He'd get information from his mom on the two women he'd just visited and then head to the casino early.

Chapter Five

There were eight cars parked around his mom's house when he arrived. He would get chewed out, but he parked on the lawn so he wouldn't have to move his vehicle for any others to leave.

He walked in the house and found his mother's printer, a piece of technology he'd purchased for her several years ago and he thought he was the only one who used it, whirring and spitting out pages. There were three women in their thirties gathered around Mimi's computer. They barely glanced up as he walked by.

In the kitchen, the rest of the visitors were seated around the table, hunched over a map of the reservation. He counted ten all together, four of them were men in their forties and fifties.

"Mom, what's going on?"

They all turned to face him and that's when he saw the flyers on the table.

"We're planning how to go out and spread the word about Sherry and talk to people. We split up into groups of two or three and take a section of the rez. We plaster the flyers everywhere and hand them to people and check all the roads and buildings in the area we are given." She glared. "If the police won't do something, we will."

"This is great, just make sure you do go out in pairs or more. There is no telling what you could come across." He looked each person in the eye, waiting for them to nod.

His mom moved away from the table. "Are you hungry? I can make you a sandwich."

"Don't worry about me. I've been fending for myself for a long time. But if you have a minute, I have some questions." He walked to the refrigerator, pulled out the tuna fish his mom always had made, and spread some between two slices of bread. While he made the sandwich and put the tuna fish back in the fridge, his mom poured a glass of iced tea from a pitcher and put a handful of chips on a plate beside his sandwich.

"Let's go out back," she said.

Hawke nodded and asked, "Where's Trey?"

"Julia West came and got him. Her son, Arnie, is Trey's best friend. He's spending the night so I can concentrate on this without him hearing what we're doing." She sat on a chair that looked out over her backyard.

Dog was busy checking out the perimeter of the drying yard.

"That's good. It might take his mind off his mom for a little bit." Hawke bit into his sandwich, chewed, swallowed tea, and started. He told her what he'd learned today and where he was going tonight. "What can you tell me about Mrs. Bolden and Ms. Alvaro?"

"Neither one has been married."

He knew the two were related. Their facial features were too close of a match for them to not be related.

"Bolden is the mother's maiden name. She never married Dela's father. Dela has her father's last name."

"That must have been awkward growing up." Now he saw why the woman had a chip on her shoulder.

"Not really. She grew up here. No one said anything about them having different last names. Ms. Bolden is a respected teacher. She's lived alongside Silas Thunder ever since she moved here, pregnant with Dela."

"And the father?" His real father was barely in his life and the reason behind it had been the root of his lack of relationships.

"No one has ever seen him. I'm not sure if he's dead or was never told." She shrugged. "It doesn't matter. Debra did a good job bringing up her daughter. Dela was in the Army. Planned to make it a career until she lost her foot." Mom glanced back at the house. "I need to get in there."

"Go. You answered my questions." Hawke finished off his sandwich and flipped through his note pad, checking to see if there was anything he needed to follow up on.

His phone buzzed. The number was the one Dela gave him.

"Hawke," he answered.

"This is Officer Red Bear. I heard about Sherry

around noon. I've been driving all the back roads looking for her vehicle." Frustration rang in the man's voice.

"Can you give me the license, make, and model of her car? I can get it out across the state."

"You think she drove off somewhere?" The anger and exasperation in the officer's voice told Hawke the man believed Hawke was like all the rest thinking she just ran out on her son.

"No. But if someone did something to her and took off in her car, maybe we can catch him with the stolen car and find out what happened."

There were a few seconds of silence. "Yeah, okay, that makes sense." Red Bear rattled off the information.

"Thanks. Did you know Sherry?" Hawke asked.

"Yeah. Good woman. Cared about her son and bettering their lives."

"That's what I've discovered with my interviews so far. Any idea what could have happened?" Hawke wrote Officer Red Bear in his notepad and waited.

"Not really. It was a Tuesday night. She didn't even go partying or drinking on the weekends. She wouldn't have been anywhere that she'd run into anyone out to cause trouble. That's what's so fucking maddening. She would have just been driving home." He paused. "When I heard she was missing, I talked to all the people along the route she would have taken to get to Mimi's. No one heard or saw anything unusual." He blew out air. "It's like one of those freakin' alien shows. Where the car and all is beamed up."

Hawke cleared his throat and said, "Nothing alien about her missing. Did you check any places a car could be hidden? A canyon, the river?"

"No, just roads. I'm off duty, but I can go take a look at a couple places. You want to go with me?"

"No, I'm meeting Dela Alvaro to check surveillance tapes at the casino. She gave me your number."

"Casino? Why would Sherry go there? She barely gambled when she took Grandpa Thunder."

"It's past tapes I'm looking at. Her friend, Morning, said a month ago there was a guy who wouldn't leave Sherry alone when she was there with Silas. I want to see if I can find him." He sighed. "It's the only thing out of the ordinary that seems to have happened to her lately."

"Okay, I'll let you know if I find anything." Red Bear ended the call.

Hawke finished writing down what he'd learned from the officer and stood, packing his plate and cup into the house.

The group had thinned. Just Mom and two others sat at the table. Hawke put a hand on his mom's shoulder. "This is good, what you're doing."

"It has to be done. No one else cares that there is someone from the rez missing." She peered up at him, a tear in the corner of her eye. "We've been on this earth for thousands of years and have always had to look out for ourselves. No one else cares if we live or die. More people these days are concerned about animals than the first people who have been shoved onto patches of land that in some instances doesn't even match were we once lived. We are treated lower than animals. If we stay strong together, we will overcome all that has been given us and be the ones on top."

He understood her anger and pain. Growing up here and when he'd joined the military, he'd always felt the disapproval from anyone who was non-Indian. What kept him going was believing they treated him this way because they feared him. That made him work even harder to be the best at what he did and not put others down. To be the bigger person in all instances. He tried, but had also failed when his anger and frustration got the better of him.

That's why he liked being a State Trooper and working the Fish and Wildlife division in Wallowa County. He could look after his ancestors' homeland and hopefully show the people he came in contact with that his culture wasn't something to be feared.

"Officer Red Bear has been out all day looking for her and her car. He's still looking tonight off duty. I'm going to check out a possible lead. Don't wait up for me. With so many people looking, we'll find Sherry." He gave her a hug.

"But will she be alive?" Mom didn't look at him, but down at her hands.

"If enough people have her in their thoughts and prayers, we could get lucky." Hawke didn't know what else to say. There was a very strong chance they would not find her alive. But giving up hope was never good for those whom the victim was dependent upon to find them.

Chapter Six

The Spotted Pony Casino sat a mile off Interstate 84. The gaming area was one of the largest in the state of the Indian run casinos. There was a twelve-story hotel, six restaurants, and a theater all on the premises. A large parking area for trucks and RVs stretched out behind the building. The casino had the prefect locale to pull in tired travelers or people who liked to gamble. Hawke had made an arrest or two here back when he was a trooper working this corridor and living on the rez with his wife. The casino and surrounding area had grown since then.

Hawke parked in the parking lot in front and walked up to the entrance admiring the aesthetics of the building and the Appaloosa horse sculpture in front. There were two sets of doors as you entered, to keep the weather outside. He stepped through the second set of glass doors and stopped. It had been a while since he'd set foot on the premises. It seemed busier, louder with voices and the machine sounds, than he'd remembered. He hadn't forgotten the acrid overtone of cigarette smoke that lingered in the air.

It was six o'clock on a Wednesday night. Then he saw the banner about a mid-week Bingo tournament. He'd never been a fan of the game, but his mom and many of her friends loved to play. It seemed so did many other people.

He glanced to the right and spotted the valet box. Hawke walked over and started up a conversation. "Is it always this busy here on a weeknight?"

A man ten or so years younger than Grandfather Thunder with fewer wrinkles but the same shrewd eyes and sun bronzed skin shrugged. "It's Bingo night."

"Other nights it's not this busy?" He persisted.

"Wednesday, Thursday, Friday, Saturday are the busiest nights. Best nights to be standing here. I make good tips." He smiled, showing two missing teeth on the left side of his mouth. "I always ask to work these nights. People feel comfortable handing the keys to their car over to an older man. These young kids who work valet, they mess with radios and take too long looking for a parking spot."

Hawke nodded. "If you work here a lot then you know quite a bit about the people who are here frequently?"

The man studied him. "Why are you asking all these questions?"

Hawke pulled out his badge. "I'm helping Mimi Shumack find Sherry Dale."

"I heard about her bein' missing. Sad. She's a nice girl." The man rubbed a hand across the back of his neck.

"What can you tell me about the people who are here when Grandfather Thunder and Sherry come once a month?" Hawke noticed a security person standing to the side watching their conversation.

"They come in, Silas heads for the poker machine over there." He pointed to a group of machines to the left of the door. "Sherry usually wanders into the gift shop then goes to the coffee shop. She has friends who work here. They stop by and visit with her on their breaks."

"That's all she does, sit in the coffee shop?" Hawke asked, wondering how a guy would have followed her around if she sat in one place.

"Sometimes she wanders around, playing a few machines. If there's a concert, she goes to that with her friend." He slid off the tall stool he'd been sitting on. "Got a customer."

Hawke wasn't finished, but he didn't want to keep the man from his work. "Thanks." He checked the layout of the casino on a big board, noticing that the building was in the shape of a bird in flight. He found the coffee shop tucked in the corner on the northwest side of the building.

A young woman, placing drinks on a table, called out, "Pick a seat. I'll be right with you."

He smiled and found one that had his back to the wall and a view out the door.

The waitress chatted with the couple at the other table before walking to the counter and coming back with a menu. "Coffee?"

He'd already turned the cup on the table over.

"Yes, please."

"Will you have anything else?" she asked, glancing over her shoulder as another couple stepped into the café.

"Pie. Which one would you recommend?" he asked, handing her the menu.

"The Dutch apple or huckleberry are the best."

"I'll take the huckleberry with some ice cream." He sipped the coffee. It was black.

"I'll get that right out." She hurried to the counter, passing the newcomers telling them she'd be right back.

Hawke peered into the kitchen. He heard music and some clanging but didn't see anyone actually back there working. For a busy night like this, he would have expected this more reasonably priced restaurant to be staffed for the Bingo players.

The waitress returned with his pie. "Enjoy."

"When you get a minute, I'd like to talk to you." He had his badge in his palm. Flipping his hand, he revealed the badge.

"Okay. What about?"

"Sherry Dale."

"Oh!" She put a hand to her mouth then dropped it. "Have they found her?"

He wasn't surprised that while the police were waiting seventy-two hours, everyone else knew she was missing.

"Not yet. I'm trying to learn more about her habits."

"She and Grandfather Thunder come in here like clockwork."

"Waitress, we'd like to order," the man who was

one of the recent arrivals called over.

"Go do your work. I'm not going anywhere." Hawke sipped his coffee.

She nodded and hurried over to the other table.

Hawke ate his pie, watching the same security guard watch him. He wondered if the guard had asked the valet about him.

The waitress walked over with a pot of coffee. She refilled his cup and sat in the chair opposite him. "I have a few minutes until their orders come up."

"The valet told me Sherry would come in here and sit while Grandfather Thunder played the slot machines. Did she visit with anyone?"

"Me, when she comes during a concert. The two usually come in midafternoon and stay until about dinner time." She glanced around when several more people entered. "I have to go. I'll come back when I can."

He nodded and picked up his warmed coffee. He didn't have to meet Dela Alvaro until eight. He'd just stay here and see what he learned. It sounded like he'd have to come back tomorrow in the afternoon to talk to anyone Sherry visited.

People started filing into the café. The waitress came by once to refill his cup and apologize for not being able to talk.

"I'll come by later. I'm meeting someone—" He didn't finish as the security guard who had been checking on him walked up to his table.

"Dela said to bring you back."

Hawke put a twenty on the table and followed the guard across the middle of the casino passing a fenced off scene of two warriors on appaloosas. They continued to a door beside the cashier cage. The guard held his ID badge up to the door lock and it opened.

This large room was filled with monitors, all showing different areas of the casino, the hotel, and the grounds around the building. Four people sat in front of all the monitors.

"I'll get Dela. Stay here." The man walked to a door at the other end of the room and knocked. Hawke glanced at the large LED clock above that door. It was 7:57:34. The woman's military career had made her more than punctual.

Hawke stood his ground, not wandering where he wasn't wanted. He hoped by not snooping the casino security would work with him and not view him as someone stepping on their toes. He already had that with the Tribal and Pendleton police.

"Trooper Hawke, you're punctual." Dela Alvaro walked toward him in a security uniform. A polo shirt with the casino logo and slacks. Her limp was barely perceptible.

"Ms. Alvaro—"

She stopped him. "Please, call me Dela, everyone does. You didn't give a precise date of the video you wanted to see. I think I have the right one. Follow me." She pivoted, leading Hawke into the room behind the door she'd appeared through.

There were two banks of monitors with a video rolling. A man in his forties sat in a chair watching it with his hand on a keyboard.

"Have you seen Grandfather Thunder arrive yet?" Dela asked the man.

"Not yet." The man continued staring at the monitors.

"Grab a seat. The show hasn't started yet," Dela said. "I'm going to leave you here with Marty. He is head of surveillance. Marty, please answer any questions Trooper Hawke has."

"Sure thing." The man never took his eyes off the monitors.

"Where will you be if I have more questions?" Hawke asked.

"I have to check the end of this shift and then do my usual nightly rounds to make sure everyone is in place and following protocol. I'll check back in an hour, no more than two, before I have to check the next shift." Dela strode to the door and disappeared.

Hawke pulled his chair up beside Marty. "Got any popcorn?"

The man glanced at him, laughed, and pointed to a microwave in the corner with a case of microwave popcorn under the cart.

"Maybe later." Hawke stared at the screen with the video of the front entrance. "You know Grandfather Thunder?"

"Who doesn't?" Marty didn't take his eyes from the screens.

"True. When I grew up here, he was just Silas Thunder."

The man glanced at him. "That was before you both grew old."

Hawke grunted. "There. That's Silas and Sherry."

The tech nodded. "I've had all the cameras booted and synced on the time. We can keep track of their movements."

The two visited a couple of minutes and Silas went to the left, just as the valet had said. Sherry went left but deeper into the casino floor. "Follow Sherry. That's who we need to watch."

"You think she met someone here?" The head of surveillance tapped keys and another area of the casino came up on the screen. Sherry walked into the frame and headed toward the Spotted Pony Gift Shop.

"Do you have a camera in the shop?" Hawke asked.

"Yeah, bringing it up."

Hawke pulled out his notepad. "Who is the person she's talking with?"

"That's Teresa Berth. She comes in to work the gift shop from two to close on the weekends." The tech sped up the film.

Hawke studied the people who purchased items as Sherry remained near the cash register, visiting after each person left. She left the gift shop twenty minutes after entering. She moved out of the frame. He blinked and Marty had the next camera up and Sherry came into view. He'd expected her to go to the coffee shop, but she walked to the middle of the casino, studied the bronze statues of two warriors on horses on what looked like a small rise, and then wandered around the scene and out of the camera.

A new view popped up. She walked through the slot machines, studying several for a few minutes then moving on. She finally sat in a chair in front of a machine and fed a bill into it.

Marty fast forwarded again. At fifteen minutes a

man sat down next to her.

"Slow it down," Hawke said, leaning forward. "Can you make them larger?"

As soon as the words came out, the two were three times the original size. The man had on a cowboy hat that hid half of his face.

"It looks like he's doing all the talking," Marty commented.

"Yeah. And Sherry doesn't look like she cares."

The woman hit a button and a piece of paper slid out of the machine. She grabbed it, stood, and walked away.

They followed her to a different area, closer to the sports bar. She sat down, put the slip she'd pulled out of the other machine into the new one, and five minutes later the same guy leaned over her shoulder.

She leaned away from him and without even getting her winnings, she stood up and walked away.

"This must be the guy Morning was talking about." Hawke leaned forward. "Can you keep an eye on both of them?"

Marty tapped keys. One monitor showed Sherry walking quickly toward the opposite side of the casino and into the coffee shop. The man in the cowboy hat came up on the other screen. He pushed a button, pulled out the slip of paper, and tucked it in his pocket. He glanced around and started wandering through the machines as if he were looking for someone.

Sherry sat down at a table in the coffee shop, ordered, and as she sat there two other women about her age joined her. One had on the uniform of the registration desk and one had on the uniform of a cleaning person.

"What are the names of those two and what are their shifts?" Hawke asked.

Marty rattled off the names and work hours. And the two screens had the same image as the man walked into the coffee shop and sat at a table across the room from Sherry.

Her body stiffened when she looked up and spotted him.

"I wish I knew what he said to her," Hawke mused, watching as the woman leaned forward, talking to her friends. One glanced over at the man, then back to their huddle.

"She told them." He studied the man. "Is he a local?"

"I don't know. You'd have to ask the techs who watch the monitors in real time. I do the playbacks and searches." Marty fast forwarded again.

The two women left, leaving Sherry sitting alone. The man didn't make any moves toward her table. She glanced his way, then put money on the table and left.

"Follow her, but don't lose him." Hawke watched the man. He knew where the cameras were and made sure his hat never tipped enough to give them a clear view. Glancing at the monitor that followed Sherry, she took a seat beside Silas. The woman on the other side of the old man leaned forward and smiled at Sherry. They said something and resumed playing.

"Who is that on the other side of Silas?"

"Looks like Lanie Porter. As much time as she spends here, she should work here." Marty tapped some keys. The man left the coffee shop headed toward the middle of the casino floor. He stopped in the middle, lit a cigarette, and continued on. He entered the Sports Bar and walked up to the bar on the far end from the bartender, where the camera was at his back.

Five minutes later, Lanie left after leaning over Silas's shoulder and saying something to Sherry.

Marty fast forwarded. Silas and Sherry remained at the same machines for an hour and then they left. Nothing out of the ordinary other than the man making Sherry nervous.

Hawke shoved his notepad into his pocket and shoved the chair back to stand. He glanced up at the monitor of the bar. The woman who'd been next to Silas walked in, scanned the interior, and walked to the end where the man stood. She said something to him and pushed up beside him like they knew each other very well.

"Can you look and see if that woman, Lanie Porter, is here tonight?" Hawke asked as the door opened.

Chapter Seven

"Have you found anything?" Dela asked, walking across the short space from the door to the bank of monitors.

"I have names to talk to." Hawke pointed to the monitor still showing the bar. "If she is here, I'd like to talk to her. And…" He held out his notebook with the names of the women Sherry had visited with.

Dela shook her head. "Teresa won't be to work until Friday. She only works weekends. Abby might still be around. You'll have to come back tomorrow to talk to Kara." She nodded toward the monitor. "Lanie is probably here. I don't think she misses a night."

"How does she afford to hang out here?" Hawke asked.

"She comes from a family with money and clout around here. She owns a clothing store in downtown Pendleton. I'm not sure how well it does. The clothing is pretty expensive for this area. Why do you want to talk to her?" Dela turned to the door, her hand on the knob.

"She talked to the man who harassed Sherry a month ago." He faced Marty. "Any chance you can pull up the videos from Sherry and Silas's visit here the last time? See if that guy hangs around her again?"

"Sure thing." Marty started tapping keys on the keyboard in front of him.

"If you find anything, give me a call." Hawke handed him one of his cards.

"Sure thing."

Dela had the door open and was already standing behind a young woman at one of the sets of monitors. "Have you seen Lanie Porter tonight?"

"Yeah. She's been bumming drinks off all the single men in the sports bar." The young employee pointed to the top right monitor.

Hawke spotted the person he wanted to question. "Thanks." He headed for the door.

The one step heavy, one step light gait of Dela followed behind him across the room full of monitors.

Hawke stopped and faced the security guard. "You don't have to come. In fact, I might learn more without you there."

She peered into his eyes and gave a slight head nod. "You're not going to tell her you're State Police."

"Usually I would, but I think I'll go at this pretending to be Sherry's friend. See what she says about the missing woman."

"You want me to round up Abby?" Dela pulled out her phone.

"Yeah. I'll meet her in the coffee shop in an hour."

"I'll let her know." Dela hit buttons on her phone and held it to her ear.

Hawke shoved the door. It swung easier than he'd anticipated, startling people waiting at the cashier cage.

"Sorry." He smiled and continued along the edge of the casino floor to the sports bar. Stepping into the bar filled with strains of country music and conversation, he stopped and scanned the room. It was good sized with a nice stage in a corner for a concert or event. He walked over to the bar, taking the empty seat alongside Lanie.

Up close she appeared to be in her early thirties, dark hair fell in waves to the middle of her back. She had on tall fancy cowgirl boots, a short dress with a wide neckline that hung off her shoulders. Her attention was on the television and the man on her right.

The bartender walked over to Hawke. "What 'cha drinking?"

"Tap beer." Hawke said, placing a twenty on the bar.

Lanie glanced over her shoulder, first at the money on the bar and then at him. She smiled and shifted, turning her stool and body to face him. "Hello stranger. Want to buy a girl a drink?"

He smiled and when the bartender returned with his beer, he motioned for the man to give Lanie another of what she was drinking.

"Thank you. Are you staying at the hotel?" She shoved her empty glass to the far side of the bar and studied him.

"No." He sipped his beer and watched her.

The bartender placed her drink in front of her and

picked up Hawke's twenty.

"Where are you staying?" She sipped her drink and leaned closer to him.

It was clear she was trying to get an invitation from him.

"With my mom."

She looked him up and down. "You don't look like a momma's boy." She walked two fingers of her left hand up his arm. "I bet she'd never miss you if you got a room here."

He picked up his beer. "Not happening. I'm looking for Sherry Dale. Have you seen her? She's not answering my calls."

The woman leaned back a bit, staring into her drink. "Why are you looking for Sherry? She wouldn't show you a good time like I can."

"Her parents were friends of mine. Heard she still lives on the rez." He set his glass down. "Do you know where she lives?"

"If you're staying with your mother, I'd think she would know. Everyone on the reservation knows everyone else's business." She stated this with a vicious undertone.

"She heard that Sherry liked to come to the casino. Thought I'd look here. See if maybe she came here to meet a man." Hawke acted like it was no big deal, but he had his gaze on the woman, who wasn't making eye contact.

She laughed and finally peered into his eyes. "Sherry hasn't wanted anything to do with men since her worthless boyfriend left her when she was pregnant."

"That's weird. Her friend told me a man had approached her here a month ago."

Her hand shook as she set the drink on the bar and rose. "I'm sorry to drink and run. I have someone I'm meeting."

Hawke watched her stride out of the bar. He could get Marty to bring up the footage and see where she went. His comment about a man approaching Sherry had upset the woman. She knew something. He pulled out his phone and texted Sergeant Spruel and Officer Red Bear asking them to see what they could find on Lanie Porter of Pendleton, Oregon.

Finishing his beer, he walked across the casino floor to the coffee shop. The waitress smiled and waved to the table he'd sat at when he'd first arrived.

Hawke sat, ordered a coffee and sweet roll, and waited. Ten minutes later, Dela walked in with one of the women Sherry had visited with in the video.

"Trooper Hawke, this is Abby Shanee." Dela made the introductions and took a seat to the side of Hawke. Ms. Shanee sat across from him.

"Pleased to meet you, Ms. Shanee." Hawke held his hand out across the table.

She shook hands. "Please, just call me Abby. Dela said you are looking into Sherry being missing."

The waitress appeared. The two women both only wanted coffee. The waitress filled their overturned cups and headed back to the kitchen.

"Yes, I watched a video from over a month ago. You, Sherry, and another woman…"

Before he could say the woman's name, Dela said, "Kara Winter."

"Yes, Kara, sat in this coffee shop talking. A man had followed Sherry in. Do you remember what she said about him?"

Abby sat forward. "Do you think he did something to her?"

"We are a long way from thinking that. I just want to know what he said, and if you knew him?"

The woman shook her head. "I hadn't seen him before. He had narrow beady eyes. Not very good looking if you ask me."

"What did he say to Sherry?"

"She said he was asking her personal questions and when she didn't answer, he said, he'd find out what he wanted to know from someone else." Abby's eyes widened. "That frightened Sherry. She has a little boy to protect."

"Did she say anything about telling the police?" Hawke asked.

The woman laughed. "Right, like the Tribals will take a woman serious about a man saying something threatening. They don't do anything unless a man nearly beats us to death. Then someone steps in."

Dela made a noise that sounded close to a growl.

He glanced at her. It was evident she had the same feelings about domestic violence on the reservation as Abby.

"Did Kara say if she'd seen the guy before?" Hawke persisted.

Abby shook her head. "Not that I remember. I can call her and ask?"

"I'll talk to her tomorrow. Thank you." He sipped his coffee. "Did you know of any men in Sherry's life?"

Dela stared at him. "Why do you ask about men? You don't think women would lure her away or do whatever you think has happened to her?"

Hawke stared at the security guard. She had a chip as big as Chief Joseph Mountain on her shoulder. "No. As antsy as Lanie Porter was when I asked about Sherry and a man together here at the casino, I think she knows something."

"Lanie?" Abby scoffed. "She wouldn't care what happened to one of us. She would only care if a man bought us a drink over her."

"I see. She doesn't approve of Indians, but she frequents an Indian casino." Hawke was getting a better feel for the woman he was sure knew something.

"That woman is full of ironies." Dela said.

Abby glanced at her watch. "I need to get back to work."

"Go ahead. Thank you for meeting me." Hawke watched the woman walk out of the coffee shop. "Can you have Marty see if he can get a photo of the man who harassed Sherry? He knew where the cameras were and kept his cowboy hat tilted to hide his face. That right there makes me wonder about him. If I have a photo, I might be able to run him through facial recognition and get a name."

"I'll have him do that. My boss, Godfrey, said to cooperate with you all I can. He's had a cousin go missing from the rez." Her eyes saddened. "Most of the people on the rez have had a family member or friend either murdered or missing. And only a tenth of them are ever solved." Her eyes grew stormy. "You can bet if Ms. Lanie Porter were to go missing they'd have the

State Police and the FBI looking for her."

Hawke felt her frustration. He'd experienced it more than once while growing up on the reservation and trying to get someone to listen to the fact his stepfather was beating his mom.

"I won't quit until we either find her or know what happened. My sergeant says I'm like a bloodhound on a scent when it comes to finding the truth."

"I was an MP in the Army. There were times when we had little to go on, but we'd dig up the truth to make sure someone stayed behind bars or was kicked out of the military." She had a determined gleam in her eyes. "I'll help you anyway I can. Sherry is a nice person. Her disappearance isn't of her making. I'm sure of that."

Chapter Eight

Hawke left the casino with plans to be back there in the morning to talk to Kara. He didn't think the woman in the gift shop would have much to say, but he planned to visit with her on Friday evening. His pickup needed fuel. He drove over to the Travel Plaza and stopped at a fuel pump. There were over a dozen semi-trucks parked around the plaza. All but two he knew the companies written on the trailers or the vehicles.

Having worked this stretch of freeway for several years after becoming a Trooper, he knew the semis and the trailers pretty well. He could tell if a trailer was full or empty by how low it sat over the tires.

He stepped out, inserted a card into the pump, and started pumping fuel into his vehicle. As the fuel flowed, he studied the activity around the parked semis. A middle-aged, chubby Caucasian woman with blonde stringy hair walked up to a cab and knocked on the door. The door opened and she climbed up inside. That was how many women of all races across the country went missing. Working as prostitutes at truck stops. A trucker either took a shine to them and drove off with them or beat the shit out of them and dumped the women along the freeway.

Relaxing his curled fists, he finished fueling and drove through the trucks before heading back to his mom's house. She lived less than ten minutes away.

The house was dark when he arrived. A glance at his watch noted it was nearly midnight. He hadn't thought he'd stayed that long at the casino after talking to people. But he'd watched the activity. Who came and went. Mainly, he was watching for the man with the cowboy hat.

Dog met him at the door. "Hey boy. You been waiting up for me?" he whispered.

"I have, too." The light by the couch came on, and his mom sat in her bathrobe, looking older than he'd ever seen her.

"You didn't have to wait up for me," Hawke said, dropping down on the couch beside her.

"I wasn't. I couldn't sleep."

"If you couldn't sleep, why sit in the dark?" Hawke put his hat on his knee and studied his mom. She'd aged more since Sherry's disappearance than she had in ten years.

"I like sitting in the dark to do my thinking. Did you learn anything?"

"Yes and no. I've learned enough to know I need more answers. Did your group find anything yet?"

"No. We'll all go out tomorrow, well, today, to ask questions and put up flyers. Someone had to have seen something."

"We'll get some answers if we aren't too tired. Come on, let's go to bed." He stood, grasped his mom's hands, and pulled her to her feet.

"It's good having you here." She leaned her head on his arm before her slippers made scuffing sounds down the hallway.

He knew he never visited long enough. He really needed to fix that.

The first thing Hawke did in the morning was call Detective Lockland to see if anyone had canvased the grocery stores.

"We can't spare men to look for a woman that will walk back into her house any day." The man's comment pissed off Hawke.

He called Morning.

"Hello?" she answered.

"This is Trooper Hawke. If Sherry planned to pick up groceries after work, do you know which store she would have gone to?" He'd go to that store himself this morning before he went back to the casino.

"She would go to the outlet store. It's on the way home. Have you had any luck?" Morning asked, sounding hopeful.

"I'm following all the leads I've got so far. Thanks." He ended the call and walked into the kitchen where his mom was filling a shopping bag with snacks for her and her partner that would be there to pick her up in thirty minutes. He'd asked her where they were going to talk to people. He wanted to make sure nothing happened to her. Some would take this group's questions as butting in.

"I'm going to the outlet store to see if that's where Sherry stopped after work. Do you need anything from there?" He liked buying items for his mom. He didn't have anyone other than himself and his animals to spend money on.

"I could use more milk and bread if you're going to be around for a while," she said it like a question.

"I know I'll be here at least a week. More if we haven't found her."

"Thank you, son. While it will be good to have you around, I'm sorry for the circumstances."

"Me, too." He ate the eggs and toast she'd made for him, washing the cold food down with warm coffee.

"I'll pick Trey up from his friend's when we finish today." She had her items packed and sat at the table with a cup of coffee.

"I'll try to come home at a decent hour, but if I'm following leads…" He left the rest unsaid.

"I understand. Just let me know."

"I will." He swallowed the last of his coffee and put his dishes in the sink. "Talk to you later. Dog, let's go."

Dog jumped up from the rug he'd been laying on by the back door.

"Say hi to Betsy at the outlet. She's a nice lady. She always makes sure someone helps me out with my groceries."

"Thanks." And that gave him someone to start with at the store.

He pulled into the parking lot of the Grocery

Outlet. There were half a dozen cars. He walked in and asked the first clerk he came to for the manager. She picked up the intercom and called the manager to her checkout.

A short, stocky woman with black hair and old-fashioned glasses walked up to the check stand. He read the name tag on her apron. Betsy.

Holding out his badge, Hawke introduced himself. "And you are?"

"Betsy Hamilton. What can I do for you, Trooper?"

"Do you have surveillance tapes?" he asked.

"Yes, they are stored by the month here. You would need proper paperwork to see them. Why?" The woman led him away from the checkout as a customer pushed a cart up.

"Tuesday night, I believe Sherry Dale, a woman from the reservation, stopped here on her way home from work. She never arrived home. I'm trying to trace her movements that night."

Betsy nodded. "There's a Sherry who usually comes in right before I go home. Do you have a photo of her?"

Hawke pulled the photo his mom had given him out of his pocket.

"Yes, that's the Sherry I was thinking about. She stops in here at least once a week on her way home from the bank. When people are getting off work this place gets busy. I usually jump on a check stand and help."

"Do you know if she was in here on Tuesday?" Hawke asked, happy the woman remembered Sherry.

Betsy stared at the photo. "I think so. Let me get

Roger to come up. He was here checking that night."
She went to the intercom and called Roger to the check
stand where they stood.

A tall, broad man with a balding head and beefy
arms walked up to them. "What 'cha need, Betsy?"

"This is Trooper Hawke. He's asking if Sherry
Dale," she motioned for Hawke to show him the photo,
"was here on Tuesday night. Can you remember?"

"Yeah, she was here. Picked up the usual milk,
bananas, and a candy bar." He shifted his gaze from the
photo to Hawke. "Why are you asking?"

"She never made it home that night."

The man's chin dropped and his mouth sagged
open for only a second. "She was having a discussion
with a man right after I checked her out."

"Discussion? As in they were arguing?" Hawke
pulled out his notepad.

"Yeah, well, I'm not sure. They didn't shout or
anything like that, but she looked upset and he was in
her space, if you know what I mean."

"He was standing close and she didn't like it?"
Hawke asked.

"Yeah, kind of like that." The man rubbed a hand
over his shiny head.

"Do you remember what the man looked like?"

"I'd never seen him before. He had on nice clothes.
You know like a business man. Slacks, a sweater. I was
thinking, man he has to be sweatin' wearing that thing."

The man from the bank who had asked Sherry out
several times was the first person that came to his mind.
He'd have to flip back through his notes for his name.
And go ask him some more questions.

69

"Did they leave together?" Hawke asked.

"I don't know. I had customers to checkout." The man shrugged.

Hawke took down his name and the information from Betsy about getting the warrant to get the tapes. "Thank you. You've both been a lot of help."

"Do you think she's still alive?" Betsy asked just above a whisper after Roger walked away.

"I don't know. We can all pray and hope for the best." He purchased the items his mother requested and walked out of the store angry that the Pendleton Police hadn't done as he'd asked, and hopeful, he'd learn something from the banker.

Chapter Nine

Hawke sat in front of the bank waiting for it to open. He called Sergeant Spruel, updating him on what he knew and asking for him to write up a warrant for the surveillance tape from the store. He gave the specifics of the day and the store. Betsy had supplied him with the store number for that company as well.

"You believe this banker may have taken her?" Spruel sounded skeptical.

"I'm just following the leads. If he didn't, he may have seen someone else she talked to either in the store or out in the parking lot." He thought a minute. "Make sure the warrant is for tapes from any camera at the store, including any that might be outside."

"I'll make sure it's worded correctly. Where do you want the tapes sent?"

"The State Police Office here."

"Have you stopped in and told them what you're doing?"

"No. I didn't even think about that. I'm sure I'd get more help from them than the city police. I'll do that after I talk to the banker. Did you get Sherry's phone log yet?"

"I'll send it to OSP in Pendleton when I do. I have someone digging up the information on the woman you sent me last night." Spruel was efficient. Hawke liked the man and the fact his superior always had his back.

"Thanks. After I check in with OSP here, I have a couple of people to question at the casino. Send me a text when the tapes and other information are available."

"Will do. Good luck."

"Thanks."

Hawke ended the conversation as the bank doors were unlocked. "Stay here and guard the truck. I'll let you out to run when we go to the OSP Office." He roughed up the hair on Dog's back and exited the vehicle.

The second he stepped into the bank everyone's gaze landed on him. He took off his hat and walked over to the office where Wade Benson was seated behind a desk.

The man glanced up. His eyes narrowed and his jaw clenched before he stood and stretched a hand out. "Trooper. Have a seat. How can I help you?"

"I've been tracking Sherry's movements after she left work on Tuesday. She stopped at the Grocery Outlet. A worker there saw her having a 'discussion' with a man in slacks, a sweater, and tie."

"You think that was me? Phil wears sweaters and ties, not me." The man tapped a finger on the desk blotter in front of him. "You need to look closer to the reservation and stop harassing me."

Hawke studied the man. He was hiding something. His eyes were twitching and by the way his jacket jiggled, the man was bouncing a leg under the desk.

"I'm getting a warrant for surveillance tapes from the store. If I find out it was you she 'had a discussion with,' I'll send a car here to pick you up during work hours. You'll be cuffed and brought to the State Police Headquarters."

Benson swallowed. His gaze dropped to his hands, now bending and unbending a paper clip. He tossed the paper clip to the side and stared at Hawke. "It was me. I hurried out of here after I'd finished with Terrel. I wanted to try one more time to get her to come to a concert with me."

"Why'd you wear a sweater? Were you hoping people would think it was Phil she was talking with?" Hawke wanted to understand how much this man had thought out about being seen with Sherry.

"What? No! I knew I'd get lots of people looking at me if I went in *that* store in my suit. I had an old sweater in the back seat. I put that on hoping to cover up my good shirt. I know the kind of people who go into that kind of store."

Hawke studied him. "What kind?"

"You know."

"People who have less money than you and have to make it spread far enough to feed a family?" Hawke wondered at the man being so interested in Sherry when it was obvious he was a snob.

"That's not what I meant."

73

"Really? Why did the store clerk say you were having a discussion? He said he wouldn't say it was an argument but more than a conversation." Hawke flipped open his notepad.

"I said, I asked her to a concert. She didn't even hear me out before cutting me off. Then I asked her why she didn't like me. She said because of the way I treated people." He rubbed a hand over his face. "I treat everyone the same."

"Obviously not, if Sherry noticed and you thought you had to dress down to go in the store." Hawke stared at him. The guy would never see his flaw. "Did you see her go out to her car?"

"Yeah. I followed her out. Only she shouted at someone and headed that direction, so I didn't really see her go to her car." He leaned back in his chair. "I got in my car and drove home."

"Was the person she called out to a man or a woman?" Hawke asked, interested in following the woman's movements.

"A woman. Probably ten years older than Sherry. Dark hair. Dressed in nice clothes. She stood by a new car. One of those fancy ones. I thought, why would someone with that kind of money shop here."

Hawke stared at him. Did the elitist not even hear what he'd just said? He could see why Sherry brushed him off.

"What?"

"Thank you for your time." Hawke stood and strode out of the office and the bank.

In his pickup, he patted Dog's head. "I need to clear my head and talk to someone at OSP."

He hoped the surveillance video would also be of the parking lot. He knew now who the man was she'd talked to, but it wouldn't hurt to see who else might have been in the store at the same time as Sherry.

They drove to the west side of town and out to the new OSP building. He'd been here not long ago to drop off something at the forensic building on another case.

He entered the main building, flashed his badge, and asked to talk to the Lieutenant in charge.

"I'll give Lt. Keller a call and see if she's available," the trooper behind the plexiglass said.

"If she's not available then anyone who has authority around here."

The trooper narrowed his eyes and put the call through. He spoke, nodded, and spoke again before hanging up the phone. "Lt. Keller will be right out."

"Thank you." Hawke was trying to remember if he'd ever met a Lieutenant Keller.

"Hawke, it's been a long time."

He turned to the female voice and grinned. "Carol, I wondered what happened to you."

The Lieutenant gave him a hug and stepped back. "Where's the uniform?"

"That's what I'm here to tell you."

"Come on back to my office. We'll have some coffee and you can tell me what's up. How's your mom?"

"That's part of why I'm here."

The woman stopped, facing him. "Is her health going?"

"No. Nothing like that." By the time they were settled in her office with cups of coffee, Hawke had relayed why he was there and what he hoped to accomplish. "The City Police are jerking me around and half of the Tribal Police think the missing woman will show up at any time. But I've done my work. She is a woman who wouldn't take off on a whim or go partying. I suspect foul play."

"I'd go with your gut any time and I have on several occasions."

"Thanks." The two had met up during incidents where she'd followed his hunches and lead every time. He was happy she'd made Lieutenant. That had always been her goal to make it up the ranks. Hawke was where he wanted to be. Working the Fish and Wildlife division in the county that he'd wanted.

"Sergeant Spruel is requesting some video from the store where the victim was last seen. I told him to have it sent here along with the woman's phone record and a person of interest's information. Could you have someone give me a call when it gets here?"

"Sure. Anything else you need from us?" She jotted a note on a pad in front of her.

"Not yet. I'm still digging for information. I have a person of interest at the casino but his face is always hidden under his cowboy hat. Once I get a name on him, I'd like it run."

"We can do that. I'll give you Sergeant Johnson's email and phone. He'll help you with whatever you need." She handed him a business card from her desk.

"Thank you. I appreciate this."

"I know what a struggle it is to get help out on the reservation. Keep me in the loop." She stood. "I have a meeting to get to. Good to see you."

"You too. Thanks!"

He left the building and opened the pickup door, letting Dog jump out and inspect the bushes and relieve himself. While Dog enjoyed his outing, Hawke leaned his back against his vehicle and stared at the freeway down below. Anyone could pull off the freeway, do something illegal, hop back on, and never be seen again. Had that happened? But who would leave the freeway to go to a grocery outlet and then pick up a woman who would never have gone anywhere with a stranger?

"Come on. We need to get back on this case. The longer it takes to find her, the less likely we'll find her alive." That was a sour ball in his gut. If they didn't find her alive, what would happen to Trey? And his mom would be beside herself with grief.

Chapter Ten

Taking the freeway to the casino, Hawke kept his gaze on the bar pit. He wondered if he could get Carol to have a trooper drive along the freeway both directions and search the sides of the road for anything that might give them a clue if the woman had been abducted, raped, and discarded.

He drove off the freeway and turned onto the road running over the interstate and in front of the casino. There were over a dozen semi-trucks parked around the travel center. The casino owned the Travel Center and more acres between and behind both properties.

On a whim, he pulled into the center parking lot, did a slow drive-by of the trucks, and parked in front of the building. He wasn't sure why, but seeing so many semis off the road and parked here seemed odd. Granted it had been nearly twenty years since he'd patrolled this area and the casino had been half the size it was now, but it just felt as if there should be more trucks on the road and less sitting idle. He noticed a couple of trailers that had been sitting in the same spot yesterday. Hard to make a living driving truck if you sat too long in one place.

The door to the store swung open. A couple in their twenties exited, climbed up into a jacked-up Ford pickup, and rumbled around to the back of the building. The Oregon plate and local car dealership logo, along with the lack of anything that made them look like they were traveling, revealed that they were locals.

He had a suspicion they were scoring drugs from one of the truckers, but that wasn't his job at the moment. He didn't need to get caught up in a drug arrest when he needed to find Sherry.

However, this was Reservation land. He'd see if there was a drug task force looking into the Travel Center. If he believed the two were off to score from a truck, any other drug officer would think what he did and check it out.

He walked inside the building. There were shelves of knick-knacks and souvenirs, shelves with snack foods and staples, and shelves with items truckers or long-distance travelers might need. A corner had hats and t-shirts with Native American images. He walked to the refrigerated drink section and pulled out an iced tea. Then he snagged a small bag of jerky and walked up to the counter.

"Did you find everything you needed?" the woman who looked in her fifties asked as she scanned his drink.

"I did. Are there always this many trucks sitting around here?"

She glanced up from scanning the jerky. "We provide showers. And they like to walk over to the casino."

"During the day, wouldn't they be on the road to their destinations?" He'd over questioned, her eyelids dropped over her eyes and her lips made a firm line.

"That will be ten-sixty-nine," she said.

Hawke paid and walked out with his purchases. He should have talked about something else to make the woman feel more comfortable before questioning the trucks. He slid into his vehicle and opened the jerky, giving Dog a piece. "I blew it in there. I forget that even though I am one of them by blood, they don't know me and see me as an interloper." He sighed and started the pickup.

The drive from the truck stop to the casino was short. Maybe half a mile. An easy walk for a person who had been driving long hours in a truck. He could see the draw to park at the Travel Center, walk to the casino, get something to eat, and do a little gambling before heading out on the road again. There was also a parking area behind the casino for trucks. Last night he'd only noticed a few back there and today there weren't any. It seemed the truckers preferred to park down at the center.

He parked at the far end of the parking lot near a grassy area. Dog leapt out and started sniffing and lifting his leg on bushes. When he'd finished his business, the animal trotted back to the vehicle.

"In you go. I'll try to not be too long. Leave me some of that jerky." Hawke rolled down the windows and closed and locked the door before strolling across the half-filled parking lot.

A different valet stood inside the doors. It was a younger Umatilla man with earbuds. Hawke tapped him on the shoulder to get his attention.

"Yeah?" The man answered, pulling a bud out of his ear.

"Do you know if Kara Winter is here?"

The valet frowned. "How would I know that? Go talk to someone at the registration desk or security."

It was evident the older valet paid more attention to the casino activity than this man.

Hawke walked across the casino floor and up to the desk. The young woman he'd talked with the night before stood at the end of the counter. He was surprised to see her this morning after working the night before. She wasn't dressed in her uniform. He moved along the counter to her.

She glanced up and her eyes widened. "Did you find Sherry?"

"No, not yet. I'm surprised to see you here."

"I came in for my check. I'll put it in the bank and then go get some sleep."

He nodded. "Is Kara at work?"

"Oh, that's right, you wanted to talk to her. She should be. I'll call back to housekeeping." Abby picked up a phone and punched a button. She asked about Kara, replaced the phone, and faced him. "She's on the fourth floor, the northeast corner."

"Thank you." Hawke walked to the elevators, pushed the button, and waited for the doors to open. When they did, he stepped in along with an older man. Hawke pressed the fourth floor and the man pressed the sixth.

"You winning anything?" the man asked.

"I haven't been gambling," Hawke responded.

"I shouldn't be," the man said as the elevator stopped at the fourth floor.

Hawke stepped off and followed the hallway to the northeast corner. An open door had to be the room where Kara was working.

He knocked quietly and asked, "Kara Winter?"

The young woman swung around, her long braid whipping through the air. "Yes?"

"I didn't mean to startle you. I'm Trooper Hawke. I'm looking into Sherry Dale's disappearance."

"Oh, yes. Abby told me you wanted to talk to me." She glanced around the room. "Can we talk while I work? We aren't supposed to loiter in the rooms."

"I understand." Hawke leaned against the door jamb. "Do you remember anything about the man that followed Sherry into the coffee shop?"

She stripped the bed, tossing the sheets on the floor and picked up folded ones from a chair. "He had on a hat. He wasn't tall. Just average. Same with his build. I looked over once and he had a weird gleam in his eyes. After Sherry had told us about his trying to talk to her, I worried he was stalking her." She stopped. "Do you think he did something to her?"

"That's what I'm trying to find out. Do you think you could describe him to a sketch artist?" Between what she said and what Abby had said the night before, they might get a decent sketch of him.

"I just noticed his eyes before he ducked his head. Now that I think about it, he didn't want anyone to see his face. But I'm sure Sherry did." The woman gasped. "Do you think he's wanted and after she rejected him, he…"

"We won't know until I find either him or Sherry. Can you think of anything else unusual that day?"

She shook her head then stopped. "Not that day. But there's been twice, I know I've cleaned a room and I get reamed out when I come into work that when guests walked into a room it appeared to have not been cleaned. Like someone slept in it and used the shower."

Hawke pushed away from the door jamb. "Do you have the days and the room number?"

Kara sighed. "Just ask my supervisor. I'm sure it's on my personnel file that I missed a room."

"Are you the only one who has had this happen?"

"No. A couple other girls said they had the same thing happen to them." She stopped smoothing the bed spread and faced him. "Do you think someone has a master keycard and uses empty rooms?"

"That's something I'm going to go ask security. Thank you, Kara." Hawke pivoted to leave.

"Do you think Sherry will be alive when you find her?" Fear crept into her voice.

"I always look on the bright side." He smiled and headed to the elevator. First, he'd get the list of rooms and the dates, and then he'd pay a visit to the casino security.

<><><><><><>

Before barging through the door to the security rooms, Hawke walked up to a security guard to ask permission to talk to the head of security. He held out his badge for the guard to see and was escorted through a door to the right of the registration desk marked "Employees Only."

A short, squat male Indian with two long braids walked up to him. "Godfrey Friday, head of security. Dela filled me in when I came on this morning. How can we help you?"

Hawke immediately liked the man. "I have a list of dates and rooms that were reported uncleaned when guests were given the rooms. I talked to one of the housekeepers who says she knows she cleaned the rooms."

"You think we might have a freeloader?"

"Yes."

"Does this have anything to do with Sherry's disappearance?" The man studied him.

"I won't know until I see the surveillance tapes."

The man nodded. "Let's go talk to Marty."

"He's still here?" Hawke was surprised he'd be working with the same person.

"He stays in a room here. Since you asked about the man in the cowboy hat who followed Sherry, he's been collecting and putting all the footage of the man onto one thumb drive for you."

Hawke followed the head of security out of the room, passed the registration desk, across the gaming floor to the surveillance rooms. They walked through the main room and into the smaller back room.

"Trooper," Marty said, tapping on the keyboard in front of him.

"I heard you've been digging up more video on the cowboy hat guy." Hawke grabbed a seat and pulled it over next to Marty.

"I am. I have video on him from last December until now. I didn't see him in any footage a month prior to that so I quit looking." Marty handed him a thumb drive.

"Any of it show his face?" Hawke asked, handing him the paper with the days and rooms he wanted video on.

"A partial on a couple. But I did see a pattern. He made conversation with several younger local women. One of them has been missing for six months."

Hawke studied the man. "And now Sherry is missing after he harassed her."

"I have shown the best photo of him we have to my staff. If they see him, they are to bring him to security for questioning," Friday said.

Hawke nodded. "Good. He is definitely a person of interest." He pointed to the paper in Marty's hand. "These are dates and rooms that I think someone borrowed without anyone knowing."

"I'll work on it." He stretched. "But first I need to get some food and a few hours of sleep." Marty stood. He was tall, thin, and dressed in casual clothes. Hawke surmised it was his tech genius that made him head of surveillance.

"Do you mind if I look at this footage here?" Hawke asked, watching the man walk toward the door.

Marty backtracked. "Go ahead. You can use this set up." He flipped on a monitor, grasped the thumb drive from Hawke, and placed it in a tower computer. "Use this to move from section to section."

Hawke placed the computer mouse the man handed him on the top of the desk as a file with other files labeled in months appeared on the monitor.

"If you need to contact me for any reason, Godfrey has my number." Marty nodded to the head of security. "He'll keep an eye on you." Marty walked out of the room.

"I trust you. I have things to deal with elsewhere," Friday said, walking to the door.

Hawke wondered at how easily the head of security walked away from keeping an eye on him. He didn't plan to sabotage the casino, so he opened the most recent file and stared at the monitor.

Chapter Eleven

Three hours later, Hawke had four videos sitting by themselves in the folder. His eyes were aching from staring at the screen for so long. He didn't know how people could sit all day watching computer monitors. A glance at his watch and the growling in his stomach said it was time to get some dinner. He'd go let Dog out for a walk and then come in and grab something to eat. After that, hopefully, Marty would be back and he could ask for a still shot to be blown up of the man in the cowboy hat from the best of the four videos he'd selected. He also wanted Marty to show him the young woman that went missing six months ago. He thought he'd found her by the way the man had interacted with a young woman in one of the videos, but he wanted to make sure.

He had also selected five videos where Lanie Porter had been talking and hanging on the man in the cowboy hat. He wanted a photo of the two of them to see if he could jog her memory about knowing the man.

Stepping into the other room, he noticed everyone was alert and staring at one screen. He walked up behind the group and studied the events unfolding on the monitor.

Friday was standing beside a dealer at a poker table. Three people sat at the table. Two men and one woman. One of the men was sweating profusely and tapping a finger nervously.

"Did you catch someone cheating?" Hawke asked, making them all jump and look over their shoulders.

"Yeah," one of the women said. "I spotted him slipping a card out of his sleeve. Don't know why he thought it wouldn't get picked up."

In the video, Friday motioned to the cards and said something to the dealer. Whatever he said, the sweating man stood up as if to leave. A security guard had him by the back of his shirt.

"I'm going to walk my dog and get something to eat. Could you tell Marty when he comes back, I'll be back to show him what I found?" Hawke asked.

Two of the people, back to watching their own monitors, waved a hand. He took that to mean they heard and would relay the message.

Hawke opened the door to the surveillance rooms and caught a glimpse of Friday, the other guard, and the man caught cheating heading toward the security offices.

At the casino entrance, Hawke noted the young man had been replaced with the older valet.

"Good to see you back. Enjoying your time with us?" the man asked.

"Yes, I am." Hawke stepped out the door and shoved his ball cap on his head.

Because it was a hot day, he'd left the windows down on his pickup. As soon as he approached, Dog popped up and hung half out of the window.

"Come," he said, and the dog jumped down to the asphalt and trotted over to the grass. Hawke opened the door, tugged the seat forward, and pulled out a dog dish and a gallon jug of water.

"Bet you're thirsty. Sorry you have to hang out in the pickup." He poured water into the dish and set it on the ground. He scanned the area between the casino and Travel Center. There appeared to be fewer trucks than earlier.

The sound of lapping water ceased.

"Do you want more?" Hawke asked, grabbing the jug.

Dog sat beside the dish, his tongue hanging out.

"I'll take that as a 'yes.'" Hawke filled the dish again and watched as Dog drank half of the water.

"Get your fill?" He picked up the dish and placed it on the floor of the cab. Replacing the water jug, he put the seat back and scratched Dog's head and neck. "Do you feel like a little walk?"

Dog wagged his tail.

"Let's go." He set off across the parking lot towards the truck stop. He wanted to see if there were any paths from the casino to the center and if they were well used. They found two. One had more foot traffic than the other one. He followed it to behind the truck stop. At the end, in the tall grass before the asphalt, were used condoms and wrappers, needles, and empty beer bottles.

It appeared partying went on back here. How come no one checked this out? He'd ask Officer Red Bear about it. He walked among the semis parked in the area.

A cab door opened and a Caucasian man in his thirties with big biceps and a tight, dirty t-shirt swung down to the ground. "What are you doing sniffing around here?"

Dog growled and sprang in between the man and Hawke.

"Me and my dog are just taking a walk to stretch our legs." Hawke patted his thigh and Dog heeled.

"Which rig is yours?" the man asked, narrowing his eyes and crossing his arms.

"A vehicle over in the casino parking lot." Hawke stared back at the man.

"What cha doing clear over here?" The man uncrossed his arms and leaned forward.

Dog growled, showing his teeth.

"Down boy, he's not going to hurt me." Hawke patted Dog on the head. "We're walking. Saw the path from the parking lot to here and thought we'd exercise our legs. I didn't know I'd be trespassing in a public parking lot."

The man tilted his head. It was as if he didn't get the jab.

"Come." Hawke turned and walked away. Why was the man so jumpy about him walking around by the semis? He definitely needed to ask Red Bear about this place.

He followed the lesser traveled path back to the casino. It went around to the parking lot behind the building.

Back at his pickup, he opened the door. "I'm going to have to go back in there. You can take another nap."

He waved his hand, and Dog leapt onto the seat. Hawke shut the door, leaving the windows down. No one would dare try to get in the vehicle or take anything with Dog, a large-sized mutt who could look and sound ferocious, on duty.

His stomach was gnawing on itself as he reentered the casino.

"Forget something?" the older valet asked.

"Nope. Hungry. Where do you suggest I eat?"

"Try the Pony Bar and Grill if you don't want a lot of noise and cheaper menu."

"Thanks." He took a right and walked into the Pony Bar and Grill. The opening was in line with the entrance to the casino to the right.

He found a tall table for two in the back of the room and sat.

A waitress arrived with a coaster and a menu. "What would you like to drink?"

"Iced tea, please."

His phone buzzed as the waitress walked away. Spruel.

"Hawke," he answered.

"The warrant was handed to the manager of the Grocery Outlet in Pendleton this afternoon and the video was taken to OSP headquarters. You'll also find the phone records and information on the woman you asked about."

"Thanks. I'll go check it out in the morning."

"Are you getting any closer?" Spruel asked.

"Maybe. Learned today that a person of interest was seen talking to another young woman who disappeared six months ago."

"That's not a coincidence."

"That's what I think. I'm hoping to get a good enough photo of him or get a woman who knows him to give me a name tonight."

The waitress returned with his drink. Hawke set down the menu and pointed to a burger basket. She wrote it down and walked away.

"Keep me posted and let me know if you need anything else."

"I should be good. Turns out the Lieutenant over here and I went through the academy and worked a few incidents together. She's got my back if I need it." Hawke was grateful he had Carol on his side. She had always been a fair, but by the book, officer.

"You must mean Lt. Keller. Yeah, she's a good one. Glad to hear you two don't butt heads."

"Copy. I'll keep you in the loop."

They ended the call and Hawke sipped his tea watching the few people who were in the establishment.

The waitress returned with his burger. Just as he raised it to his mouth, Dela walked into the grill and straight toward him. He bit into his sandwich and chewed as the woman sat down at his table and a waitress brought over a cup of coffee.

He swallowed. "You're on duty early."

"Heard you were here and wanted to see if you needed any help." She sipped her coffee.

"I'm going to see if Marty can make me some stills from videos I looked at and I need to visit with Lanie

Porter. I found her conversing and snuggling with our guy in the cowboy hat several times."

"That doesn't surprise me. There aren't enough eligible men around here for her."

Hawke caught disdain in the woman's comment. "I take it you know Lanie beyond her visits to the casino?"

"I went to school with Lanie. She was very popular with the boys and not so much the girls."

"I see. She had a habit of taking boys away from other girls?" Hawke watched the woman's facial expression.

She winced as if a bad memory flashed in her mind. "Yeah. She didn't care if a couple were going steady or even engaged. If she decided at a party or dance that she wanted a certain boy, she went after him."

"What is she doing hanging around the casino? I'd think she would have sunk her nails into someone with money by now." Hawke took a bite of his burger.

"Oh, she did. He died about two years ago, leaving her a wealthy, lonely widow who has gone back to her ways of enticing horny males into her lair." Dela set her cup down so hard coffee sloshed out. She cleaned it up with a napkin, not looking at him.

Hawke had a feeling Lanie had seduced someone who meant a lot to Dela at some point.

"She prowls around here looking for excitement?" he asked, picking up his iced tea.

"Yeah, I guess you could call it that. Most nights she leaves alone. However, there are some nights we see who she leaves with." She tossed the napkin into her cup. "You ready to go make some still photos?"

He understood she was done talking about the other woman. "Sure." He slipped money under his basket and slid off the chair. "Lead the way."

Following Dela across the gaming floor, he couldn't help but notice how she carefully placed the prosthetic leg. But he had to give her credit, her pace never wavered. He wondered how long she'd been disabled. She seemed to not let it stop her. He'd wondered the same seeing her at her mother's house when it had looked as if she'd just come from jogging.

She pressed her ID card to the lockbox at the door to security and they walked in. It appeared to be a shift change as people gathered belongings while others settled into the chairs.

Dela opened the door into Marty's office. She took one step in and stopped. Hawke bumped into her back and scanned the room.

A man who screamed Fed from his shiny black shoes to his short-cropped hair and dark suit sat in one of the chairs talking to Marty.

Chapter Twelve

Marty glanced over as Hawke ushered Dela into the room and closed the door. "Trooper Hawke, meet Special Agent Pierce. He's from the Pendleton Field Office."

Hawke held out his hand and shook.

"I don't know who you talked to but I got the memo at noon to be here tonight, some hot shot trooper was trying to show up the tribal and local police," Pierce said.

Hawke crossed his arms and studied the man, trying to decide if he was joking or serious. "I'm trying to find a woman before the others will even start looking."

Pierce held up his hands. "Hey, I'm here to help. Lt. Keller called our office and said you were making headway even while the local P.D.s weren't calling it a missing person's case yet. I'm here to help. If that's what you want."

Carol. He should have known she'd use whatever clout she had to get him help. "If Lt. Keller sent you then I can use the help." Hawke took a seat next to Marty. "Did you find the videos I took out of folders?"

"Yeah. I have the stills over there." He pointed to three eight by ten photos sitting on the table to his right.

"Good. Any of them give us a decent view of the guy's face?" Hawke stood up and grabbed the photos.

"Not really."

"The other one. Of the man and Lanie Porter. Can you print one of those. I plan to have a talk with her tonight." Hawke watched as the skilled computer tech pulled up the video, selected a frame and had the printer whirring in seconds.

"Did you get any videos yet of those rooms?"

"What rooms?" Pierce asked, from behind him.

Hawke went on to explain about rooms being used after they'd been cleaned but before they'd been used by patrons.

He whistled. "That would mean either someone in housekeeping was letting someone use the master key or someone at the registration desk or someone made their own master keycard."

Hawke glanced over his shoulder at the man, then shifted his attention to Marty. "Is that possible to make a master keycard?"

Marty nodded. "That's why we have surveillance on all the floors. And to answer your question, no, I haven't had time to locate the video and look."

Hawke nodded. "I've kept you busy."

"I can bring in one of our techs to help you," Pierce offered.

Marty shook his head. "No outside people are allowed to use our equipment."

Just today Marty had allowed Hawke to use a laptop, but he wasn't going to say anything. He knew he was an exception. He was Mimi's son, an Umatilla member, and the first person to come to the aid of a missing woman.

"I'm going to hang out and wait for Lanie to arrive," Hawke said, standing and moving toward the door.

Pierce stood.

Dela stepped in front of Pierce. Her eyes narrowed. "Since when do the Feds care about a missing Umatilla woman?" Anger darkened her face and hardened her lips.

Hawke wondered if this FBI agent had been on the team looking for Dela's friend. "Come on, Pierce. I have a job for you."

The agent followed him out of the surveillance area and to the casino floor. "Thanks for getting me out of there."

"You and Dela have history?" Hawke asked, walking over to the older valet.

"A little. But I think it's more she just doesn't like the FBI. Since I work for them…" Pierce stopped beside him.

"Has Lanie Porter arrived yet?" Hawke asked the valet.

"Looks like she's headed this way now." The older man smiled. "You interested in keeping her company tonight?"

"Not me. My friend. But don't tell her. It's a

surprise." Hawke led Pierce away from the door and behind a bank of slot machines.

"What is this all about?" Pierce asked.

"The woman I'm going to point out to you is a person of interest. She knows the man I think had something to do with Sherry's disappearance. Lanie, the woman coming in now." He waited while Pierce got a good look at her. "She likes men with money. You, in your suit, look like a man with money. She's met me and I didn't take her bait."

Pierce studied him. "I take it she is a barracuda?"

"You could say that. Anyway, just keep her busy, talking, drinking. I'll come find you in an hour and pull out my photo of her and this man. I want to see how she reacts. I already know she won't answer me straight. Maybe after I leave, if she doesn't tell me anything, she might say something to you that will help us."

The man nodded. He undid his tie. "Long day and all that," he said, walking away from Hawke.

He hoped Lanie didn't peg Pierce as FBI.

After an hour of moving around the casino floor, keeping an eye out for the man in the cowboy hat, Hawke headed to the bar and grill.

Pierce and Lanie were cozied up at a tall table in a corner.

Hawke walked up, barely giving Pierce a once over, and slapped the photo of Lanie and the cowboy hat guy on the table in front of her. "Have you remembered his name yet?"

She startled at his actions. Her gaze landed on the photo and she immediately shifted it to her drink. "I told you before I don't know his name."

"But you know him. I have video of half a dozen times you and he were cozy in this bar on different nights. Are you telling me you can get cozy with a man and not know his name?" Hawke stared at her.

She twitched, kept her gaze on her drink, and didn't say anything.

"Hey, I think you need to leave her alone. She said she doesn't know anything." Pierce made as if to stand and defend her.

Hawke glared at him. "Did she ask you your name?"

Pierce glared back. "I offered my name just as she offered hers."

Slapping his hand on the photo before picking it up. "See. You should know this man's name. Don't you care that Sherry Dale's life could be at stake?"

The woman jumped when he'd slapped the table. She shook her head. "I'm worried about Sherry, too, but I can't help you." Her gaze never left her drink. Not even when Pierce stood up for her.

She was scared. He had a feeling the man in the cowboy hat had threatened her to keep her mouth shut.

"Her death is on you," Hawke said, shoving the photo in his pocket and striding out of the bar. Now he had to wait to see if she'd confide in Pierce. He was tired of wandering around the smoky casino floor. He asked a security guard to let him into the surveillance area. If he was lucky, Marty may have found something of interest in the case.

Dela joined Hawke in Marty's office. "Did you learn anything from Lanie?"

"Not me. I'm hoping she thinks Pierce is someone she can talk to." Hawke noticed anger or contempt, he wasn't sure which, flicker in Dela's eyes. She and the FBI agent did have more history than the Fed fessed to.

"I found part of the videos for the rooms that were used without permission," Marty said.

"Pull them up," Dela said. "This is as much a matter of interest to security as it is to Sherry's disappearance."

Marty started the first one. At 1:30 AM stamped on the video, two people approached and stopped at the door of the room.

"That's the man in the cowboy hat," Hawke said, leaning closer. "See that. He knows where the surveillance camera is and keeps his hat tipped so his face isn't seen. Do you know who that woman is?"

"Enlarge the image," Dela said.

The video zoomed in. "She's not a local. At least not one who frequents the casino. Marty, can you get a still of her face?"

"Yeah." Marty tapped the keyboard and within seconds the printer whirred. "Here's the next date."

"Damn! It's Cowboy Hat again. With another young woman." Hawke rubbed a hand over his face. "I'm seeing a pattern."

The fourth video, both Marty and Dela reacted.

"That's Meela Skylark who went missing at the time of this video." Dela stood. "That man has to be found."

Hawke shot to his feet. "I know the person to ask." He strode out of the room, across the other room, and out to the casino floor.

He strode to the bar and found Pierce sitting by himself. "Where's Lanie?"

"She excused herself to go to the restroom and hasn't returned."

"Shit!" He pulled out his phone and called Dela. "Dela."

"Hawke. Have surveillance see where Lanie went. She left the bar." He hung up. "Come on."

"Where are we going?" Pierce asked, pulling on his suit coat and tightening his tie.

"To find Lanie. The guy I asked her about was seen sneaking into a room with a young woman that went missing at that same time." He strode over to the nearest restrooms. As he stood there debating how to proceed, Dela passed him and walked into the women's side.

She came out within minutes. "She's not in there," Dela said into her mic. Then to Hawke and Pierce, "That's the last place they saw her on surveillance."

She cocked her head listening to whoever was talking to her through the ear bud attached to the microphone. Nodding, Dela said, "Lanie came out of the restroom dressed in a blonde wig, leggings, and a tunic. She didn't change her shoes. That's how they noticed her."

Hawke started to leave. Dela put a hand on his arm and asked into the shoulder mic, "Which direction did she go?"

Dela nodded and waved a hand toward the other side of the casino and the theater complex. "She went toward the theater then ducked out the side entrance. Cameras outside lost track of her. They believe Lanie must have stayed close to the side of the building."

"Take me to the door she went out." Hawke strode through the slot machines to the other side of the building. He stopped, waiting for Dela and Pierce to catch up. He noted Pierce kept his stride with Dela's.

"This door." The door Dela pointed to was an Emergency Exit with an alarm.

"Why didn't the alarm go off?" Pierce asked.

"Good question." Dela was on her mic asking to speak to Custodial Services.

Hawke shoved through the door with Pierce right behind him.

"What are you looking for?" the agent asked.

"Which direction she went." Hawke wished he hadn't parked so far away from the building. He could use Dog and a flashlight.

The door opened. "Here." Dela handed him a flashlight. "I have to stay here. Let me know what you discover."

"I will. Thanks." Hawke slowly swept the beam of light on each side of the door. He saw a faint scuffing of the dirt on the left side. "She headed that way." With the light on the ground, he studied the scuff marks and heel prints.

"That's the area where the semis and RVs park," Pierce said.

"Yeah. Looks like we'll be checking out who is staying in them." He lost the tracks at the cement walkway between the landscaping around the casino and the asphalt of the parking lot. "She was either picked up or is out there in one of those vehicles."

Pierce pulled out his badge. "Guess we narrow it

down. Want to do this together or split up?"

"Considering the suspicious trucker I ran into earlier today, let's check it out together. That way we have backup." Hawke pulled his badge out from under his shirt and they headed to the RV parked closest to the building.

Chapter Thirteen

Hawke entered the casino with Pierce.

"What do you want to do now?" the agent asked.

They'd checked all the trucks and RVs in the parking lot. No sign of Lanie or anyone who knew anything about her.

"We need to get her picked up as soon as possible. She could end up a victim." A thought came to Hawke. He walked over to the valet. "Is Lanie Porter's car still out in the parking lot?"

"Last trip I made it was."

"When was that?"

"Ten minutes ago."

Hawke glanced at Pierce. "Where's it parked and what's the model?"

"It's the teal mini cooper convertible. Walk straight out and you can't miss it. She always parks under a light."

"Thanks." Hawke and Pierce exited the casino, and

sure enough, the shiny teal car was like a beacon.

"I'm surprised she leaves the top down. Anyone could steal it," Pierce said.

Hawke chuckled. "Anyone who wanted it could grab some friends and lift it onto a trailer."

"She had to have called someone to pick her up." Pierce stood with his hands on his hips, scanning the parking lot.

Hawke watched a semi-truck pull out of the Travel Center. His phone buzzed. "Hawke."

"Dela. Our parking lot cameras picked her up walking toward the Travel Center."

"Copy." He shoved his phone in his pocket and took off across the parking lot at a jog.

"What's up?" Pierce asked. His fancy shoes keeping cadence with Hawke's boot heels hitting the asphalt.

"I'm getting my dog. Dela said the parking lot cameras picked up Lanie heading to the Travel Center." Twenty feet from his vehicle, Hawke whistled. Dog leapt out of the open window and ran to him.

"Come on, boy. We need to find a woman." Hawke glanced back at the casino. "I wonder if she ditched any clothes in the restroom."

"Not if Dela didn't come out of there with them in her hands."

Pierce knew the security guard better than he did. If he said the woman would have found them, then Lanie took everything with her. Which meant she'd done this duck and run before.

"Let's go." Hawke led the way to the path between the two businesses. Dog trotted ahead of him.

"How do you plan to find her?" Pierce asked.

"I'll go inside the store and look around. If I don't see her, I'll ask. Then we'll knock on semi doors."

As they approached the back of the truck stop's property, Hawke stopped. "You stay here in the dark, until I come back from checking inside."

"Why do I need to stay here?"

"Because, I'll have to charm the clerk. I can't do that with a Fed at my elbow, and if the people back here around the semis see you, they'll start shooting. I saw a drug deal go down back here this afternoon. This is where I ran into a burly driver who didn't like my walking around." He started across the asphalt toward the front of the building. At the corner, he glanced back but didn't see Pierce. He hoped the agent had enough sense to stay put.

Hawke and Dog walked through the door. There was a different clerk on duty. This was a young man, he guessed to be in his mid-twenties.

"How's it going?" the young man called out.

"Good. You?" Hawke continued to the refrigerated drinks and pulled out a soda. He grabbed a bag of jerky and some chips.

"It's been a slow night. I hate nights like this." The young man rang up his purchases.

"I hear ya." Hawke held out money. "Did a blonde lady come in here this evening? Long legs, wearing those tight legging things?"

The young man grinned. "If that had happened it wouldn't have been a boring night. She a friend of yours?"

"I met her over at the casino. She wandered off and

I thought maybe if she came in here, you might know her name." He raised an eyebrow as he picked up the bag with his purchases.

"Sorry. Only a few local women were in here. Good luck."

"Thanks." Hawke walked out, pulled the jerky out of the bag, opened it, and tossed several pieces to Dog. When a car pulled up to the front of the store and a man near Hawke's age stepped out, he walked over and handed him the bag with the soda and chips. "Enjoy."

The man looked in the bag and thanked him.

Hawke tossed the open jerky bag in the trash and walked to the back of the building. Before he reached the back corner, Pierce joined him.

"Anything?"

"The kid hasn't seen her tonight." Hawke walked up to the first semi and knocked on the driver's door.

The cab wiggled and a head popped out of the sleeper. "What'cha want?"

Hawke held up his badge. "Trooper Hawke. I'd like to search your truck."

"Hell. You want to what? I was sleeping. I need to be on the road by five in the morning." The man crawled out in a t-shirt and boxers. He opened the door and studied Pierce holding up his badge. "Shit. I just pulled in an hour ago. I need to get some sleep."

The man looked as if he'd been driving for days without sleep.

"What are you hauling?" Hawke asked.

"Furniture that's to be delivered to Portland tomorrow by noon."

"Anyone in the sleeper with you?" he asked.

The man stared at him. "No. I was sleepin' and I'm a happily married man." He showed his left hand and the ring on his finger.

"Sorry to bother you." Hawke closed the door and watched as the man climbed back into the sleeper.

They continued on down the line, finding either empty cabs or sleeping drivers, until they came to the spot where his burly truck driver friend had been earlier. The spot was empty. "Guess the guy who was threatened by my presence earlier today is gone." Hawke walked by his empty spot wondering what he'd been hauling that had him jumpy. The company name wasn't one he was familiar with.

After going to each truck, they didn't find Lanie. His gut told him she was in trouble. Why else would she have left like she did?

They walked back to the casino on the path. At the parking lot, Hawke held out his hand. "It was good meeting you and I look forward to working with you."

Pierce shook. "Likewise. I'll get Lanie Porter's description out on NCIC. That way every law enforcement entity will be looking for her."

Hawke stared at him. "You need to do that for Sherry Dale."

"I already did as soon as I was told what was going on here." Pierce nodded toward the casino. "What do you need me to do tomorrow?"

"I'm going to OSP to look at video surveillance from the store where people last saw Sherry. They also have her phone records and info on Lanie Porter. I'll be going over that in the morning."

"I'll see you there at nine." Pierce walked off.

Hawke patted Dog's head and they walked over to his pickup.

The lights were still on at his mom's when he parked in the driveway. One extra car sat in the driveway.

He and Dog let themselves in the front door. Talking in the kitchen drew him through the house.

Mom and another woman were drinking coffee and eating cookies.

"Gabriel, I'm glad you made it home before Thelma left." His mom stood, grabbing a cup and filling it with milk. She placed it on the table in front of a chair.

"Thanks. Pleased to meet you, Thelma," he said, sitting and picking up a cookie from the plate in the middle of the table.

"Mimi has told me so much about you, I feel like I know you already." The woman's smile lit up her eyes.

"What are you two talking about so late at night?" Hawke asked.

"We wrote down what the other teams told us that they'd learned today," his mom said.

"Was there anything helpful?" He picked up the paper laying on the table.

"Robert and Tiny talked to a man who said he was at the Travel Center that night when a car he thinks was Sherry's raced around to the back of the store. He said when he came out, it was loaded on a car carrier. He figured the person had been late getting there to deliver their car."

"Did they get the name of this man?" Hawke read

down the sheet looking for the names and information Mom said.

"Yes. It's there." She pulled the paper down and plopped her finger on a spot about two-thirds down the page.

"Good. Anything else?"

"Some were wondering if this had anything to do with Meela Skylark's disappearance." His mom stared at him.

"When did she go missing?"

Thelma pulled out a photo. "She was my granddaughter. She went missing six months, one week, and five days ago."

Hawke stared at the face of the young woman Cowboy Hat had taken into a hotel room without registering. He peered into the older woman's eyes. "I believe it does. A person of interest was seen talking to both the missing women."

Tears shone in the woman's eyes. "If you find out what happened to Sherry, we could find out what happened to my Meela?"

"I believe so." He took the woman's hand and held it. "I'm doing everything I can. A friend of mine called in a Federal Agent. He was helping me tonight."

The woman spit to the side. "Feds. They never do anything to help. When Meela went missing, they just took down the information and left. No one. Not the Tribals or anyone tried looking for her."

"We did. Members of the community did the same as we did today. We asked questions and put out flyers. But any information we gathered and gave to the police they just looked at and didn't follow up." His mom also grasped one of Thelma's hands. "This time we can make them see it matters to start as soon as someone is missing. Look what Gabriel has learned and the police are still waiting for their seventy-two hours to start doing anything."

"We gained some solid leads tonight. And tomorrow morning I'll be looking at surveillance tape from the grocery store." Hawke stood. "I'm tired. See you in the morning Mom. Thelma it was good to meet you. I hope we can solve your granddaughter's disappearance as well." He walked out of the kitchen, the burden of two young women's disappearance on his mind.

Chapter Fourteen

The next morning, true to his word, Special Agent Quinn Pierce was waiting for Hawke at the OSP building.

"The young woman missing from the reservation six months ago, were you the one who took down the information?" Hawke asked. If Pierce had been the one, why hadn't he given it as much attention as he was giving Sherry's case? Was it because Lt. Keller called him or because Hawke had done most of the leg work?

"Six months ago, I was on a case back East. I didn't know there had been a report." Pierce stopped and grabbed Hawk's shirt sleeve. "Is it the young woman we saw your cowboy hat guy take into a room and you asked for confirmation if it was the other missing woman?"

"Yes. Meela Skylark. I met her grandmother last night at my mom's house. She has nothing good to say about the Feds or the Tribal Police. Everyone in law enforcement ignored her. She and tribal members went out putting up flyers and asking around. They didn't come up with anything. The young woman is still missing and her family has no idea what happened to her. The grandmother said an FBI agent came and took down the information about Meela and they never saw him again." Hawke pulled the side entrance to the building open and walked in. "My mom and other community members canvassed the reservation yesterday. They discovered a man who saw a car like Sherry's drive in fast and go around the back of the Travel Center building the night she went missing. When he came out, the car was on a car hauling trailer."

"You think whoever kidnapped Sherry brought her to the truck stop and then sold her car?"

"It sounds like it."

"Hawke, Quinn, good morning," Carol met them as they came abreast of the breakroom. "We have the tapes and other information you wanted set up in here." She led them to one of the interview rooms. "Sorry, it's all we had."

"This will work. Thanks." He noticed there was a carafe of coffee and two cups. All they needed was a bag of cookies and they were set.

"Lieutenant, do you have any of the information about the woman who went missing six months ago?" Pierce asked Carol.

"I don't remember anything about that," Carol said.

Hawke growled and they both stared at him. He relayed to Carol what he'd learned about another woman since looking for Sherry.

"And no one has been looking for her?" Carol

asked. Her hands were on her hips. She looked like a mama bear ready to take on anyone who came near her.

"As far as I can tell the Fed who took down the information, never did anything." Hawke stared at Pierce.

"I'm going to see what I can get on that case." Pierce pulled out his phone and walked to a corner of the room.

"You think the two are connected." Carol watched Hawke.

"Yeah. The same guy with the cowboy hat was seen with both. Meela, the night she disappeared. I'm going to have Officer Red Bear go talk to the family and see what else we can learn that might be the same, other than the casino."

"Good idea. I'll leave you to this." Carol left and Hawke pulled out his phone.

"Officer Red Bear," the man answered.

"This is Trooper Hawke. I have reason to believe the disappearance of Meela Skylark could be related to Sherry Dale's disappearance."

Red Bear cursed.

"Yeah. I'd like you to go talk to Meela's family. We need to see what similarities we can find between the two."

"I can do that. When Meela went missing all they did was call in the FBI and that agent didn't want to be here." The resentment in the officer's voice told Hawke what he felt toward the FBI.

"Also, is there a drug task force staking out the Travel Center?" Hawke didn't want to step on any toes if that turned out to be where the cowboy hat guy was coming from. He had a feeling, since the guy wasn't around all the time, that he was a trucker.

"There is supposed to be someone keeping an eye on the place. Why?"

"I'm sure a drug deal went down there yesterday. When I walked back around the trucks, I was warned to stay away by a burly driver who drove for a company I've not heard of before." Which reminded him to have Pierce look into the company.

"I'll talk to the Chief. He'll send someone out there—"

"I don't want them rousted yet. I just thought there might be someone who watched the center on a regular basis who could give me info on the trucks and drivers." Hawke interrupted him.

"You think a trucker is taking our women?" Anger punctuated the words.

"I'm not certain, but a person of interest who Special Agent Pierce and I wanted to question disappeared and her tracks led us to the travel center."

Red Bear cursed again. "Many of us have mixed feelings about the casino. The profits have given us more organizations and better facilities for our medical help, but it has also brought in people who abuse our land and our people."

"Go talk to Meela's family and don't tell anyone what I've told you. The fewer who know the easier it will be to catch the person." Hawke hung up as Pierce walked over to him.

"Special Agent Dobbs said he didn't see any reason to follow up when he'd learned the woman's boyfriend was a musician." He rolled his eyes. "There are incompetent members of every law enforcement group."

Hawke nodded. "Can you see if you can learn anything about this trucking company?" Hawke read the name off from his notes. "I've never heard of them and it's the company the guy who didn't like me looking around was driving for."

"I'll get on it." Pierce wandered back to the corner he'd occupied before.

Hawke sat down to the laptop with a flash drive on top. He put the drive in the slot and the screen came to life. A few clicks and he opened up the video marked *Inside*. He fast forwarded to 5:30 p.m. and then slowed down to check out everyone who entered and left the store. He spotted Sherry entering. She nodded to a couple. Then hurried about the store retrieving the items she came for. Leaving the checkout, she had her discussion with the banker. The clerk had been correct. It wasn't an argument. Just the two trying to get their points across. She left, and he followed immediately.

Clicking out of that video he opened the one marked *Parking Lot* and fast forwarded to the time Sherry arrived at the store. When he spotted her walking toward the store, he slowed the speed and watched the cars coming and going. Lanie Porter's fancy little convertible pulled into the parking lot three cars over from Sherry's.

Sherry walked out of the store in a hurry. She glanced over her shoulder, then as she hurried forward, waved and shouted. Lanie waved back. Sherry walked over to her, they talked, and Lanie got into Sherry's car and they drove off.

That was why the woman had rabbited last night. She was up to her eyeballs in Sherry's disappearance. He fast forwarded. The store closed and the teal convertible was the only car in the parking lot. At two in the morning a car pulled up beside it. Hawke slowed the speed. Lanie got out of the car, entered hers, and started it up, driving away. The other car followed.

He backed it up and no matter how hard he stared, he couldn't see who the driver was. He wrote down the car color, make, and model. He didn't see a license plate on the front or the back. Another dead end.

"Damn!" He leaned back in the chair.

Pierce came over. "What did you find?"

"Lanie Porter was part of Sherry's disappearance. We need to find her to get answers." He went back to the point on the tape that showed Lanie getting into Sherry's car and ran it forward to the other car dropping the woman back off.

"I can see if my tech guys can get facial recognition on the driver." Pierce pointed to the screen.

"You can't see whoever the driver is. What did they say about the trucking company?"

"It's owned by several different corporations. They are still digging through the red tape."

Hawke stared at the agent. "Isn't it odd for a trucking company to have multiple corporations owning it?"

"Not necessarily. These days corporations look for places they can lose money. You know, for tax deductions. But a trucking company would be the least likely of a place."

Standing, Hawke slipped the flash drive in his

pocket and grabbed the folder with the other information. "Let's go see if we can find Lanie. I have her address."

They walked out of the building and stopped between the two vehicles.

"You driving, or am I?" Pierce asked. "It doesn't make sense to drive separately."

Knowing they'd end up back on the reservation at some point, Hawke pointed to his pickup. "I can get more people to talk to me if I don't drive up in a government vehicle."

Pierce nodded. "Do I need to get out of my suit?"

Hawke studied him. "You can do that while on duty?"

"If it makes obtaining information easier, I will."

"I have to say, you are the first Fed I've come across who actually seems to care about justice on the reservation." Hawke slid in behind the steering wheel of his pickup.

"I joined the FBI to help make a difference. To me that means doing my job anyway I need to. I'll grab my bag and run in and change out of this suit."

Hawke nodded, opening the file that had been left for him. He scanned Sherry's phone records. The last call she made was at noon. He recognized it as Morning's number. The other bank teller had confirmed the call. They had been talking about the baby shower. Nothing else in or out since that call. Going over the list of numbers, she'd only called the bank, his mom, Morning, Silas, and the neighbor, Debra. Sherry had led a very secluded life.

He moved on to the report on Lanie Porter.

Daughter of a local rancher and aspiring politician. She went to school in Pendleton and college in Portland. Came back here, married an older man, he died leaving her a rich young widow. She opened a clothing store. It was Friday. She should be at work. If she wasn't there, they'd go to her place and then her parent's.

Pierce came out of the OSP building followed by Lt. Keller.

Hawke stepped out of the vehicle. The scowl on Carol's face meant there was bad news.

Pierce threw his bag into his car. He was dressed in a long-sleeved plaid shirt, open over a t-shirt, jeans, and cowboy boots. Hawke had to admit he looked like he'd fit in around here.

"Hawke, Mr. Wilson, Lanie's father just called. He wanted to report his daughter as missing."

He couldn't help himself. "Has she been missing seventy-two hours?"

Carol glared at him. "I know that it is eating at you that no one will move a finger to help with Sherry Dale's disappearance until tonight, but this is a person who can make life hell for us if we don't do something."

"We're headed to her store and residence right now anyway." Hawke motioned for Pierce to get in the pickup.

"Keep me posted on what you find. I'll tell Mr. Wilson we're working on it." Carol pivoted and strode back into the building.

Hawke slammed his hands on the steering wheel, letting out the frustration that was perking inside.

"Just keep digging for the answers to Sherry. We

know Ms. Porter had something to do with it. She's probably on the run."

"She's our only lead unless the guy in the cowboy hat comes back to the casino." Hawke started the vehicle and pulled out of the parking lot, headed to the clothing store in downtown Pendleton.

Chapter Fifteen

The clerk at the clothing store said Lanie hadn't shown up that morning and hadn't called. She'd been trying to call her to ask about an order, but the owner wasn't answering her phone.

A knot twisted in Hawke's gut. He had a bad feeling about the woman's disappearance.

"Let's go see if she grabbed clothes and took off," Pierce said, as Hawke pulled away from the curb in front of the store.

"I hope there are signs of her leaving quickly." He drove to the Southgate area. Pulling up in front of the house, he spotted a woman standing on the porch. The build was similar to Lanie's.

He and Pierce exited the vehicle and walked up to the woman.

She studied them and held out her hand. "I'm Mrs. Wilson. Lt. Keller said you'd be coming by to see if you can figure out what happened to my daughter."

Hawke shook hands even though he still had aggravation gnawing at his insides. If it weren't for his mom calling him, Sherry Dale wouldn't have anyone looking for her, yet this woman's daughter had barely been missing twelve hours and she had the State Police looking into it.

"Trooper Hawke and Special Agent Pierce," Pierce said, taking her hand. "Could you open the house so we can have a look around?"

She smiled at Pierce and unlocked the door.

"Ma'am, we'd appreciate it if you stayed out here," Hawke said, leading the way into the house.

It was a far cry from the trailer Sherry and Trey lived in. It was so new you could smell the paint and wood. Hawke headed for the bedroom to look in the closet and see if any clothes were missing.

Pierce peeled off into the master bathroom.

Three suitcases stood side by side on the top shelf of the closet. The hanging clothing didn't have any spaces and there were only two empty hangers. He walked over to the dresser and pulled open the drawers. Clothing was neatly stacked. It didn't appear to have had any taken out in a hurry.

He dug around, looking for a diary or documents.

Pierce entered the bedroom. "There doesn't seem to be anything missing."

"Here too." Hawke sighed and headed out of the room and into one that appeared to be an office. "See if you can find a phone bill. That will give us access to her phone information and we can pull her records. See who she's been calling. Maybe even find out where she is with GPS."

Hawke found her bank statements. He rifled through them to six months ago. A sum of $5,000 was put in her savings two days after Meela went missing.

He pulled out his phone and dialed Carol.

"Lt. Keller."

"Hawke. We need warrants to get Lanie Porter's bank records. She deposited five grand two days after Meela Skylark went missing. I bet she did the same a couple days after Sherry disappeared. Nothing is gone from her closet or dresser. I've got a bad feeling she went to the person who paid her for help."

"I'll get those records. Don't you dare say what you just told me to Mrs. Wilson or anyone. Not until we have confirmed it to be true." Her order rankled, but he understood her position. She had to work with the father and his friends in the area.

"It's between us until I get my hands on her." Hawke hung up and glanced at Pierce. "What are you reading?"

"Her date book has initials and cryptic wording. Why would someone who had nothing to hide do that?" Pierce held the book up for Hawke to study.

"Bring it with us." Hawke strode out of the house.

Mrs. Wilson stood on the porch. "What did you find out?"

"She didn't take anything with her." Hawke walked over to his pickup and slid in behind the steering wheel.

His next stop was the truck stop. With Pierce as back-up, he was ready to question every single driver.

<><><><><><>

At the truck stop, Hawke parked in front. "Let's

walk in separately and see what's going on inside, then meet up outside and talk with the truckers."

Pierce nodded, remaining in the vehicle as Hawke exited and walked into the store. There were more customers wandering around at mid-day than at night. Travelers grabbing snacks and souvenirs. The clerk was the middle-aged woman who'd shut down on him the day before. He grabbed a bottled iced tea, bag of chips, and a hot dog. It was near noon and he was hungry.

He waited in line behind a man who smelled of diesel fumes and sweat. The guy was fidgeting. Couldn't just stand and wait, he shifted his purchases from arm to arm, moved his feet side to side.

"Got a deadline?" Hawke asked.

The man swung around. His eyes were wide and vibrating. His dilated pupils stared as if he didn't see Hawke.

Pierce sauntered by the line as Hawke asked again, "Got a deadline? You act like a trucker with somewhere he needs to be."

The guy nodded. "Yeah. I got a load that has to be in Spokane by tonight."

Studying the trucker's eyes and nervousness, it was obvious he was on something and shouldn't be driving. "Good luck getting that load there on time."

The trucker nodded and moved up to pay for his things.

A couple stood behind Hawke. The man whispered, "He looked too strung out to be driving."

Hawke twisted sideways and quietly said, "Have your wife pay for your goods while you see what truck he gets in. Write down the license plate and company, then call the State Police and report him."

The man nodded. He handed all the stuff to the woman with him and when the trucker left, he followed.

"We won't get in trouble for calling, will we?" the woman asked as Hawke walked up to the counter.

"You'll save lives." Hawke smiled at the grumpy woman behind the counter. "How's your day going?"

She grunted at him, rang up his purchases, and mumbled, "Eight-ninety-seven."

He gave her a ten and pulled out his photo of Sherry. "Have you seen this woman around here?"

The clerk narrowed her eyes. "Why are you waving Sherry Dale's photo around?"

Hawke pulled out his badge. "Because I'm trying to find out what happened to her."

"I heard she was missing. She only came in here once in a while to buy smokes for Grandfather Thunder when he was at the casino." The woman handed him back his change and looked around him to the woman who was next in line.

Hawke gathered up his items and moved to the side. "Did anyone ever talk to her when she was in here?"

The clerk scanned the woman's items. "Not that she'd pay any attention to. A couple of truckers tried to talk to her one time. But she ignored them."

"Were they rude?" Hawke wanted to know what went on in here.

She recited the price to the customer. "I don't allow for no bad talk to our girls. I told the truckers to shut their mouths or leave."

Hawke nodded. "I thank you for that. Did they follow her out of the store?"

"No. They bought tokens to take a shower." She handed the customer her purchases and the woman left.

Pierce stepped up to the counter.

"*Qe'ciyéw'yew'*," Hawke said, grabbing his lunch items and walking out the door. He leaned against the side of the pickup eating the hot dog, waiting for Pierce to exit.

"Whatever you said before leaving, got the clerk all worked up," Pierce said, opening his bag and pulling out a packaged sandwich.

"I thanked her in Nez Perce." He shrugged. "Just because I don't live on the rez doesn't mean I don't retain what I've been taught."

"I heard what you said to that couple. That trucker looked dangerous behind a wheel." Pierce bit into the sandwich and grimaced. He spit the bite back into the package and pulled out a bottle of water.

"Yeah. It would be better if they turn him in than us. I didn't want anyone seeing us wandering around by the trucks before we were ready." Hawke opened the bag of chips and started crunching them down.

Pierce opened a bag of chips. "Are we showing our badges to talk to the truckers?"

"Not if we can help it. I think if we pretend to be truckers who pulled in here for the first time, we might get more out of them." Hawke crumpled up his empty chip bag and tossed it in the bag with the paper boat from his hot dog. He tossed that into the garbage can, twisted the top off his drink, and walked to the side of the building.

Pierce dumped his trash and followed. The first truck was locked up, no sign of a driver. The second truck the driver sat behind the wheel filling out a logbook. His truck was idling to keep the air-conditioning running while he sat.

The driver rolled down his window. "Yeah?"

"We just parked and wondered if this is a safe place to leave our truck while we wander over to the casino?" Hawke asked.

"It's as safe as any other truck stop on the freeway. If you have a fancy truck or a load of high-end stuff, you'd have surveillance cameras over at the casino parking lot." The driver started to raise his window.

"You're saying this isn't a safe place to spend the night?" Hawke asked.

The man nodded and closed the window.

They walked to the next truck. It was a female driver. Pierce took the lead.

"Hi. We just parked and wondered if this is a good place to leave our truck while we go to the casino?" Pierce sprung a tooth sparkling smile and the woman patted her hair.

"If you don't have anything worth stealing, you're safe. Me, I carry low-end cargo that no one wants and I truck on a low budget. No one bothers me."

"But you've seen shady things go on here?" Pierce asked.

Hawke glanced down the line of trucks and saw the burly guy from the day before.

"Yeah. There's a truck that sits here a lot. I think he's dealing. Then there's a group that steals from the cargo in some trucks. I've seen them offloading in the middle of the night when I've pulled in late."

"Doesn't anyone call the cops?"

"It's better to let whoever you're hauling for collect insurance than deal with the cops."

Hawke tapped Pierce's arm as the burly guy headed their direction.

"Thanks for the information. I think we'll move to the casino parking lot." Pierce faced him.

Tipping his head towards the man approaching them, Hawke walked out to meet the trucker.

"What are you doing sniffing around here again?" The trucker asked.

"I'm trying to figure out what it is you're trying so hard to keep me from seeing."

The man looked over his shoulder.

Hawke didn't see anyone coming. He also realized Pierce had disappeared. "Want to show me your truck?"

"Get the fuck out of here." The trucker swung at him. Hawke ducked the fist and twisted to wipe the attacker's feet out from under him with a leg sweep.

The burly man landed hard on the ground. Hawke didn't have any handcuffs, but he had a knife in his right boot sheath and his backup Glock in his left boot sheath. He'd started for his knife when he spotted a 9mm sticking out of the back of the man's waistband. He grabbed that and stuck it in the man's face. "I don't like it when someone tells me where I can and can't go." He grabbed the back of the trucker's shirt. "Get up!"

The trucker rose to his feet.

"Let's go have a look at your truck." Hawke racked the slide of the 9mm to see if there was a bullet in the chamber. The sound made the trucker flinch. "Move it."

The man started walking. Hawke followed, scanning the area for Pierce.

Seeing the cab again, Hawke realized this was the truck he saw leaving the travel center last night when he and Pierce walked over from the casino. "Where did you go last night that you are back here so early today?"

The man didn't say anything.

Hawke did a quick scan of the area, still no sight of the FBI agent.

"Open your cab." He shoved the gun in the man's back.

The trucker dug in his pocket for longer than was necessary.

"Pull the keys out, or are you waiting for an accomplice to show up?" Hawke kept the weapon pressed to the man's back and dug in the opposite pocket, finding the keys. "Funny how you forgot which pocket you put the keys in."

He glanced around again, hoping Pierce would show up to watch the trucker or search the cab.

"You steal my truck I'm calling the cops," the trucker said.

"I don't want your truck. I want to see what you're trying to hide." He pulled the man away from the cab and over to the back end of the cab chassis. "Don't move. I'd rather put a bullet in you than fight with you."

Two bungee cords held the air hoses up. He undid those while holding the handgun on the man. He wrapped a bungee around the trucker's wrists, tying his hands behind his back, then toppled him to the ground and bungeed his feet together at the ankles.

Once the man was trussed up, Hawke unlocked the cab and looked around. The sleeper smelled of perfume. Not the cheap kind prostitutes wore. It was expensive. A fragrance he'd had a whiff of recently. Where he wasn't sure.

He checked the logbook. The man had been parked here since Monday. But he'd seen him leave last night. That trip wasn't in his logbook. He pulled out his notepad and wrote down the VIN number, the driver's number, and the phone number on the business cards in the ashtray. He also scanned the trip sheet to see what he was carrying. It said furniture.

No drugs in the cab. Nothing he could find that was illegal. He climbed out, leaving the gun and the keys in the cab.

"Hope you find someone to help you out of those cords," Hawke said, closing the door on the semi and heading to the front of the building.

Chapter Sixteen

Returning to his vehicle, Hawke climbed in behind the steering wheel. Five minutes later Pierce came around the side of the building.

"Where the hell were you?" Hawke asked, starting up the vehicle as the FBI agent slid into the passenger side.

"I didn't want him to see me if we needed to roust him again. I saw you had things under control and continued down the line asking questions."

Hawke pulled out of the Travel Center and headed to the casino. "What did you learn?"

"That trucker and his truck have been here all week. One other guy who said he was here on Monday saw the truck sitting in the same spot as he found it when he came back here today. He wondered how that trucker makes any money sitting in one spot all the time."

"He left here last night when we were walking

from the casino to the travel center," Hawke said. "And his sleeper smelled of perfume. Not the cheap stuff."

He felt Pierce's gaze on him. Hawke glanced over as he turned into the casino parking lot. "Did you happen to see what type of perfume Lanie wears?"

"Yeah. She had a bottle of Jade something. I didn't look at it more than a glance. Didn't think her perfume would be necessary."

"It's almost two. I need to go have a chat with the woman in the gift shop. And see if Dela has learned anything more about the guy in the cowboy hat." Hawke parked and exited his vehicle.

Pierce was beside him as they entered the casino. The younger valet stood at the stand with his earbuds in. He didn't even notice their arrival.

Before Hawke crossed the casino floor headed to the gift shop, a security guard stepped in front of him.

"Godfrey wants you and your pal to come to Marty's office."

Hawke nodded. He and Pierce changed direction and followed the security guard to the locked door. The guard held the door open. They walked into the room full of monitors and across to Marty's office.

Friday waited for them. "Have you learned anymore about Lanie?"

"She's missing." Hawke glanced at the monitors.

Marty spun in his chair. "She spent two nights in a room with Cowboy Hat."

Hawke swore and stared at the video playing. "Did you notice if the man in question contacted Meela Skylark before the night he took her to the room and she disappeared?"

"The month before, I found him talking to her in the sports bar." Marty handed him a photo.

"What was the day and time this happened?" The bartender would have had a good look at the guy as many times as he'd been in the casino.

"I've been going through footage and from what I can tell the guy comes in late afternoon and stays until early morning, if he uses a room, or leaves around one."

A thought slapped Hawke. "When did he, or they, come out of the room the night he went in with Meela?"

"That's what I can't figure out. There is no sign of him or her coming out of the room before a couple enter the next afternoon."

Hawke studied Marty and Godfrey. "You have someone in surveillance who is tampering with the camera and someone from security who could be helping Cowboy Hat gain access to the rooms."

"I can vouch for all of my staff." The head of security's face deepened in color and his eyes shot daggers at Hawke.

"I'd like a list of all your employees. Security and surveillance," Pierce said. "I'll run them through the federal database."

Friday grumbled. "You'll have to go over to the security offices. I can have someone make a copy of them for you to pick up." Friday pulled out his phone.

Marty tapped on the computer. "What email do you want them sent to?"

Pierce rattled off an email address.

"Can you tell me the bartender on duty in the sports bar the last night the guy in the cowboy hat was here?" Hawke wanted to get this cleared up. There were now three women missing, if you counted Lanie. He had a bad feeling she'd ran to the man for help and he'd silenced her.

"It's Dexter Bane. He'll be in tonight at seven," Marty said.

Hawke nodded. "Is Teresa Berth working the gift shop now?"

The monitor on the left switched to the gift shop. "Looks like it."

He glanced at Pierce busy messing with his phone. "I'm going to have a visit with her. Let me know when Bane shows up."

Marty nodded. Friday grunted.

"I'll go to security and get that employee list," Pierce said, following him out the door.

Hawke walked through the other room and stopped. "If any of you notice a man with the build of the guy in the cowboy hat paying extra attention to a specific young woman, let me know."

The group of monitor watchers either nodded or raised a hand to acknowledge they heard him.

If Lanie had run to the guy in the cowboy hat, he'd be an idiot to come in here, now, when they had figured out he was taking young women. But what Hawke didn't understand was why this man had drawn in so many people to help him if he was just raping and killing the women. That didn't make sense. And why pay Lanie to help him? Most serial killers worked alone. Part of the thrill of killing was knowing they did it all by themselves and could do it again. Too many other people were involved in the women's disappearance.

A buzzer sounded as he stepped into the gift shop. Three other people were milling around. Hawke noticed a display of perfumes. He walked over and picked up one that had Jade in the name. A whiff and he knew that was the scent he'd smelled in the truck. Flipping a box over, he glanced at the price. Not the ten-dollar stuff he'd purchased for his wife years ago.

He carried the display model up to the counter.

"That's not for sale. You need to get an unopened box," the clerk said.

Hawke grabbed the chain around his neck and pulled his badge out from under his shirt for the clerk to see. "Are you Teresa Berth?" He knew she was, but didn't want her to know that.

"Yes. Are you the trooper looking into Sherry's disappearance?"

"Yes." Her friends or Dela must have told her he'd be by.

"Have you discovered anything?"

"I'm getting closer. Can you tell me, did Lanie Porter ever buy this perfume?"

"Why do you want to know about Lanie? You should be looking for Sherry." The woman glared at him.

"I can't give you details, but I need to know if Lanie wore this perfume."

"Yes. She would come in here and buy a bottle every year on her birthday."

"Thank you. Now, did you get a good look at the man Sherry told you about that had followed her into the coffee shop two months ago?"

"Abby told me you were asking her and Kara about

him. He had a narrow face, small eyes…I want to say he had freckles but the shade from his hat made it hard to tell."

Hawke's heart raced. This was the first person to give him a halfway decent description of the man. "Height, weight?"

"He was average height. And average build. Nothing to look at really." She shrugged.

"Thank you. Would you be willing to work with a sketch artist?"

"I can try but I didn't look at him that close."

"You have described him better than anyone else I've talked to."

"Did he have something to do with Sherry's disappearance?" She glanced over his shoulder.

Hawke moved to the side to let a woman with several items in her hands walk up to the counter. "We think so. If you see him, contact security."

He walked out of the gift shop feeling a bit of a spring in his step. Now, if he could get a corresponding and more detailed description from the bartender, they might have a way to find their suspect.

Hunkered down in a booth in the back corner of the sports bar waiting for Dexter Bane to come on duty, Hawke flipped through his notes on the disappearance. Pierce kept checking his phone for a reply to the security and surveillance employee's information he'd sent to the Feds.

Hawke's phone buzzed. Carol.

"Hawke."

"A body was called in. It was dumped up at

Deadman's Pass."

Hawke's gut twisted. "Lanie Porter?"

"How'd you know?" her tone indicated he'd been withholding information.

"Gut feeling. She hadn't taken anything when she disappeared and I believe she ran to whoever was paying her to help him get women. She drove off with Sherry the night she disappeared and Lanie ran to the Travel Center when she thought we knew what she'd done. A truck cab that I saw leaving there last night had the scent of her perfume in it today."

"Give me his information and we'll pick him up."

Hawke rattled off the information he'd written down while checking out the truck. "When you get him, see if he knows who the guy in the cowboy hat is. I'll send you the only photo we have."

"Will do." The line went silent.

Hawke sent her the photo.

"They found Lanie's body?" Pierce asked.

"Yeah. Dumped along the highway up on Deadman's Pass." He set his notepad down. "That's a half hour drive from here by truck."

"Do you want to go grab the truck driver or check it out?" Pierce shoved his phone in his pocket.

"I doubt the truck is still sitting at the center's lot. But I would like to see the dump site after we talk to the bartender."

The waitress came over to top off their iced teas. "Dexter just walked in." She pointed to a tall, long haired man in his thirties.

Hawke and Pierce walked up to the bar and waited for the man to come to them.

"Can I help you?"

"We hope so." Hawke pulled out his badge and the photo. "Can you give us a description of this man? We know he frequents this bar and he never takes his hat off for the surveillance cameras to get a good photo of him."

Dexter took the photo and nodded. "He thinks he's God's gift to women." He snorted. "Most of the women who hang around him just want free drinks."

"What does he look like?" Hawke repeated.

"Narrow face, big ears, big nose, small eyes, freckles all over his face. His front teeth even protrude a bit, if I remember right. Thin reddish mustache on his upper lip."

"Would you be willing to talk to a sketch artist?" Pierce asked, tapping on his phone.

"Sure."

"Good. She'll be here in twenty minutes."

Hawke glanced over at Pierce. "How can you get one here so fast?"

"When we began this hunt for the man in the hat, I had one of our agents who does sketches travel to Pendleton." Pierce grinned. "Thought it might be of help."

"Are you going to wait here for her to arrive while I go to the crime scene?" Hawke pushed away from the bar.

"I'd like to go with you if you can wait twenty minutes."

"I'll grab something to eat. Text me when you're ready." Hawke walked out of the bar and around the corner to the bar and grill. He found a table to his liking and sat.

Waiting for his order, he watched Dela and Officer Red Bear enter the establishment, scan the room, and walk toward him.

"Did I miss a memo about a meeting?" he asked, trying to find some levity in a shitty day.

Dela rolled her eyes, and the officer's lips twitched.

"No. Jacob came to me with some information he'd dug up, and I wanted to get up to speed with you." Dela took the seat to his left and Red Bear sat across from him.

Hawke leaned back, peering at the officer. "You go first."

"You asked me about drug trafficking at the Travel Center. There is a task force, but they have been shorthanded and haven't been keeping tabs on the center. They do know that the truck you asked me about has been through here at least once a month for a year. It sits at the Travel Center for several days, to a week, before it moves on." Officer Red Bear ordered a coke when the waitress arrived with Hawke's dinner.

"That truck may now be involved in a murder." Hawke told them about Lanie.

Dela shook her head. "She was always a thrill seeker in school. But I never thought she'd end up tossed on the side of a road."

"I have a pretty good description of our guy in the cowboy hat from the bartender in the sports bar. Pierce has a sketch artist coming to see if she can render a likeness." Hawke picked up his burger.

"We should have thought of that," Dela said,

scowling.

"As soon as we have a likeness, I want to use all our resources to find out who this guy is." Hawke put his burger down and picked up a fry.

"I'm sure your FBI friend can use facial recognition." Dela had been professional until this comment. It sounded as if she were jealous of either the Feds or a certain FBI agent. He wasn't sure which.

"I hope so. The sooner we know who he is, the quicker we'll find him and discover what happened to Meela and Sherry." Hawke picked up his burger and took a huge bite. He chewed, swallowed, and waved a hand at Officer Red Bear. "The State Police are looking for that truck. You might do a drive by the Travel Center and see if it's still sitting there."

The officer downed his drink, nodded to Dela, and left the bar and grill.

Dela cocked her head to one side. "Did you do that on purpose?"

"Yes and no. I'm pretty sure the truck is gone, but on the off chance it isn't, it will give him points with the State Police." Hawke started to pick up his burger and stopped. "What do you have against the FBI, or is it just Special Agent Pierce?"

Chapter Seventeen

Hawke continued eating his burger while Dela stared at him. He had all the time in the world until Pierce arrived.

She sipped her coffee and cleared her throat. "I take it one of my comments gave you the impression I don't care much for the FBI."

He nodded, hoping she'd continue.

"When my friend was missing, the FBI came, barely talked to anyone, and then said if something happened to her it was my fault for leaving her." She put the cup down and looked away. She swiped at a tear trickling down her cheek. "I've blamed myself every day since then. I didn't need the Feds telling me what I felt in my gut."

"It wasn't your fault. Your friend should have gone home with you and chose not to. What happened to her, wasn't her fault either. It was the fault of the person who she came across that sought to do wrong." Hawke finished his food and shoved the basket to the middle of the table. "In your job you will have times, like now, when you need to work with the Feds. Tuck that anger away so you don't overlook something important."

"Is that what you do, when you are treated differently for who you are?" Her direct question and gaze confused Hawke.

"What would you know about being an Indian in a White world?" he asked, noting her comment wasn't far off the mark.

"I've lived my whole life, other than my military years, on this reservation and even though I grew up here, I'm still treated as an outsider by many. In the military, it was my gender and Hispanic last name that made others treat me differently. And now." She barely glanced down at her right foot. "I have other things that set me apart."

"Always turn the other cheek and then prove you deserve to be here." Hawke had learned that long ago, the hard way.

She nodded as Pierce walked into the bar and grill.

"Ready?" the Special Agent asked, his gaze landing on Dela.

"I am." Hawke stood. "Did you get the bartender to sit down with the sketch artist?"

"They are working as we speak." Pierce faced Dela. "I told Special Agent Tuma to get the sketch to security when she was finished so you can make copies for your people and surveillance to have."

"Thank you. Where are they working at?" Dela stood.

"In the back corner of the sports bar." Pierce's gaze

remained on her.

"I'll go see if they are about finished and take the agent to the office to make copies." She walked out of the bar and grill.

Hawke had been watching Pierce, whose gaze had followed the woman. "You ready?"

"Yeah." Pierce kind of shook himself and followed.

When they were outside of the casino, Hawke asked, "Were you the agent who told Dela her friend's death was her fault?"

"What? No! I would never tell that to anyone. What made you think that?"

"You and she seem to have something going on, but I can't tell what it is." Hawke usually stayed out of people's lives. He hated anyone meddling in his.

They climbed into his pickup and left the parking lot. He turned onto Interstate 84, heading up Cabbage Hill toward Deadman's Pass. The ascent of curves and views of the farmland below usually soothed Hawke. Today, there was too much unsettled in his mind.

Pierce stared straight ahead, then said, "We do have a backstory. But it's not what you think. We both served in Iraq. She was an MP in the Army. I was intelligence in the Marines. We had a difference of opinion over someone she had in custody. He was my informant, and she wasn't about to let him go. He'd raped an Iraqi female."

Hawke scowled.

"I didn't condone the man's activity, but I had to get intel off to my commander and the only way I could get that was to have my man released." Pierce let out a long, tired sigh. "I had to go over her head, and she has never forgiven me for not making that man pay."

"You've run into one another in your jobs stateside before?" Hawke now understood the woman's coldness to the FBI agent. It wasn't every agent, he didn't think. Just this one.

"Only one other time, when I came to the reservation for an altercation that started at the casino and ended in Washington State." Pierce waved a hand. "Could we talk about the case?"

"It helps we now have a sketch of the cowboy hat guy."

"Yeah. Agent Tuma will run it through our facial recognition when she gets back to the motel. Do you think the trucker you harassed this afternoon killed the Porter woman?"

"We won't know until we ask him. I don't think he'll get too far. Not with Lt. Keller wanting to do right by Porter's father and the local government entities." Hawke just wished more people in those places cared about what happened on the reservation.

"I'm sure she is working just as hard on helping find the missing woman." Pierce leaned forward as Hawke slowed and turned down into Deadman's Pass rest area.

Lights flashed on a Tribal Police vehicle. A body bus disappeared under the interstate to make the loop back onto the road headed toward Pendleton. Hawke parked next to the tribal vehicle and exited.

"Why are the Tribal Police here?" Pierce asked as he and Hawke ducked under the crime scene tape.

"This is Reservation land," Hawke replied.

"No one is allowed in this area," the Umatilla Tribal officer said, walking toward them.

They both pulled out their badges.

"We're working another case that this woman was involved in. Who is the officer in charge?" Hawke asked.

"Over there. Detective Jones." The officer pointed to the detective Hawke had cornered at the tribal station.

"Thanks." Hawke strode over to the man, followed by Pierce. "Detective Jones." Hawke held out his hand. "If you don't remember, I'm State Trooper Hawke, and this is Special Agent Pierce."

The man scowled. "Lt. Keller told me you were interested in my vic. You think this has something to do with the Dale woman?" He led them away from where a State Police forensic team was combing the ground.

As they stood, facing the movements of the evidence collecting team, Hawke filled him in on what they knew and suspected about the victim.

"I see. You think she ran to whoever has been taking women, specifically the Dale woman, from the reservation and he killed her?" The skepticism in the man's voice irked Hawke.

"We have proof she has been consorting with the man who we believe has taken two young women from the casino. And she was the last person seen with our latest missing woman," Pierce said.

"I see. Not much here to tell you. No one that we know of saw anything. A person who pulled off the interstate to use the facilities and walk their dog found the body. I got the call about two this afternoon." He waved his arm. "As you can see, the body wasn't where everyone coming to the rest area would see her."

"Have you picked up any evidence a semi-truck drove near the dump site?" Hawke asked.

"Not in the dirt, there's no sign. I guess someone could have carried her over and dumped her."

"How was she killed?" Hawke asked.

"Strangulation."

That was why there hadn't been any blood in the sleeper of the truck. Just the lingering scent of the woman's perfume. But that was little to hold the trucker on. They would need more proof.

"Strangulation by hand or with a ligature?" Pierce asked.

"Ligature. M.E. thinks it was a piece of clothing. He'll know more after the autopsy." The detective started to walk away.

"Send a copy of your report to the OSP office in Pendleton," Hawke said.

The man spun around. "You do the same with your investigation."

Hawke waved a hand and headed back to his vehicle.

"You're leaving?" Pierce asked, following.

"This isn't where she was killed. If I'm right about it being the truck I saw leaving the Travel Center last night, then we need him and his truck. This was just the dump site." Hawke slid into his vehicle. "There has to have been more than the person driving the truck working with the man in the cowboy hat. We need to take a closer look at the videos Marty dug up of our main suspect."

His phone buzzed before he turned to head back on the interstate. Mom. He pulled over and answered.

"Is everything okay?"

"Yes, but no. Trey keeps asking for his mom, and I don't know what to tell him." He heard the tears in his mom's voice.

"The truth is always the best. She's missing and the State Police and FBI are trying to find her." He glanced at Pierce.

"You have FBI involved?" Mom asked.

"Yes, Special Agent Pierce is with me. We think we have a lead, but I need to go back to the casino and look over more tapes."

"You have to find her. Sherry is a beautiful butterfly who finally shed her cocoon and was using her wings to fly and gain independence for herself and Trey." Her words were filled with pride.

"I know. We're working as fast as we can with what we know. Tell Trey we are going to find her. Look Mom, I gotta go. But call me if you learn anything that might be helpful. Or if you need to talk."

"I will. And Gabriel...Thank you for doing this for Sherry and Trey."

"I'm doing it because it's the right thing to do. Good night." He ended the call. "And the right thing for you."

"Is Trey your son?" Pierce asked.

Hawke put the vehicle in gear and headed onto the interstate back to the casino. "No. He's Sherry Dale's son. He's staying with my mom." Hawke told Pierce about how his mom watched the children of Umatilla tribal members who were single and needed a helping hand.

"She sounds like a wonderful woman."

"That she is. Sometimes over the years, I've told her, her heart is too big. But then she wouldn't be who she is if she didn't have a big heart." Hawke eased down the hill, seeing the casino in the distance. "She's an advocate for the Missing and Murdered Indigenous Women cause. They've been putting up posters and asking questions. They came up with the witness who saw Sherry's car loaded on a car hauler. Everything seems to have happened around the casino and Travel Center. More out of towners go in and out of there than locals. Some on the reservation think the casino is a blessing, allowing them to put up new buildings and bring in more jobs. Others think it's a curse, bringing gambling and outsiders onto the reservation. If the casino is the center of the missing women, it will take a hit from the community."

Pierce nodded. "But I'm sure the good will outweigh the bad. If you can crack down on whatever is happening here, then the security at the casino will know to recognize the activity next time and stop it before it happens."

"I hope so." Hawke pulled into the casino parking lot and entered the building. He was pleased to see the older valet on duty. Hawke stopped, facing Pierce. "Did Agent Tuma send you a photo of the sketch?"

"Yeah." Pierce pulled it up on his phone.

Hawke walked over to the valet.

"Hey, hey. You are becoming a regular," the man grinned.

"Not the way I would like." Hawke motioned for

Pierce to show the man the sketch. "If you see this man enter or walking about, contact security. He's a person of interest in Sherry Dale's disappearance."

The man studied the sketch. "I don't remember seeing him at all."

"He usually wears a cowboy hat." Hawke hoped to jog the man's memory.

"I don't think he comes in through this entrance. I would remember him, hat or no hat." The man nodded.

"Thanks, even that is helpful." Hawke headed to the surveillance area door, gathering a security guard along the way to gain entrance.

Chapter Eighteen

In Marty's office, Hawke asked the head of surveillance to pull up one of the videos of the man in the cowboy hat. "I want to see how he comes into the casino, and if we can see him in the cameras in the parking lot. Maybe see what he drives."

Marty tapped the keyboard and the man in the cowboy hat came into view on the middle screen. The video moved backwards in fast motion. The man came in through the door by the cineplex where Lanie ran out.

"That's why that door was disabled," Hawke muttered.

"Yeah." Pierce tapped Marty on the shoulder. "How can we get a list of the maintenance men for the casino?"

"Either ask Godfrey to get it or go ask at the personnel office." Marty kept the video rolling.

"Where's Godfrey?" Pierce asked.

"Ask next door."

Pierce left the room, and Hawke continued watching the monitor.

"You lost him." Hawke leaned forward studying the shadow along the building.

"Let's try another one," Marty said.

"How about the night Meela disappeared?"

Marty ran a finger down a notebook beside his keyboard, typed in a date, and a video popped up with the cowboy hat guy in full view. "Something I noticed picking out these videos, the guy never plays the tables. And he only stays at a slot machine long enough to chat with women. The bar is the only place he lingers and that's usually because he has a woman with him. He never talks to a man."

The video ran backwards rapidly. The man came in a different fire door.

"What the hell!" Marty picked up a phone as Hawke continued to watch the man walk around the corner and out of sight.

"Can you get a visual on him?" Hawke asked.

The video stopped as Marty spoke into the phone. "We have a huge breach in casino security." He replaced the phone. "I'll have to pull up the whole set of cameras from that time and date. It's going to take a bit."

"Who did you just call?" Hawke asked.

"Godfrey. Both those doors are supposed to be no admittance from the outside. They are fire doors. Someone tampered with them more than just taking out the batteries."

"Is that why the one by the cineplex didn't go off

when Lanie went out of it?" Hawke asked.

"Yeah. Dela had a maintenance man check it out while she stood there. It didn't have any batteries, but I don't know if they checked if it locked."

"Dela was here earlier. Any way I can find out if she's still around?" Hawke wanted to see what she thought of the security guards and maintenance staff.

"I'll give her a call and see." Marty picked up the phone and hit one button. "Hey, Trooper Hawke wants to talk to you." He listened. "I'll send him out." The tech replaced the phone and said, "She's down at the offices behind the registration desk helping the FBI look through the personnel records on the maintenance staff."

"Thanks. Call me when you get that set up to see more."

"Will do."

Hawke walked through the open room with all the monitors. He realized this was a new crew. He'd returned after a shift change.

He walked along the casino floor, headed for the hotel registration desk. As he approached, Pierce and Dela appeared through a door behind the counter.

"You wanted to talk to me?" Dela asked, leaving the area behind the counter.

"Yeah. I'm surprised Friday hasn't contacted you. Marty and I just watched our cowboy hat guy enter through the fire door by the conference rooms the night Meela disappeared. All of the fire doors and exits that should be locked need to be checked right away." Hawke studied the woman. Her face had deepened in color and a scowl wrinkled her forehead.

"Double frickin' shit! After finding the door last night, I should have gone around and checked all of them. I'll grab a maintenance man and do it now."

Hawke stopped her. "Make sure it's one you trust. And would you know if the door was tampered with?"

"I know which one to ask. He isn't on anyone's payroll but the casino's." She smiled and strode off at a brisk pace.

"I faxed this list to Agent Tuma as soon as we had it. She's running it through for priors and to see what she can find on the employees. There has to be more than one who is being paid to allow this man in. What is he doing that is so lucrative he can pay people?" Pierce said, staring at the casino floor.

"You know he didn't drag people into this to kill the women. He must be part of a human trafficking ring. That's the only thing that makes sense." And it gave Hawke the hope they would find Sherry alive. But when they'd find her was another problem. He had a feeling that even if they grabbed this guy, he'd never talk and would be bailed out before they learned anything.

"We have to come up with a way to get inside the organization." He searched all the people milling around.

"We know it has to be the one truck that sits here, probably collecting the women." Pierce touched his arm. "Let's go to the coffee shop."

Hawke followed the man over to the coffee shop and sat in a booth across from the special agent. "What do you have in mind?"

"I can contact other agents, see who is working

human trafficking in the Pacific Northwest. They may
have an idea of someone we can use to get hooked up
with the cowboy hat guy." Pierce pulled out his phone.

Hawke was thinking something more local. "What
if we discover who the person is that has been helping
him on the inside here? Then we get them to tell us
what they know and possibly get him to ask for a more
profitable job with the cowboy hat guy?"

"That's too risky. You don't know who the guy is
they have in here or if he'd help us." Pierce punched
numbers on his phone. "My way is less risky."

Hawke shook his head. "But it will take longer."

"Bringing down large crime syndicates takes time.
You have to get someone on the inside that they don't
suspect and gather the information that will bring them
down."

"I'm going to find Dela. You do what you think
you need to do. I'll do what I think I need to do." He
grinned. "I'm not on the clock for this one. I'm on
vacation."

Hawke stood and walked out of the coffee shop
dialing Dela's number.

"Yeah?" Dela answered.

"Where are you?" he asked.

"Checking the fire door at the end of the hall by
the gift shop."

"I'll be right there." He hung up and strode to his
left, past the gift shop and headed down the hallway.

Dela and an older Umatilla man were examining
the fire door.

"Is that one not working, too?" Hawke asked.

"So far, every fire door on the ground floor isn't

locking." Dela straightened. "This is distressing, not only for the scum that has been getting in this way but because the whole facility has been compromised."

Hawke nodded. He held out a hand to the maintenance man. "Gabriel Hawke."

"Clarence White." He shook hands. His grip was firm and his smile genuine.

"How easy is it to leave the doors unlocked and rig them to notify security?" Hawke asked. "But not let anyone but us three know that's what was done?"

"It's still a security breach to allow them to remain unlocked," Dela stated.

"Just until the man we want comes in. After that, you can get them all locked up." Hawke glanced from the security guard to the maintenance man.

"I could do it, but not tonight. I'd need to get some parts," White said.

"Can you get what you need locally?" Hawke asked.

"Yeah. First thing in the morning." The man finished screwing the plate back on the door.

"Could you come here straight from getting the parts and fix the doors? I think the person who dismantles them is on the night shift."

"How do you know that?" Dela moved closer to him.

"Because our suspect comes at night, took Meela out of here at night, and no one on the security team saw our suspect come through one of the doors. That means someone provided cover on a security camera for the suspect to take Meela out of the hotel."

"Double Frickin' Shit!" Dela had caught on to

what Hawke had been trying to make her understand. The person they could get to help them catch the guy in the cowboy hat was upstairs watching them fix the doors. What Hawke asked White to do had to be done during the day shift.

"I need to talk to Godfrey," she pulled out her phone.

Hawke put a hand on it. "Let's keep all of this between the three of us."

"But the day shift is going to know Clarence is doing something to the doors if we don't say something." She didn't raise her phone. "Unless, I can get Marty to redirect the feeds at the doors until Clarence gets done."

"I think he's okay to have in the loop. If he were working with our suspect, he wouldn't have pulled up everything he has." Hawke nodded. "But not a word to anyone else."

Clarence put his tools in his box and straightened. "Can I have tomorrow night off for working a double shift?"

Dela smiled at the man. "Going to your sister's birthday party?"

"If you can make it work." He studied her.

"I can get you off the roster to work tomorrow night, but I'll have to wait to actually get you the over time until we have the man we're after. I don't want the wrong people putting two and two together. If you just come in and work with no record of it, then no one will know you are helping us." Dela put a hand on his arm. "But I promise, you will be paid for the double shifts."

"I know you'll make it right. And I'll keep my

mouth shut."

"Thank you," Hawke said, to both of them.

Clarence wandered down the hallway, speaking into a walkie talkie that he was finished with his project and was available.

"Why do you trust him?" Hawke asked.

"He's my friend's uncle. He wants to help find Meela and Sherry as much as the rest of us who have had a missing or murdered loved one." She stared at him. "There are many families on the rez who are hurting. It's just a matter of getting them all together to make noise about this atrocity that no one off the rez wants to address."

"I agree. I think I know what we're dealing with. Let's go ask Marty to take care of the fire exit cameras tomorrow, then I'll fill you in on my take and what I have planned."

"Let's grab a coffee to go. It's going to be a long night. I came in early because Godfrey had some paperwork to catch up on and couldn't get it done and take care of everything else." She led him up the hall to a small deli at an angle from the hotel registration desk.

"Dela, who is the handsome man with you?" a middle-aged woman, who was as wide as she was tall asked, and giggled.

"Rosie, this is Trooper Hawke. You might want to put your tongue back in your mouth. He's Mimi Shumack's son," Dela said, grinning at Hawke.

"Ohhh, then according to Mimi, he's a catch." Rosie winked at him.

Hawke smiled. "Could we get two black coffees to go?"

"Sure handsome." She giggled and spun around to pour coffee into two paper cups.

Hawke reached in his pocket to pay.

"Security doesn't pay for coffee. It helps us stay awake." Dela took the two cups, handing one to him. "Thanks, Rosie."

"Any time."

As they walked toward the door to the security offices, Dela said, "Rosie likes men, in case you couldn't tell."

Hawke laughed. "No, I couldn't tell."

Dela tapped her ID on the surveillance door lock and held the door for him to go first.

Inside the room, he scanned the people sitting at the monitors. He figured the person working with their suspect could be sitting here right now since the cowboy hat guy always seemed to show up in the late afternoon, early evening. Which gave him another idea.

Dela moved by him headed to Marty's office. Hawke followed.

Marty leaned back in the chair, his eyes closed and his mouth open.

"Do they pay you enough?" Hawke asked, drawing the man out of his nap.

"Huh? What?" Marty sat up and stared at them. "Man, I've been putting in too many hours."

"I asked if they pay you enough to work around the clock?" Hawke repeated.

The computer tech grinned. "They do. But I need to train someone else to take over for me when I take that money I've saved up and go on vacation." He winked.

"We have one more thing we need you to do and not tell anyone outside of the three of us," Dela took the chair beside Marty.

"What about Godfrey?"

Dela shook her head. "It's better he doesn't know about this. He's loyal as can be, but he can't hide anything."

"True. What am I doing?"

"We need you to make sure the camera feeds on the fire exit doors don't show on the monitors tomorrow until Clarence White calls you." Dela eased back in the chair, propping her right leg on a box under the table.

"Okay, I can make that happen. What's he doing?" Marty started tapping the keyboard.

"He's putting a silent alarm system on the doors so only those of us in this room know when one has been breached from the outside."

Marty smiled. "We're going to catch our guy in the cowboy hat coming in."

"Yes."

"Why the secrecy?" He stopped moving his fingers and studied both of them.

"Because we have reason to believe one of your surveillance people is helping our suspect," Hawke said.

"Shit! One of ours?" Marty said it as if he couldn't believe that was true.

"That's what it looks like. Now you know why we can't let Godfrey know." Dela said.

"Yeah, he'd be making everyone nervous staring at them." Marty started typing again.

"How long until you finish fixing those feeds?" Hawke asked.

"About ten minutes." The tech never looked up from the keyboard.

"Then I'll sip my coffee and wait." Hawke found another chair and pulled it up beside Dela.

"It's getting late. Don't you need to go home and get some sleep?" Dela asked.

"I'm not sleepy." Hawke smiled and sipped his drink.

"Do you work this hard when you're being paid?" she asked, taking a swallow of her coffee.

"Yep. I'm a tracker by nature. Once I get on a trail, I can't stop until I satisfy my curiosity. Right now, it's finding Sherry. And if we're correct in our assumption, this is human trafficking—"

"Shit, you think this is one of those sex-slave rings?" Marty asked, staring at him.

"For the whole process to be so well thought out, and this guy is paying people to help him, there has to be a big payoff in the end for him. So, yeah." Hawke made a triangle between him, Dela, and Marty. "This is just between us. We don't need to get anyone else involved or scared."

"What about the Fed?" Marty asked.

"He's working it from his angle." Hawke hid the grin behind his cup. If he were a betting man, he'd bet on this room of three to figure it out before Special Agent Pierce.

Marty smiled. "Gottcha. He's going to do all the paperwork, and we're doing the ground work."

"Something like that. Are you done?" Hawke

leaned forward.

Marty tapped a few more keys and raised his hands with a flourish. "Done. Now what did you need?"

"I'd like to see all the footage you found with cowboy hat guy. I want to see who he mingles with here besides women."

Marty shook his head. "Knock yourself out, but all I saw were women, including Lanie."

Chapter Nineteen

Three in the morning. Hawke stared bleary eyed at his watch. He'd watched all the videos Marty had provided him of the cowboy hat suspect. The only people the guy talked to more than once were the waitresses and bartenders in the sports bar. But it wasn't long enough to do more than ask for a drink and then he didn't converse with them again.

He wiped a hand across his eyes and stopped. A man entered the sports bar. "Can you rewind that?"

Marty snapped out of his chair. "What, huh?"

"Sorry I'm keeping you up, but can you rewind this back about five minutes, please." Hawke leaned forward, drinking the last swallow of cold coffee in his cup. Dela had gone to make sure the gaming tables were all closed down and the money and chips locked away.

The keyboard clacked and the video rewound and started again.

"There. That guy who walked up to the waitress. Who is he?" Hawke watched as he slipped something under the glass that the waitress handed to cowboy hat.

"Jerome Marks, he works surveillance. You think he's helping?" The tech's tone insinuated the surveillance man was above board.

"He slipped a note to our suspect." Hawke stood. "Is he still here? Marks?"

"He should be here until seven."

"Then he'll be gone when White fixes the doors. Good." Hawke slapped Marty on the shoulder. "I'm done. Go get some sleep. That's what I'm going to do."

He walked out of the office, noting Marks sat at a monitor near the exit. Not wanting to draw any attention to the fact he was studying the man, he asked, "Any idea where I can find Dela?"

Marks shrugged. One of the female members pointed to her screen. "She just came out of the vault. It's behind the Change Cage."

"Thanks." He headed out the door, and across the casino. There were very few machines making noise. It seemed this casino wasn't an all-nighter for most gamblers.

Dela moved out from behind the Change Cage as he walked up. "Going home?"

"Yeah. But I'll be back here tomorrow." He grasped her elbow, leading her away from employee ears. "I think I found our surveillance personnel on the take."

"Who?" her voice said what he already knew. She didn't like traitors.

"Marks. He passed a note to cowboy hat in the

sports bar. I'd like all the information on him that you can round up and text or email it to me."

She nodded. "I'll do that as soon as I finish getting the gaming all closed up."

"I'll see you back here tomorrow night. By then I might have something figured out to get cowboy hat to show." Hawke started to walk away.

"When can I let my boss know what's going on?" Dela asked.

"When you trust he won't blow it." Hawke walked across the casino floor, nodded to the valet, and walked out into the cool night air. He drew in a deep breath, filling his lungs, and recharging his tired brain. The scent of diesel fumes tingled his nostrils. He glanced over at the Travel Center and saw smoke pluming out of one of the semi's exhaust.

Hawke slid in behind the wheel of his pickup, started it up, and left the parking lot, turning left toward the Travel Center. There were several vehicles parked in front of the store. Busy for this time of night. Moving at five miles an hour, he drove alongside the building and around to the back. The truck idling behind the store wasn't one that had been there earlier. He had a feeling it was a legit trucker who had stopped to get a few hours of sleep before moving on. His cynical brain told him to stop and see what the guy had to say.

Parking in front of the truck, he exited his vehicle and walked up to the door.

The driver sat behind the steering wheel, a metal logbook case open. The window was rolled down.

Hawke knocked on the door. "Can I ask you a couple of questions?"

The driver jumped and peered at the window. "What'cha doin' scarin' a body like that?"

"Sorry. I just wondered when you arrived?" Hawke pulled his badge on the chain out from under his shirt.

The driver squinted, reading it. "I have nothing to do with the drug selling back here."

Hawke grinned. "Mind if I step up?"

"Come on aboard."

Hawke walked around to the passenger side, opened the door, and climbed up into the passenger seat. "You stop here often?"

"Every week like clockwork. I have a good gig hauling from Portland to Nebraska." The man picked up a large paper soda cup and slurped.

"You've seen the drug dealing going on here?" Hawke asked.

"Yeah. They don't try to hide it. Aren't you cops watching them?" The driver asked.

"It's not my job. But I happen to know the place is under surveillance. I was wondering if you could tell me about a truck I saw here two days ago."

"I wasn't here then."

"I know, but it seems to hang out around here and doesn't really go anywhere." Hawke went on to describe the truck and driver and the logos he'd noticed on the trailer.

"That guy. I had a run in a while back with him. He doesn't like anyone going near his rig."

"Is he one of the drug dealers?" Hawke asked.

"No. Not that I've seen. I did see a guy in a cowboy hat shaking hands with the driver once. They seemed all buddy, buddy."

Paty Jager

. Hawke leaped on that. "When was that?"

"Hard to say. Maybe two, three months ago. Like I said, I land here once a week, but I can't really tell you when I saw that."

Hawke pulled up a photo of Lanie. "What about this woman? Have you seen her hanging around with either the truck driver or the guy in the cowboy hat?"

"Her. Yeah. I couldn't figure out what someone who looked like she had money would be doing hanging around back here with truckers."

"Did you see her with anyone?" Hawke needed to connect her to the truck, the driver, or the cowboy hat suspect.

"She always parked in front of the truck you were asking about."

"What's your name and a way to contact you?" Hawke pulled out his notepad.

The man cooperated. "This something other than drugs?"

"The body of the woman I showed you was found at Deadman's Pass this morning. I believe she was taken there by the truck I asked you about." Hawke closed his notepad. "Don't say a word to anyone. We are looking into two missing Umatilla women."

"I'm headed to Portland and won't say a word. Good luck finding those women."

"Thanks. This information will help me get the warrants I need." Hawke climbed down out of the semi and slid behind the wheel of his pickup. He could call Carol tomorrow and request a warrant for the truck in question. He was surprised he hadn't heard from her about their finding it or the company on the truck.

Driving home, he ran all he knew through his mind to keep from falling asleep. They were getting closer, but if Sherry and Meela were taken by this man, and he was part of a human trafficking ring, they could be anywhere. Especially Meela who had been abducted six months ago.

The sun threw an ethereal glow as he pulled up to his mom's house. He needed four hours of sleep. Six would be better. After hitting his fifties, he'd realized that sleep was the best remedy to rest. However, in situations like this, it wasn't always easy to do.

He let himself into the house. Dog greeted him whimpering.

"Shhh… we don't want to wake the others," he whispered and walked down the hall to his old room.

"Gabriel, is that you?" his mom said from her bedroom.

He entered the room. "Yes. I didn't mean to wake you."

"I've not slept well since Sherry disappeared." She patted the side of her bed. "Are you getting closer to finding her?"

"We are. However, it's not that simple." He went on to tell her what he thought had happened. "If it is human trafficking, we are going to have to find a way to get close to the group and discover where she was taken."

"But that means she is still alive," Mom said, with relief.

"She should be. They deal in live people. Unless she fights them too much. Then…" He left it unsaid. She could become another Jane Doe in a city somewhere.

"I will pray for her quick return." She patted his arm. "When would you like me to wake you?"

"I would like noon, but get me up no later than ten if I'm not up." He leaned over, kissed his mom's cheek and went into his room.

Lying on the bed, his hand dangling over the edge, petting Dog on the head, he drifted to sleep.

Hawke's phone buzzed, vibrating the thin wood nightstand next to the bed. He reached out, grabbed the irritating thing, and narrowed his eyes, trying to see who was calling. Dani. He glanced at the time. Eight. He hit the ignore button and drifted back to sleep.

The buzzing started again. Hawke slapped his hand on the phone and pulled it to him. Pierce.

He scrubbed a hand over his face, rolled to his back, and answered. "Hawke." His voice croaked liked he'd been swallowing sand while he slept.

"Wanted to get you up to speed." The younger special agent sounded well rested and ready to take on the bad guys.

Hawke shoved the two pillows behind him. "I'm running on three hours sleep. Want to fill me in slowly."

Pierce chuckled. "I can let you sleep some more and you call me when you're ready."

"I'm awake now. Go ahead."

Trey appeared in the door of the bedroom with, from the steam and aroma filling the air, a large mug of coffee. The boy walked over and set it on the nightstand.

"Thank you," Hawke said, picking it up and drinking.

"I haven't told you anything yet," Pierce said, a question in his voice.

"Trey brought me a cup of coffee. Go on. Tell me what you learned and I'll tell you what I found out last night." Hawke sipped and listened as Pierce said they were sure they had found the surveillance team member on the take. The name he mentioned wasn't Jerome Marks.

"Why do you think it's this person?" he asked.

"Because she has deposited several larger amounts of money into her bank the last three months."

"You're wrong. I want you to look into Jerome Marks. Watching videos, I saw him pass a note to cowboy hat. The only people who know it's him are me, Dela, and Marty. They didn't want to tell Friday because, I guess, he can't hide his feelings. Which would tell Marks we are on to him if the boss is kept in the loop."

"Marks? Really? He came back clean. No priors, no outstanding bills, no extra money in his account."

"Keep digging. Then cowboy hat has something on him to get him to help." Hawke swallowed the rest of the coffee and started to feel somewhat awake. "I talked to a trucker who knows about the drug activity at the Travel Center and he placed Lanie with the truck I believe she was dumped from."

"You have been busy. I got a hit on the cowboy hat. His name is Rory Hughes. He had some misdemeanors in his teens and twenties but after that he is squeaky clean. Almost too clean. We're digging up information in the Seattle area. That's where he's from."

"Where does he work?" Hawke asked.

"He's a salesman for a company that sells equipment to China and the Middle East."

"That's where the women are going. Seattle, Portland, or San Francisco would be the closest ports to ship to China." Hawke was feeling like they needed to move faster. Before Sherry ended up in China, and they couldn't get her back.

"We believe the truck and driver that may have dumped the body is headed to Seattle. I have agents watching the business's warehouses and the port. If the truck arrives, it will be searched."

"There's no guarantee she's on that truck." Even as Hawke played Devil's advocate, his gut told him she was. But what about Meela? Now his hunt was no longer for one woman—it was for two.

"Any chance someone can find out if that truck dropped anything off during the week following Meela Skylark's disappearance?" he asked.

"We're working on that, too. Just hard to do when we don't want to alert them that we know what's going on."

"I understand." Hawke told Pierce about their discovery of the fire exit doors and how they were setting them up to alert them of anyone coming in through the doors. "Again, only Dela, Marty, Clarence White, and I know about the doors."

"I get it, the fewer that know, the easier it is to keep it quiet," Pierce said. "Are you trying to catch Hughes?"

"Yeah. I was going to swap ideas with you this morning on how to get him to come to the casino." Hawke stretched and sat up on the side of the bed. Dog woofed and spun in a circle. He wanted Hawke to get up.

"Meet you at the casino buffet in one hour," Pierce said. "We can figure it out there. I'll have Agent Tuma put together a file on Marks, my person of interest, and Hughes."

"See you then." Hawke stood up, grabbed clean clothes, and headed to the shower. Hopefully the shower would wake him up some more.

Chapter Twenty

The buzzing of Hawke's phone stopped him in front of the casino. He didn't recognize the number.

"Hawke."

"Is this Trooper Hawke?" the woman's voice asked.

"Yes."

"I'm Officer Prentiss with the Pendleton City Police. I'm calling to say we would like to talk to you about the missing person's report for Sherry Dale."

Hawke started laughing. "You're kidding me, right?"

"No. Did Ms. Dale return home?"

"No. The FBI, the Oregon State Police, Umatilla Tribal Police, and myself are all working the case to find her. You can tell the city police to not worry about it. They should have started Wednesday morning like I did." He hung up and stomped into the casino and over to the entrance to the Sunrise Buffet.

He stood at the entrance, fuming that the city police were just now beginning an investigation. Shit. It was twelve hours past the seventy-two hours. That was last night.

His phone buzzed as a hostess walked up to him. He glanced at the phone. This time it was Carol. "Hawke. Just a minute," he answered, then said to the woman, "I'm meeting someone."

"He's here."

As he followed the woman, he returned to the call. "Carol, how are things going on your end?"

"That's what I was calling to ask you. Did you get a chance to go to the drop site?" she asked.

"Yes. Did forensics come up with anything to find our killer?"

The woman leading him glanced over her shoulder at him.

He spotted Pierce and a woman who must have been Agent Tuma. "I've got it from here," he told the hostess and veered away from her.

"There were some fibers around her neck. The M.E. believes she was strangled with a piece of clothing. It wasn't found with the body."

"Maybe the suspect kept it as a souvenir," he said, sliding into the semi round booth.

"Could be. We're also working on the truck you think she was dumped from. Haven't seen it yet."

"I'm having breakfast with the FBI. They have a lead on the truck. We're slowly getting this figured out. I'll come by later today and fill you in."

"You can't talk now?" she asked, curiosity in her voice.

"Not for the reason you're hinting at. Just lots of ears. Talk to you this afternoon." Hawke ended the conversation and held his hand out to the woman. "Trooper Hawke."

"Agent Tuma." She shook with one hand and slid files across the table toward him with the other.

"Who were you talking to?" Pierce asked, picking up a cup of coffee.

"Lt. Keller. She said the victim yesterday was strangled. They've recovered some fibers. If we catch up to the truck and driver, we may be able to match them to him or the vehicle."

"Good news." Pierce shoved a napkin wrapped around silverware over to Hawke.

He pushed it to the side and picked up the top file. The one on the FBI's person of interest who worked security. "Did you figure out where the money was coming from?"

The waitress arrived, filled the cup in front of him with coffee and topped off the other two cups. "Just walk up to the buffet, grab a plate, and fill it up. I'll be around to top off your coffees." She walked away.

"The same account, but we haven't been able to figure out exactly where it's coming from. Looks like an oil company." Agent Tuma frowned.

Hawke pulled out his phone and dialed Dela. He'd planned to leave a message, but she answered.

"Dela. What's up?"

"You've had less sleep than me," he replied.

"Comes with the territory. What did you need?"

"Do you have any idea why…" He read off the name, "would be getting a check every month from an oil company?"

"Yeah. Her folks put oil wells on their property and have the money from them split among the three kids. Why?"

Hawke grinned. "It stumped the FBI."

She laughed. "Make sure they eat crow. Is that who they thought was the leak in security for the cowboy hat?"

"Yeah. But we have a name for him. Rory Hughes. Pierce, Agent Tuma, and I are working on a plan to get him to the casino. I'll let you know how that goes."

"Sounds good. I'm sleeping a few more hours." The line went dead.

"Lucky you," he mumbled, putting his phone back in his pocket.

"What did whoever you were talking to have to say?" Pierce asked, sliding to the edge of the booth.

"The money that is in this person's account every month comes from family oil wells. It's dispersed among her and her siblings." Hawke waved for them to go ahead and get their food. "I don't want to pack these or leave them here." He opened the next file. Jerome Marks.

The two walked off, and he read all the man's information. He'd been married, divorced now. He didn't see any mention of kids. Did he owe alimony or child support? That would be a reason for him to need money. If it was given to him in cash, he'd just hand it over to his ex-wife. It would never have to touch a bank. If he were smart, which he seemed to be, to keep his relationship to Hughes hidden for who knew how long, there could be another reason he was helping—

blackmail.

The agents returned. Pierce's plate was heaped up. Agent Tuma's plate had food evenly spaced and all the same amount.

Hawke shoved the folders to the center of the table and stood.

Friday, the head of security, walked into the restaurant, didn't even look around as he strode over to the table with the FBI agents. He must have been told that the FBI and Hawke were gathering in the Sunrise Buffet.

After piling his plate with all the foods he liked, Hawke returned to the table.

Friday stood at the edge of the table. "What you're telling me is you have some new information but it's not anything I need to know?"

"It's not so much that you don't need to know, it has nothing to do with the casino," Pierce said.

The man stared at Hawke. "I was told you, Dela, and Marty spent five hours in Marty's office last night. What were you doing?"

"I was watching the videos of the nights Cowboy Hat was in the casino. I was trying to see who he had for an accomplice, besides Lanie Porter." Hawke wasn't lying. He just wasn't sharing everything he knew.

"I see. And what did you determine?" Friday continued to stare, his arms crossed, and his right jaw flinching as if he clenched his teeth.

Hawke understood why Dela had suggested not telling this man about Marks. "That someone here at the casino had to be helping him pick the women. But I'm still working on that." And he was. He didn't think Hughes picked these women out of the blue. Marks had to have noticed the two were usually alone and then done a check on whether a boyfriend or husband would come looking for them.

He nodded. "You'll let me know what you determine from this," he swirled a hand over the table, "meeting?"

"Yes. Once we get it all figured out." Hawke sat down. A cue that the man could leave.

And he did. Striding to the entrance.

"That was some fancy footwork," Pierce said. "He's bound to figure out something is up with so many of us keeping him out of the loop."

"Did you see his agitation when he was talking to us? Dela was right to keep him from knowing everything. But we'll need to make sure he gets credit for this." Hawke picked up his fork.

"Why should he get credit for work you and Dela have done?" Agent Tuma asked.

Hawke studied her. "Because his position is a matter of pride to him and his family. Dela isn't going around him to take his job, she wants to make sure justice is done."

The woman stared at him. "But if she does the work, she should get the praise and accolades."

Hawke had figured out Dela enough to know she grew up surrounded by the Umatilla people. What he'd seen of her so far, she honored them and their way of life. She would never do anything to one up anyone to try and upset the unity and work relationships. "She'll know in her heart that she did a good job and that she kept her working environment favorable."

He could tell the agent still didn't understand. Pierce was nodding. He got it.

Hawke thumped Marks's file. "We need to dig on him. Here are my two scenarios that may have put him in his predicament." He rattled off his thoughts on divorce and blackmail.

"Agent Tuma will go talk to his neighbors. Best to leave the family out of this to keep him from getting suspicious," Pierce said.

"I agree. Once we understand him, we can work at getting him to contact Hughes." Hawke had a feeling they were going to need Hughes to find the women.

"How do you know Hughes is even still in the area?" Pierce picked up his coffee cup.

"I don't. Especially with his truck transportation gone. But I'm sure if Marks calls him saying he is going to turn or… whatever we come up with, he'll come back to either keep Marks quiet or to see how much he's blabbed."

"That makes sense. Unless he sends someone else?" Pierce held a piece of bacon in front of his mouth. "What if he just sends someone to kill Marks?"

"Then we catch him and see if we can get him to tell us what we want to know."

"It all sounds risky," Agent Tuma said.

"Everything in life is risky. It's how you deal with the risk that makes the difference." Hawke smiled at the woman and dug into his food. All the time he ate, he thought maybe he should do the interviews of Marks's neighbors. He didn't like Tuma's need for praise.

Chapter Twenty-one

Pierce paid for the meal, while Hawke asked Agent Tuma to wait for him. "I'd like to join you when you interview Marks's neighbors. I'll meet you in the parking lot." He wandered to each of the fire exits and found Clarence working on the one by the cineplex.

"How many more do you have to go?" Hawke asked.

"Just one more and they'll all be wired. Marty gave me the gadgets to make it alert his computer." Clarence held up a small device.

"Good. Go home and get some sleep when you finish," Hawke said.

"I plan on it."

Hawke exited the casino and found the two agents standing by a rental car. "You want to ride with me?"

"I thought you were going to fill in the OSP Lieutenant," Pierce said.

"I can do that later." Hawke motioned to the

woman agent. "I'd rather go along with her. Someone who looks more like a local will get more information out of the neighbors than someone looking like a Fed."

Pierce nodded. He was in his suit and tie today.

Tuma was dressed like someone from a large city.

"I don't understand why I need to go along with Trooper Hawke. He will be doing all the talking and I'll just stand there." Her arms crossed, her eyes narrowed, and she scowled at Pierce.

Hawke hid his amusement. She was acting like a spoiled child. He was glad he didn't have to partner up with anyone for work.

"Then you can go back to the motel and see what else you can dig up on Marks, and I'll go with Hawke to interview the neighbors." Pierce handed her the rental car keys.

She huffed, clicked the unlock button, making the car beep, and slid in behind the wheel.

"Let's go," Pierce said, pulling off his tie.

They found the small house where Marks lived. They would have to be careful. The man was home sleeping from his shift the night before and getting ready for his shift tonight. The house was located on the end of a block.

"I'll park around the corner, and we'll walk around the block and start at the other end." Hawke parked his pickup at the curb on the next street and they exited.

"If he's sleeping, it's unlikely he'll see us talking to the neighbors," Pierce said. He'd shed his suit coat, put his shoulder harness and gun in the glove box, and rolled up his sleeves.

Hawke locked his vehicle and walked up to the house directly behind Marks's house.

He knocked. The sound of daytime television could be heard. He knocked a little harder.

"Coming!" The voice sounded like an older man.

The door opened and a short, round man with a bald head looked up at him. "You Jehovah's Witness?"

"No." Hawke flashed his badge. "Oregon State Police. Could we come in and ask you some questions about your neighbor?"

The man backed up opening the door wider. "You here about the bunch across the street that blast music half the night?"

The house was small and filled with furniture and boxes. Hawke wound his way through the boxes to what appeared to be the living room.

"No. We're interested in Jerome Marks. The neighbor behind you." Hawke pulled out his notepad.

"Jerome? I hardly see him. If he isn't at work at the casino, he's sleeping. That's what he's probably doing right now." He narrowed his eyes behind thick-rimmed glasses. "What are you looking into him for?"

"We're doing a background check for the casino." Not quite a lie but it would keep the man from being so skeptical. "Your name?"

"Bernie Trower. I would have thought they did that when he started working there?" The man wasn't going to be easy to get information from.

"We do follow ups every so often. When a person works security and surveillance at a facility that deals with money, they have to be checked up on." Hawke wanted to roll his eyes at himself. "Has he changed any of his routines lately?"

"No. He moved in there right before he got his job. His days off, he sleeps, does laundry, and goes to the store." The man slowly shook his head. "He has less of a social life than me."

"I see. You talk to him often?" Hawke asked.

"No. Maybe once a month."

"How do you know his routine on his days off so well?" Hawke wondered if there was a fence between the two lots.

"You can hear his old washing machine thumping, and I've met him at the store getting groceries on a day when he wasn't working."

"Have you or other neighbors visited with him?" Hawke asked.

"Like I said, maybe once a month I run into him either at the store or he's in his backyard when I am. That's mostly in the summer, like now." The man pulled his glasses off and wiped them on a handkerchief he pulled out of a pocket.

"Is he friends with any other neighbors?" Pierce asked.

Mr. Trower glanced at him. "Not really. I know Mavis has been taking him casseroles. She wants to fix him up with her daughter." The man chuckled. "It would take more than a casserole to get a man interested."

"Where does Mavis live?" Hawke asked.

"Across the street from Jerome. The yellow house with green shutters." The man cringed.

"Thank you, Mr. Trower." Hawke stood. "There's no sense saying anything to Mr. Marks about this. It's just routine. I wouldn't want him thinking he's in trouble."

"Sure. I get it. No sense making him worry when it's just routine." Trower walked them to the door.

"Right," Pierce said, and they stepped out of the door.

"Mavis?" Pierce asked.

"Yeah. Then we'll talk to the others." Hawke walked around the corner, and wondered at how he hadn't noticed the buttercup yellow house with the nearly neon green shutters when they drove down the street earlier.

"Wow! I wonder how the neighbors sleep with this house glowing at night," Pierce said, following him up the sidewalk to the small porch and green front door.

Hawke knocked and waited. This time the door opened right away. A woman, he would guess around forty, with a long, angular face, and taller than the door, peered out at him.

"Hello, we're looking for Mavis," Hawke said.

"That's my mother. Come in. I'll get her." The woman left the door open and crossed the room in four strides.

"That is one tall woman," Pierce said, stepping into the house behind him.

"Hello? Gretchen said you wanted to speak with me?" A woman in her late sixties, with streaks of brown in her graying hair, walked into the room. She was just under six feet and stouter than her daughter. Where her daughter's face was long and narrow, the mother's was round.

"Mr. Trower sent us over," Hawke started.

"Why would Bernie send you over here?" She was smiling at Pierce. He was a couple inches taller than Hawke's six feet.

Hawke grinned inwardly. The woman was sizing the special agent up for her daughter.

"We're doing a background check on your neighbor, Jerome Marks, for the casino." Hawke held up his badge, but the woman wasn't interested in him.

"Gretchen, bring these two men your special lemonade," Mavis called over her shoulder.

"That's kind ma'am, but we won't be staying that long," Pierce said.

"What's your last name?" Hawke asked.

"Davis." She glanced at Hawke. "I thought you said Bernie sent you over here. How come you didn't know my last name?"

"He only told us Mavis." Hawke motioned for them to sit. He took the stiff-backed chair and Mavis took the recliner. That left the couch for Pierce.

When Gretchen entered the room with a tray laden with a pitcher and glasses, her eyes lit up. She sat on the couch next to Pierce and smiled at him.

"Mrs. Davis, what can you tell us about Jerome Marks?" Hawke pulled out his notepad, writing down her and her daughter's names.

"Jerome is a nice young man."

Hawke shot a glance toward Pierce. The man in question was in his forties. Not really a young man.

She continued. "I send Gretchen over with a casserole once a week. Always the first day of his work week. That way he doesn't have to worry about cooking with those awful hours he puts in."

"How do you know his work schedule?" Hawke asked.

"Gretchen works for the employment agency that sends applicants to the casino. She knows all the jobs and shifts. Don't you Gretchen?"

The younger woman smiled and watched Pierce.

Hawke turned his attention to the daughter. "Gretchen, did the casino hire anyone new in the maintenance department about six months ago?"

She stared at him, her eyes blinking. "Yes. There was an opening in maintenance. We sent three people over, but they hired someone who walked in off the street."

"Do you know the person's name?"

"No. You'd have to ask casino personnel."

"Thank you." His mind was wrapping around who had disabled the doors. It had to be another person on Hughes payroll. "Does Mr. Marks ever have any friends come visit him?"

Mavis pursed her lips. "The only person I've ever seen is a dark-haired woman in a small blue convertible."

Hawke's gaze met Pierce's. Hawke pulled out his phone and found the photo of Lanie Porter. "This woman?"

"Yeah, that's her. She pulls up, honks her horn, and they take off in that little car on his days off."

"Did anyone else ever come by?" Pierce asked.

"No, I've never seen anyone."

Gretchen nodded her head. "There was a man who pulled up one day after I'd delivered the casserole. I was standing on our porch. He was in a fancy car. He had on a cowboy hat, nice western cut jacket, and boots. That's what made me turn and look, his heels clacked on the sidewalk as he walked up to Jerome's door."

This information could place Hughes with Marks. "Did Jerome look happy to see the man who'd arrived?"

She shook her head. "He looked nervous. He glanced up and down the street, saw me watching and pulled the man into his house."

Pierce held his phone up to Gretchen. "Is this the man?"

"I didn't get a good look at his face, but that's how he was dressed."

He held the photo out for Hawke to see. Mr. Cowboy Hat, Rory Hughes. They had their connection between the two.

"Can you remember when this was?" Hawke asked.

She again batted her eyes as if information was flickering through her brain like circuits in a computer. "It was early January…I believe around the sixth. Yes. Because I'd asked Jerome how his trip he'd taken over Christmas had been. It was the first time I'd seen him since he'd arrived home. And that was a week after he'd returned."

"Where did he go for Christmas?" Hawke asked.

"He didn't really say. Just it hadn't turned out as well as he'd thought." Gretchen's face screwed up in a puzzled expression.

"How long has he been seeing the woman with the blue convertible?" Pierce asked.

"The first time I saw her was in January. Only the car didn't have the top down then," Mavis said.

Hawke couldn't wait to contact Dela and see if anyone in security or surveillance knew where Marks had gone for Christmas. He had a feeling something happened that now had him helping a human trafficking ring.

"Thank you for all of this information." Hawke stood. "Let me remind you this is all confidential. Don't tell Jerome that we were here, or anyone else."

Gretchen stood. "But shouldn't he have the right to know his work is checking up on him?"

Pierce put a hand on her arm. "No. We do this to make sure they are suitable for their jobs. If he heard we were checking him out, he'd worry and that could jeopardize his employment."

She smiled at Pierce. "I understand. Will you be coming back?"

"I doubt it." Pierce held his hand out to Hawke. "Give her a card in case they think of anything else."

While Hawke knew they hadn't introduced Pierce as FBI and he wanted it kept that way, he was reluctant to give the woman giving Pierce doe eyes, his phone number. Handing the card to the special agent, he said, "This number is only to be used if you think of anything else that might enlighten us about your neighbor."

Gretchen nodded, but she only had eyes for Pierce.

"Come on." Hawke headed for the door.

"What's your name?" Gretchen asked Pierce.

"Quinn. Thank you for your time." He nearly pushed Hawke out the door.

"Come on, if you stayed behind, you'd have learned a lot more," Hawke kidded the special agent.

"I think we have more than enough to confront Marks." Pierce strode down the sidewalk faster than he had earlier in the day.

"Trying to put distance between you and your new girlfriend?" Hawke chuckled.

"Not funny. She's nearly a foot taller than me. Did you see the size of her hands and feet?" Pierce opened the passenger side door of Hawke's pickup. "I like my women daintier."

"Can you see if there are any surveillance or front door cameras on houses within five blocks of Marks's house? Then get some officers to go to those places and see if they can get any footage that shows a fancy car and possibly a photo of Hughes headed that way?" Hawke started up his vehicle. "We really need something to show Marks if we want him to talk and help us."

"Drop me off at the motel. I'll get Tuma on it and see what I can dig up." Pierce rolled his sleeves down and put on his suit coat, before looping his tie around his collar.

"I need to check in with Lt. Keller and make a call to Dela." Hawke headed to the Interstate to catch it over to the FBI building in downtown Pendleton.

"What are you calling Dela about?" Pierce asked. His voice wobbled a little.

"You afraid I'm going to tell her you had a giant woman interested in you?" Hawke grinned. While Pierce and Dela acted as if they didn't like one another, he'd picked up on a different vibe between them.

"No. It just seems like you keep going to her for help rather than her boss or even the tribal police." The man protested too much.

"Because she cares that we find the two missing women. She has a passion for justice that I've not seen in a very long time. And she's lived on the reservation her whole life other than her military service. She has ins that even though I lived here as a kid, I'm a stranger to most. She can get people to talk to her." He pulled into the parking lot near the FBI building and pulled out his phone.

Pierce remained in the vehicle while Hawke called Dela.

"Hawke, what's up?" the security guard answered.

"We learned more about Marks. Do you happen to know where he went over Christmas?"

"No. I remember he took a week off, but not where he went. I can ask around. Rosie at the deli might know."

"That would be great. I should get to the casino about when you do. There's a lot to go over."

"Sounds good. See you then."

The line went silent. Hawke glanced at Pierce. "She doesn't know where Marks went but will ask the others."

Pierce nodded and exited the pickup. "I'll call you when I know anything on this end."

"Same here." Hawke put the vehicle in gear and headed back to the interstate and the OSP headquarters.

Chapter Twenty-two

Entering the OSP building from the back, Hawke made his way to Carol's office without informing her he was there. He knocked on the door.

"Come in," she called.

He walked in, and she looked up.

"I'll call you back later." Carol rolled her shoulders and leaned back in her chair. "I don't know what you said to the city police this morning, but they called me wanting to know where you get off telling them what to do." She raised her eyebrows.

"I just told the officer who called wanting to start the investigation into Sherry Dale's disappearance that the state police, myself, and the FBI were already working on it." He shrugged. "They were eighty-four hours too late."

She laughed. "Well, they weren't happy." She leaned forward, picked up a file, and flipped it toward him. "Forensics on Lanie Porter."

He opened the file and didn't learn much more than what she'd told him earlier. "We have a witness who saw Rory Hughes, our cowboy hat suspect who was seen with both missing women, with a member of the casino surveillance we suspect of helping him."

"I see. Is the FBI working on the Hughes suspect?"

"We're working on it together. We think something happened when Marks went on vacation around Christmas that got him linked up with Hughes. The assistant head of security at the casino is working on that angle. We hope to get Marks to help us lure in Hughes. Then we'll concentrate on finding the women when we can get more information."

"You believe they are still alive and you can find them?"

He nodded. "We, Special Agent Pierce and I, believe they were taken by a human trafficking ring. We plan to find out where they were taken and get them back. Of course, Pierce wants to also take down the whole ring."

Carol shook her head. "You never did do anything the easy way."

Hawke grinned. "You know me, I have to follow the leads all the way to the end." His phone buzzed. He glanced at it. Dani. Damn! He'd forgotten she'd called earlier. "Hold on a minute," he said, answering the call. He stood and said to the Lieutenant, "That's all I have for you now. I'll let you know the outcome of what we're looking for."

Carol nodded. "Good luck!"

He walked out of her office toward the back of the building. "Hi. Sorry about that. I was in a meeting with

Lt. Keller." He stepped out of the building.

"Were you working this morning when you didn't answer my call?" Dani asked.

"No. I was sleeping. I didn't get to bed until five this morning. Long day and night yesterday." He walked toward his pickup but didn't get in. The sunshine and fresh air were welcome after as much time as he'd been spending in the smoky casino.

"I know you're at the reservation to help find a woman your mom said is missing. How is all of that going?"

She must be at her place outside of Eagle to have called him. On the mountain all they had for communication was a radio.

"It's a long story. Did you fly out for supplies or more customers?"

"Both! When there are additional people staying and eating, we need extra supplies. We've had more people visit so far this summer than we had all of last summer." Pride filled her voice.

"Good. Then you are fulfilling your dream of making Charlie's Lodge a destination place." Hawke knew Charlie would be excited for his niece, but unhappy so many people were treading through his lodge and around the mountain. While he'd enjoyed catering to the hunters and fishermen, they were enough company for him. The old man had been set in his ways. Dani was all about getting more people on the mountain to enjoy nature.

"Yeah. Any idea when you'll be back in Wallowa County?" There was a bit of wistfulness in her words.

"Not sure. This is getting complicated. When we

dig up new evidence it makes the situation more critical. My vacation ends a week from tomorrow. If we don't have the women or enough to get them by then, I'll take another week. Special Agent Pierce and I have it figured out. We just need to get people to play along to help us find the women." As he stated what had to happen it sounded easier than it was going to be.

"I thought you were there to find one woman. You just said women." Her quick mind, as always, intrigued him.

"We've discovered the person who took Sherry also took another woman from the reservation six months ago. Our goal is to find both of them."

"Did you run across human trafficking?" The disgust as she said the last two words made him smile.

"Yeah. We believe they are alive, but not sure if the first one is still in the country." That was his fear. That Meela had already been shipped to China.

"Is there anything I can do to help?" There was her military training kicking in. Ready to help at a minute's notice, to defend.

"I'll let you know. Right now, it's just leg work and finding the right trigger to get someone to turn on the man in charge."

"Be careful." Her voice held concern.

"I have the FBI at my back. I'll be fine. Say hi to everyone at the lodge for me."

"Will do. Kitree has been teaching the kids who come all about the wild plants. I told her not to talk about the poisonous ones. All I need is a lawsuit because a kid went home and killed a sibling with a plant she told them was poisonous." She laughed, but he understood that wouldn't be good. There was always someone on the lookout to cause another person harm.

"Glad you told her that. I really have to go. It was good talking to you." He didn't want to end the call but there was still a lot to do.

"I understand. Let me know how things go and if you need help."

"I will."

Silence filled the line. He was glad she'd called. When he became consumed by a case like this, he forgot there was a world outside of his trail. He slid in behind the wheel of his pickup wishing Dog had come along. He liked talking things out to the animal. Made him look less crazy if someone noticed him driving and talking. However, as he'd left the house this morning, his pal was curled up next to Trey watching cartoons. He'd decided the boy needed his friend more than he did today.

His phone buzzed. Mom. "Hawke."

"Gabriel, Moss Smith said he saw something strange the other night when he was closing the golf course." She took a short breath and continued. "He said he thought he saw a car pull up to the back of a truck, and two people put something that looked like a body in it. He said the car looked like the kind Sherry drives."

Hawke put his vehicle in drive. "Where can I find Moss Smith?"

"He's sitting here at my table drinking coffee." Her tone was smug.

"I'll be there in fifteen minutes." He hung up and headed to the Interstate.

Stolen Butterfly

The minute Hawke sat down at his mom's kitchen table, she set a cup of coffee in front of him.

"You left here so quick this morning, I didn't get a chance to tell you what we learned yesterday," she said, sitting down alongside of him.

"The tribal members you brought together found this man?" He studied the Umatilla man in his forties, with shoulder length hair, wearing a t-shirt and jeans.

The man grinned and nodded. "I was working on the golf course, just like usual, and two women walked up, showed me pictures of a woman and a car. I remembered seeing that car."

"When and where did you see the car?" Hawke pulled out his notepad.

"It was Tuesday evening. Close to dark. I'd gone out to check all the holes, make sure there wasn't any garbage, and check to see what needed watered. The last group had left about a half hour earlier. I was out on the ninth hole when car lights flashed. I looked to see where it came from. That's when I saw the car pulled up at the back of a semi-trailer. A person walked around to the passenger side, and another larger person opened the back of the trailer and they put something, either a body or a rug, in the back. I'm thinking body, because it wasn't stiff like a rug." The man nodded.

"What happened to the car?" Hawke asked.

"That was the strange thing. They drove it up onto a car carrier. Not a semi. It only held three cars. And it drove off."

Hawke wrote all the information down. "Mr. Smith, I'd like you to go to the state police headquarters in Pendleton. Ask for Lt. Keller. Then tell her what you just told me. She'll have you sign a statement. And thank you for coming forward. This could be what we needed to find Sherry."

Putting an arm around his mom's shoulders, he said, "Your group discovered how they got rid of the car and where Sherry was taken. I have to go meet up with the FBI. We're getting close."

"Does this mean Sherry is alive?" his mom asked, peering at him through teary eyes.

"I'm sure of it. We just have to catch up to her before she's out of our reach." He held out his hand to Mr. Smith. "Thank you for coming forward."

As he strode out of the house, Dog fell in step behind him, jumping into the vehicle as soon as the door opened.

"Had enough cartoons for one day?" Hawke asked, roughing up the hair on Dog's head and starting the pickup. As he drove out of Mission, he dialed Pierce.

"Where are you?" the special agent answered.

"Headed to the casino. I have an eyewitness to Sherry being put in a semi-trailer and what happened to her car." Hawke went on to tell him about what Mr. Smith had seen.

"That's good. I'll work on getting the paperwork to search all of the trucks and get information about which trucks were there that night."

Hawke turned into the casino parking lot. "I'm going to see what I can get on Marks. Do you want to be present when I confront him?"

"Yeah. Text me when you're ready to do that."

"Copy." Hawke ended the call and parked at the far

side of the lot, away from the casino. He rolled the windows halfway down and put a dish of water on the floorboard for Dog.

"Hopefully, I won't be too long. We might need you when we check out the trucks." He patted the dog's head and exited the vehicle.

Crossing the parking lot, he noticed there were a lot more cars. Saturday seemed to be a busy day for the casino. It was mid-afternoon. Too early for Dela to be at work. He remembered she'd made the comment Rosie at the deli might know something about Marks's vacation.

His stomach grumbled as he entered the building. Walking through the colorful slot machines, the sounds of games and winning clanged and rang in the air. He had to dodge more bodies than earlier in the week. While during the week the gamblers were alone or with one other person, now they were gathered in groups of three or more around carousels of slots.

The half dozen tables in the deli area were full. He didn't want to stand by the counter eating and talking to the woman who manned the cash register.

"I wondered if you'd come back without Dela." The woman winked at him.

"Hi Rosie. I'd like an iced tea and a ham sandwich with chips." Hawke ordered and pulled out his money.

She took his money, gave him back his change, and picked up a paper cup. "I'll get your drink and bring your sandwich out to you."

He glanced around and spotted people leaving one of the tables. Hawke walked over, cleared the table, and retrieved his drink from the counter before sitting down. Now to get the woman to sit with him and visit.

Five minutes later, Rosie sauntered out from behind the counter with his sandwich and chips.

"Do you have a few minutes to talk with me?" he asked.

Her cheeks darkened. "I can make that happen." She walked over to the counter and called, "Cathy, watch the counter." Then she walked over to the drink station, filled a large cup with soda, and sat across from him. "What did you want to talk to me about?"

"Dela told me you visit with all of the casino employees." He took a bite of his sandwich.

"I do. The security and surveillance people come by for free coffee to help them stay awake during their late shifts." She sipped her drink.

"I suppose they tell you things like where they go for vacation or what's happening in their families." He took a swallow of tea and another bite.

She laughed. "They do. I'm told I'm easy to talk to. You have anything you want to tell me?"

He grinned. "No. But I was wondering if Jerome Marks told you where he went on his vacation over Christmas."

"That was over six months ago. Why would I remember?"

He could tell by the way she'd closed her eyes before saying anything that she did remember.

"It's important for me to find out."

"Why don't you ask him yourself?" She studied him.

He really didn't want to tell her he was a suspect in a kidnapping. "I have reason to believe he might have been caught up in something that could be detrimental to his job. I want to look into it discreetly before confronting him."

She listened as she sipped her drink. "What do you mean detrimental to his job?"

"Could put a bad name on the casino."

Her eyes widened. "We can't have anything discredit the casino. The money raised here built a new community center for everyone on the rez. They have plans to improve streets."

"Then you understand why I'm investigating quietly?"

She nodded. "He won a trip to Crystal Mountain Resort in Washington."

"Did he say if anyone was going with him?" Hawke asked.

"He said we, but he's not married and he never really talked about any friends or family. But when I asked him how his trip was when he returned, he said, he skied. That was it."

Hawke nodded. "I appreciate your help. And keep this between us."

"I love my job. I'm not going to do anything to mess that up." She stood. "I need to get back to work."

"Thank you." He finished his food while texting Pierce to see what could be dug up at the resort and surrounding area during the week before and during Christmas.

Chapter Twenty-three

Before Hawke finished eating, Godfrey Friday, the head of security, walked into the deli and straight toward him.

"I'd appreciate it if you would fill me in on what you've uncovered about the missing women," he said, standing beside Hawke's table.

"Have a seat." Hawke figured it was best to give the man something instead of leaving him out of the loop. He was the head of security after all.

Friday sat down, put his forearms on the table, and waited for Hawke to speak.

"Special Agent Pierce and I have figured out that the man we've been trying to identify works for a human trafficking ring." He stopped there. Let the man ask the questions that would reveal if he had deduced the same.

Friday leaned back, rubbing a hand over his face. "You're telling me that a criminal element is using this casino to get women?"

"We believe they have taken two. We watched the man take a woman, who has been missing for six months, into a room in the hotel. That was the last anyone saw of her. Marty is working on trying to figure out why the surveillance camera in that hallway went blank after they entered the room." Hawke let that sink in.

The head of security scanned the deli area. "You're telling me that you picked up on the discrepancy and the others didn't?"

Hawke shrugged. "They weren't following the man's actions like I was."

"And the second woman. The one that brought you here. Was she taken from here?"

"No. But she was targeted here by the same man."

Friday's big hand came down hard on the table, ringing through the small area. Everyone swung their attention to him and Hawke.

"No one in my security group knew this was going on?" The man seemed to be baffled that his group hadn't seen anything out of the ordinary.

Hawke wondered if Friday was doing this to see if he was going to point a finger at one of his employees.

His phone buzzed. Hawke pulled it out.

Dela texted. *On my way to the casino. Found info on Marks.*

Here already. Your boss is with me.

She sent him an unhappy emoji.

Meet in coffee shop. He sent back.

"I have a call I need to make. We'll bring you up to date as soon as we have more." Hawke stood.

The head of security studied him while standing. "I need to know if there is a person under my supervision who is working with this man you're after. From what you've said it sounds like there is."

"The FBI have been doing thorough checks on your employees. We should know something in a few hours. When they show up, we'll come straight to you." Hawke strode out of the deli and over to the coffee shop. There he found a table in a corner and called Pierce.

"We found a story in the news about a party that got out of hand at a condominium at Crystal Mountain Resort. Names were collected of those present. Rory Hughes, Lanie Porter, and Jerome Marks stood out as names we're interested in."

"Fits my source saying that Marks won a trip there and took someone. That someone was Lanie. She and Hughes set Marks up to be able to blackmail him into doing what they needed here." Hawke ordered a coffee from the waitress. "Dela is headed here with info she gathered about him, too. And I just had an uncomfortable visit with the head of security wanting to know what we've learned."

Pierce made apologetic sounds. "I'll grab up all the intel I have and head to the casino. Wait until I get there to share with Dela. Once we ask to question Marks, we'll fill Friday in."

"That works. Just get a move on. The longer it takes the farther away our butterflies have flown." Hawke ended the call and sipped his coffee.

The waitress was refilling his cup when Dela hurried into the coffee shop dressed in her security uniform. She slid into the booth across from Hawke.

The waitress came over and they exchanged pleasantries while she filled Dela's coffee cup. Once the waitress left, Dela picked up the cup, drank heartily, then peered at him over the rim. "I found out that—"

"Pierce is on his way. He wanted us to wait to tell what we each found out until he arrived."

She frowned and placed the cup down harder than was necessary. "Why is he telling us what to do? You started this investigation."

"Because he has more contacts and a larger resource to dig things up." Hawke sipped his coffee and set the cup down. "We believe the women were transported in trucks to a port on the west coast."

"Seattle, Portland, or San Francisco?"

"Most likely Seattle since that is where the company is that Hughes works for."

"That makes sense. I see why you are letting him call the shots. This could turn international." She picked up the cup. "But it doesn't make me any happier."

Hawke grinned. "Me either. But you play ball with whoever can get you the results you want."

"*T'ikú'.*"

Hawke studied the woman. She'd just used a Nez Perce word his mom used all the time for a form of yes. "Who are your people?"

She shook her head. "Danish on my mom's side and Hispanic on my dad's. I picked up that word growing up on the rez."

"I thought my mom said you weren't Native but when you said the word so well, I thought maybe she'd been mistaken."

"I always wanted to belong to one of the tribes. If I said that growing up, I was made fun of. But having only a mother and living surrounded by this culture, I wished to belong."

He saw the longing in her eyes. "Is that why you joined the Army? To belong."

"Yeah. I would have stayed in thirty if I hadn't been hit." She glanced at the door. "There's Pierce."

He could tell she was happy to change the subject.

Pierce strode over to their table, several files in his hands. "Sorry it took so long. Agent Tuma wanted to come. I told her she would serve better keeping tabs on the company in Seattle." He plopped onto the bench seat where Dela sat, making her scoot over or be sat on.

"Tell me what you've uncovered and we'll see how it works with what I've learned about Marks." He glanced at Dela first.

The waitress arrived, refilled Hawke and Dela's cups and filled one for Pierce. "You three have been spending a lot of time in here lately. Want me to put a reserved sign on your booth?"

"Thanks Gloria, we're fine," Dela said, giving the woman a nod of her head to move along.

The waitress stood there a few seconds more glancing from Dela to Pierce and back to Dela before returning to the counter.

The color had deepened on Dela's cheeks as the waitress made up her own version of what was going on.

"Dela, fill us in on what you learned," Hawke said, to break the awkwardness.

She slid all the way to the wall and shifted so her

back was against it as she spoke to them both. "I put out some feelers to other security and surveillance members who were on the chummy side with Marks. They all said since he came back from his vacation he's been withdrawn and made excuses whenever they talk about going out. They also said they noticed he'd been spending time with Lanie. Which we know was because she was helping keep him in line for Hughes." She glanced back and forth between Hawke and Pierce.

"Correct." Pierce picked up the conversation, adding what he'd already told Hawke about the Crystal Mountain Resort.

"And all I learned was where he'd gone and he'd been secretive since he'd returned." Hawke ended.

"That's how you knew to look into the resort, Hawke gave you that information." Dela studied Pierce.

"Yes. He called after he discovered the information and Agent Tuma and I did the digging into police reports." Pierce picked up his coffee and guzzled.

"Anything else of interest come up?" Hawke asked.

"We were able to get any shipments by the company Hughes works for from leaving our shores until we get a federal judge to sign a warrant to look."

Hawke released a huge sigh. "That helps." He glanced at his watch. "Do we wait for Marks to show up or go get him?"

"He's coming in early. I called and asked Marty to tell Jerome another employee was sick and he was needed sooner." Dela smiled at him.

"I like a woman who can think on her feet," Pierce said. "When is he arriving?"

"In fifteen minutes. Shall we all go to the security office to greet him? I have a guard at the door to bring him to us." Dela stared pointedly at Pierce.

"I think she means, move out of the booth." Hawke translated for the special agent as he stood and shoved money under his coffee cup.

Pierce stood, picking up his files and walking toward the door.

Dela fell in step beside Hawke. "Thanks. He has a really thick skull."

Hawke chuckled. "When are you two going to realize you like one another?"

She stopped.

Hawke kept on walking. Dela caught up to the two of them at the security office door. They walked in and she motioned to a door to the right. "We can set up in this room." She opened the door, walked in, and picked up a file sitting on the table. "This should be still shots of Marks with Lanie and Hughes. I asked Marty to send it down here. The photos should help to prove we have the goods on him."

The room had a long table with three chairs on one side and one chair on the other.

"Your boss is going to want in on this," Hawke said.

"I'll handle him. You two wait here. I'll bring Marks back." Dela walked out of the room.

Hawke took a seat. He wasn't sure Dela would be able to keep her boss out of the room. It was already three against one. Marks would see he was doomed the minute he walked in.

Chapter Twenty-four

Marks entered the room. The second his gaze landed on Hawke and Pierce, he stopped.

"Come on in. We have a lot to talk about," Hawke said, pushing the chair across from him with his foot.

Dela must have given the man a push because he stumbled forward and grasped the back of the chair for support.

"Have a seat, Marks," Pierce said, in a congenial tone.

Dela put a hand on the man's shoulder, pushing him down in the chair. "Take a load off."

It appeared she was going to be the bad cop. Hawke stopped his lips from twitching and decided to let the other two do their thing. He'd just jump in when he had something relevant to add.

"Do you know why we asked you to come in early today?" Pierce asked.

"Marty told me Oscar was sick." He narrowed his

eyes. "I'm thinking that's not true."

Dela opened her file and plopped photos of Marks slipping the note on the barmaid's tray and leaning close to Lanie talking.

Pierce opened a file he had and plopped a photo down of a car parked in front of Marks's house.

The way the man's face grew pale, Hawke had a feeling it was Hughes's car.

"We know you were put in a compromising position in December at Crystal Mountain Resort," Pierce began. "And that led to you working for Rory Hughes, who we believe kidnapped two women from the reservation with your help."

The man deflated right before their eyes. "When I heard Lanie was murdered, I knew it wouldn't be long before someone put it all together. I didn't want to help him, but I didn't want to lose my job either." He stared at Dela. "I didn't know what to do."

She wasn't buying his pleading tone. Her face was as solid as a granite boulder.

"You're going to do what's right, now that it's out." Pierce said. "How do you contact Hughes?"

The man shook his head. "I don't. Lanie would tell him when she'd picked out a woman. She'd contact him and then she'd give me my directions."

Hawke and Dela exchanged glances. This man was a pawn. Disposable. Hawke nodded toward the door. The other two stood and they walked out into the main room. A security guard stood outside the door of the smaller room.

"Did you get a copy of Lanie's phone record?" Hawke asked.

"Yeah, but there weren't any calls other than local ones. And Marks wasn't called. I double checked," Pierce said.

"Then she had another phone. If it was on her, they have it," Dela said.

Hawke studied the woman. "If you were running from police would you want to have the phone you'd been contacting a trafficker on in your possession?"

"She ditched it somewhere in the casino." Dela walked over to a computer with a large monitor. "I had Marty give me all of the footage pertinent to this investigation in case we had to look up something." She dug through several flash drives and shoved one into a USB port. More typing and Lanie leaving the sports bar and entering the closest restroom popped up on the monitor. The video then showed a blonde in a tunic and leggings exit the restroom. She went straight for the fire exit by the cineplex.

"The phone has to be in the restroom. Were the clothes she changed out of picked up?" Hawke asked.

"When I went in looking for her, I didn't see any." Dela frowned. "I didn't look in the garbage."

"But if she planned to come back for the phone, she wouldn't have put it in the garbage," Pierce said.

"It has to be in the restroom." Dela grasped her mic and change the channel on her radio. "Mary, this is Dela. Go to the women's restroom near the sports bar and set up a cleaning sign. I'll be there in five minutes." She headed to the door and spun around. "Come on. I'm not the only one going to dig through the toilets."

Hawke grinned at Pierce and followed behind.

They encountered Friday just outside the security

offices.

"What's going on? I've been told you took Jerome into the holding room."

"Keep him company. We'll be right back," Dela said, patting her boss on the shoulder as she passed.

Hawke followed the woman through the gaming tables with Pierce on his heels. They crossed straight for the women's restroom.

A woman in her fifties stood guard.

"Thank you, Mary. Would you remain here while we look around?" Dela asked, as she continued on, not waiting for a reply.

Hawke nodded to the woman, following the security guard into the restroom. Dela stood in the middle, scanning the area.

"If the phone was used only for contacting Hughes it would be a burner phone. Most likely only about this big," Pierce made the sign of an object about two inches by three.

"A flip phone," Dela said, to give more clarity. Her tone implied she and Hawke weren't dummies.

"Yeah." Pierce glared at Dela.

Hawke didn't care to watch their contest of wills, he walked into the first stall and looked to see if there was a space the phone would fit. Coming up empty there, he picked up the lid of the toilet tank and looked inside. Nothing. He plunked the lid down and stepped out. The other two had entered stalls. The three of them went through all the stalls. No phone.

Hawke picked up the garbage can. Nothing was under it or taped to the bottom of it.

"The cleaning crew would have noticed if it were

in the garbage can," Dela said. Her gaze drifted up to the feminine products box hanging on the wall. "Mary, could you come in here please?"

The woman hurried into the restroom. "Yes?"

"How often are the tampon machines filled?" Dela asked.

"Every Monday unless someone complains they are empty."

"Do you have the key?" Dela held her hand out.

"Yes." The housekeeper held up a small group of keys.

Dela took the keys and opened the box. Sitting on top of the tampons was a small black phone.

Hawke pulled a latex glove out of his back pocket and picked up the phone. "Good catch."

"Mary, please close this and open the restroom back up." Dela led the way out of the restroom and back to the security offices.

"Did she have a key to get into that box?" Pierce asked.

"Anything you can fit in the keyhole will open it," Dela replied. "Any woman who has ever been desperate knows how to get in one of those boxes if they don't have change."

Pushing through the door to the security office, they found Marty sitting in a chair.

"I came to see what you were finding out about my guy." His gaze fell on the phone Hawke still carried with a glove. "What do you have there?"

"We found the phone Lanie used to call Hughes," Dela said, pulling on a pair of gloves and taking the phone from Hawke. She flipped it open and scrolled the contacts with Hawke looking over one of her shoulders and Pierce the other.

"She has three numbers on here that she called." Dela read them off.

Marty wrote them down then started typing on the keyboard. "The last number belongs to Jerome. Still working on the other two."

Hawke headed to the door of the small room. They hadn't asked enough questions. He opened the door and the head of security shot to his feet. Marks looked like he had been given the news he was fired.

Dela and Pierce followed Hawke into the room. It was crowded with so many people.

Hawke pointed to the phone Dela held. "You're going to call Hughes and tell him you have Lanie's phone and you're going to take it to the police if he doesn't come meet you face to face and hand over ten thousand dollars."

The man's head snapped up from staring at the table. "He won't bring money. He won't even show up. He'll just send someone to kill me."

"Lanie had three numbers on this phone. Yours, Hughes, and who was the other person?"

Marks shook his head. "I don't know."

"You spent time with her at the ski resort and after you returned home. You have to know who she was talking to on that phone." Pierce sat down across the table from him. "Think about it. Did you see her having conversations on that phone?" He pointed to the phone that now sat on the table between them.

"I didn't know she had a second phone. I tried to find Rory's number on her fancy phone one night, but all I found were locals."

"Why were you trying to find the number for Hughes?" Hawke asked.

"To tell him I didn't want to do anymore work for him. I haven't been able to sleep or eat. When I'm at work, I know everyone is watching me. Then at home, I'd never know if Hughes would go through with his threat of hurting me if I didn't do what he said." The security guard ran a hand over his sagging face. "I should have just confessed to the police in Washington."

"What brought the cops to the condominium?" Hawke asked.

"It was a loud party. I only had a couple of drinks but the next thing I know, I woke up on top of some girl that didn't look old enough to be partying. She shoved me to the floor and ran out of the room. I was sitting in the room, trying to make sense of things and Rory came in congratulating me for 'breaking in' a new girl." The man's face became pasty and sweat beaded on his forehead. "I'm sure I didn't do anything with her, but when I walked out of the room, she cowered behind Lanie. I felt horrible. Then the cops came. Lanie took the girl in another room and came back out. She and Rory talked to the cops, agreeing they were too loud and would tone it down." He rubbed a hand over his face, again. "All I wanted was for them to go away so I could figure out what happened. After the cops left, Rory said he'd make sure the girl didn't say anything. He knew her family and would make sure this didn't get out." He blew out air. "Then on the drive back home, Lanie told me that I owed Rory and all he needed was for me to fix a couple doors on the casino and stop surveillance cameras from filming while he was entertaining women."

He glanced at each person in the room. "I honestly thought he was just trying to keep his wife from finding out he was a playboy. He would take women up to a room I'd find out wasn't being used and fool around, then come back down and leave by the door he came in. But then after the night he took Meela into the room, she was missing. I asked Lanie and she said the woman got drunk and must have went off with the wrong person." Marks shook his head. "I wanted to believe that. Not that I had any hand in her disappearance. But then he had tried to start up a conversation with Sherry twice when she was in here. He was more tenacious with her than the others. I didn't know why, but then she disappeared. And now Lanie's dead." He dropped his head into his hands.

"I'll get someone to work on finding the girl. I'm pretty sure you didn't do anything. They probably drugged you and then staged it all. Right now, we need you to help us stop Hughes from taking any more women." Pierce motioned to Dela. "Go see if Marty has figured out which number belongs to Hughes."

She glared at Pierce but left the room.

Hawke sat down. "Was a large Caucasian man, with arms like tree trunks and a tattoo of a hula girl on his bicep, one of the people at the party?"

"No. But I saw him, here, talking to Lanie outside near a semi twice." Marks studied him. "Do you think he is the other number?"

"The paranoid truck driver?" Pierce asked.

Hawke nodded. The man they believed killed Lanie.

Friday stood when Dela reentered the room.

"Marty said the number ending in seven-seven belongs to an Adrian Newcomb. The other number is unlisted, and he can't find it no matter what system he uses."

"That would be Hughes's number," Hawke said. He shifted his gaze from Dela to Pierce. "I would bet Adrian Newcomb is an employee of the company Hughes works for."

Pierce pulled out his phone and stepped out of the room.

"Are you ready to call Hughes?" Hawke asked.

Chapter Twenty-five

In the end, to not have Marks thinking he was going to be killed, they suggested he offer to tell Hughes that an Oregon State Trooper was looking into Sherry's disappearance. He could fill him in on what he'd heard if they met up.

Hawke didn't mind being the target. He had more confidence in the Feds and Dela than Marks did. "Did he agree to come?"

"Yeah, but he doesn't want to meet at the casino. He wants to meet at my house tomorrow morning." The man's hands shook as he reached up to rub his face, again.

"I'll have my guys set up around the neighborhood," Pierce said.

"He's been to my place before. He'll know if there's anything different." Marks was looking scared.

"We'll be discrete. Stay here until your shift is over. If he has anyone watching you, he'll know if you change up your routine." Pierce stood. "I have phone calls to make."

Hawke motioned to Marks. "Keep him here until his shift is over." He studied Dela. "What time does he get off?"

"Six."

"I'll be back here at five-forty-five to follow him home." He walked out of the small room.

Dela followed. "What do you plan to do until then?"

"Enjoy one of my mom's dinners and get some sleep. Any chance I can get the number of the truck driver?" He stood beside Marty.

The tech wrote it down and hand it to him.

"Thanks."

"What are you going to do with that?" Dela asked.

"Make sure Marks's story to Hughes holds up." He grinned and walked out of the security offices and across the casino floor.

With the number in his hand, he walked out of the casino and straight to his pickup. "Come on, Dog, let's go for a walk." He let the animal out of his vehicle and they started across the parking lot toward the Travel Center.

When he was at a spot where he could see the trucks parked behind the building, he dialed the number.

"Hello?" answered the voice he remembered telling him to get lost.

"This is your favorite Oregon State Police Trooper. I'd like to have a talk with you."

"Go to Hell—"

"Don't hang up, or I'll tell your boss, Hughes, that you are working with me."

"You don't know what the fuck you're talking about." The man tried to sound tough, but his voice raised a pitch. He was scared of his boss.

"I have your phone number and I have your boss's. But I'd rather help you, because I think just like poor Lanie, who I believe you killed—"

"Prove it!"

"—I think you are a pawn, and Hughes would have you killed just like he had you kill Lanie. Would you rather go down for first degree murder or manslaughter?" Hawke waited while the man on the other end of the conversation breathed heavily.

"What's the difference?"

Hawke grinned. "One you go to prison with the chance of parole and the other you spend your whole life in prison."

"You think there's a chance I could get the one with parole?"

"If you work with me. You need to be punished for killing Lanie, but the person I really want is your boss. How about meeting up with me and we can talk about it?" Hawke hadn't expected it to be this easy. He was wondering about the people Hughes picked to help him pull this trafficking off. Maybe he wasn't the big fish given his poor choices of cohorts.

"Let me think about it. I'll get back to you."

"You have my number." Hawke hung up.

Smoke from a truck's stack spewed in the air in the line of trucks. He heard the revving of an engine. A couple minutes later a loaded three-vehicle car carrier pulled out from behind the building.

"Dog, do you think that's our pigeon taking off?" Hawke asked, keeping his eyes on the vehicle. Now he wished he'd driven down to the Travel Center. Or had a pair of binoculars. He did the next best thing.

Hawke dialed Carol.

"Lieutenant Keller," she answered.

"Hawke. There's a three-vehicle car carrier leaving the Travel Center headed west. I only have a partial plate." He recited the letters. "Can you have a trooper pull it over? If it's Adrian Newcomb, you'll have Lanie's murderer."

"I'll get on that. Thanks."

The line went silent. He had no doubt if it was Newcomb, he was already on the phone with Hughes, thereby giving the security guard's information for Hughes more credence.

Hawke smiled and patted Dog on the head. "Come on. Let's go grab a good meal at Mom's."

They walked back to the casino parking lot. Hawke opened the driver's side door and Dog jumped in. Hawke slid behind the wheel and headed toward Mission and his mom's place. Pulling up to her house his phone buzzed.

Carol.

"Hawke."

"They picked him up the other side of Pendleton. All three cars on the truck were stolen. We have him in custody here. He's saying a cop named Hawke said he'd get an easy sentence. Any idea what he's talking about?" the Lieutenant asked.

He filled her in on his conversation with the man.

"You'll have to use your forensics and the fact I smelled Lanie's perfume in the cab of his semi the day after he killed her. He's looking for a deal because his boss would have him killed if he finds out Newcomb is in custody and might talk."

"You don't want to do the questioning? You know the case better than anyone."

"If you can hold him until tomorrow afternoon, I'd appreciate it. I was up all last night and I have to be up early tomorrow. I plan on eating one of my mom's dinners and going to bed."

"Okay. I'll let them know you'll be by tomorrow to talk to Newcomb."

"Thanks."

The front door opened and his mom stepped onto the porch, waiting.

Hawke slid out, let Dog jump to the ground, and walked up to the porch.

"You look tired," she said.

"I am. But we're making progress." He inhaled. "Smells like I made the right choice to come home for dinner."

She smiled. "Your favorite. Chicken and dumplings."

He put an arm around her shoulders and they entered the house.

"Can we eat now?" Trey called from the kitchen.

"He still has an appetite," Hawke remarked.

"He's doing well, considering his mom didn't say good-bye. I told him she's at a banking conference." His mom didn't look the least bit upset at having lied to the child.

Hawke understood her thinking. If the boy thought his mom was just away on business, he wouldn't worry.

"He did ask if he could call her. I told him she didn't have her phone and I didn't know the number of where she was staying." His mom did look guilty this time. "I hate lying but he would be so grief stricken if I told him the truth. This way he can play with his friends and watch TV and not be making himself sick."

They entered the kitchen. Trey sat at the table, waiting impatiently. He'd already placed carrot sticks on his plate.

"How was your day?" Hawke asked the boy as he washed his hands.

"Good. Watched cartoons with Dog. He's nice."

Hawke nodded as he sat down.

"Then played outside with my friends." The child looked at him with big eyes. "I miss mommy. Mimi said she doesn't know when mommy will come back."

"In a few more days." Hawke bowed his head as his mom said the prayer.

When she finished, he dished up chicken and dumplings for her, Trey, and himself. If all went well tomorrow, he hoped to have Sherry back by the first of the week.

After dinner, Pierce called. He had agents in place around Marks's house. Hawke told him about his call to the truck driver and that said driver was being held by OSP for stolen car violations until he could question the man about Lanie and the trafficking operation.

"Want me to be there for the questioning?" Pierce asked.

"Only if you aren't hauling Hughes somewhere to

question." While Hawke thought this was a foolproof plan to take Hughes into custody, he had a bad feeling that the man wouldn't be this easy to catch.

Chapter Twenty-six

At five-thirty Sunday morning, Hawke turned into the casino parking lot. It had more cars than his previous morning visits and it was earlier. He'd texted Dela the night before asking where the employees parked and what Marks drove. Driving around behind the building, he found the employee parking. A quick lap through the cars and he spotted Marks's vehicle.

The pickup was parked on the end of a row. Hawke nodded toward a spot over by a semi and asked Dog. "Does that look like a good place to watch?"

Dog glanced toward the truck and back at him. He took that to mean the animal liked his choice.

Hawke parked, facing the parking lot, and waited.

Ten till six, cars started arriving and parking. The next shift was showing up. At exactly six, a back door opened and people headed toward vehicles. Some cars held up to three people and others had single occupants as they drove out of the lot.

Hawke waited for Marks. Had Dela kept him back for some reason or was the man ducking out on helping them?

The door opened. Dela and Marks walked out together. It must have been a busy night. Dela's limp was more evident. She said something to him and walked over to a compact car.

Marks walked toward his vehicle, unlocked the door, and slid behind the wheel. Hawke was close enough to see the man inhale and let the breath out slowly. Then he reached down and started the car.

BOOM!

The explosion made Hawke's pickup rattle and a piece of metal hit his hood. He glanced over at Dela. She'd started to back up, but was now hurrying toward the vehicle on fire.

Hawke shoved his door open and ran toward the burning vehicle. He grabbed Dela as she jumped back from the heat of the flames.

"We can't help him." Hawke pulled out his phone and called 9-1-1. After reporting the car fire, he called Pierce.

"You can call off your people. Marks's vehicle just blew up with him in it."

Pierce swore then asked, "How did they get someone there so fast to place the bomb?"

"I don't know, but I don't like it. There is someone else in the casino who has Hughes's number." Hawke glanced at Dela.

She'd heard what he said. "The only people who know we were talking to Marks are the night shift security people. No one else in the casino would have known." She scowled. "I don't like thinking there are two people in security and surveillance that are working for Hughes."

Hawke drew her farther away from the flames as the gas tank caught fire. "There is one person who Hughes was in contact with a lot. The bartender."

"The one who gave the FBI the sketch of Hughes?"

"What do you want to bet he did that to get rid of Hughes and take over the business himself?"

Dela shook her head. "No…Why would he help take Native women? He's Native as well. That's bad karma."

Hawke shrugged. He'd known many who took advantage of their own people. He also knew it wasn't the way of his people, but no matter the culture or ethnicity, there were always people who preyed on anyone they could. "Can you think of anyone else?"

"The only other person I can think of who was left alone with Marks was Godfrey." She turned sad eyes toward him. "He took me in and gave me a job when no one else would. But he should have picked up on the rooms being used and the fire exit doors not working."

The emergency vehicle sirens grew closer. The fire truck and a Tribal Police vehicle arrived at the same time. Followed close behind by Pierce and Agent Tuma.

The tribal policeman was Officer Red Bear. He walked up to Dela. "What happened?"

She explained what happened from her point of view and then the officer asked who else was present when the car caught on fire.

Hawke offered what he saw.

"And the reason for, you say, a bomb going off on his vehicle?" Red Bear asked.

"Because he was working with the people who abducted Meela Skylark and Sherry Dale," Hawke said.

Pierce glared at him. Hawke didn't care. He was tired of acting like they didn't know what had happened to the women. They just had to either prove it or find them.

Red Bear stared at him. "You believe they were kidnapped? Who? Why?"

"I'll fill you in later. Right now, we need to see if there is a camera on this lot?" He glanced at Dela.

She nodded. "We had some thefts from the employee vehicles last year. Cameras were installed then." She started walking toward the building.

"We can get Marty to help us," Hawke said, jogging to catch up to her. "You worked all night and need to go home."

"Sunday and Monday are my days off. I can hang around and help. Sleeping is for slackers." She gave him a faint smile.

"I take it that you are calling me a slacker because I slept instead of sat in the parking lot watching Marks's vehicle?" Hawke asked.

"No. Just repeating something my sergeant would say when someone complained they needed sleep." They stopped at the employee entrance. Dela pulled out her employee ID card, tapped it on the card pad, and the door opened.

By this time, Pierce and Tuma had caught up. They followed Hawke and Dela through the security check point and the employee breakroom, lockers, and supply rooms. Dela pushed on a door and they stepped into a hallway that went three directions.

"Ahead are the security offices. To the right are the laundry services and maintenance." She continued straight. They stepped into the security offices. "I really need to grab some coffee before we go to the surveillance room," Dela said, detouring toward the coffee shop.

Hawke thought the deli would be faster but noticed it was closed this early in the morning. He followed Dela and heard the footfalls of the Feds behind him. Catching up to Dela, he steered her to a booth.

"Might as well catch each other up on what was accomplished overnight before we tackle the videos," he said, sliding into the booth and giving Dela the outside.

She smiled at him.

He'd witnessed the other day how sliding out of the booth after Pierce had blocked her in, had given her discomfort.

Tuma sat on the inside of the booth across from Hawke and Pierce took the outside. "Why did you stop here?" Pierce asked.

"Dela hasn't slept like the rest of us and needs some caffeine. And we might as well compare notes." Hawke waited for the waitress to take their orders of black coffee before starting the update.

"OSP has Newcomb in custody waiting for me to question him." Pierce already knew this, but Hawke felt it was something Dela should know since it was her fellow employee who was just blown up.

"How did they catch him?" Dela asked as the

waitress placed their coffees in front of them.

Hawke told her how it had come about.

"Do you think Hughes has enough pull to get someone inside the jail to silence him?" Dela asked.

Hawke glanced at Pierce. That was a solid question given how the people who worked for Hughes were dying.

Pierce stood. "I'll go make some calls to get a few FBI agents at the OSP headquarters." He walked out of the coffee shop.

"How did your people feel about having been pulled from Marks's house?" Hawke asked the agent sitting across from him.

She shrugged. "It happens more than you think. We strategize and get set up then have someone turn themselves in, or like today, the person goes a different direction."

He glanced at Dela. She was studying the woman. He'd love to know what was going on in her head.

Pierce returned. "What did I miss?"

"Nothing," Dela said. "I can't add anything other than helping you look through last night's video of the parking lot."

"Did you learn any more about the cargo waiting to go to China?" Hawke asked.

Pierce shook his head. "Still working on getting a Federal order to open them. Someone up in the courts must be in the pocket of the company. I'm having an agent knock on doors today to try and get it signed."

Hawke nodded. He'd already set his mind that if he didn't get anything helpful out of Newcomb, he'd have Dani fly him to Seattle. He'd sneak onto the dock and open the crates himself. The longer the women sat on the dock, the worse their conditions could become.

"Let's get to those videos," he said, picking up his coffee and guzzling it.

Dela picked up her paper cup and stood. "Let's get this whole thing over with." She headed out of the coffee shop with Hawke and the agents behind her.

He had a thought and caught up to Dela. "Did Friday leave when he was supposed to last night?"

"Yeah. I thought it was weird considering one of his employees was on the line for aiding an abduction." She flashed her ID at the lock outside the surveillance offices. The door opened and she leaned against the door, waiting for the agents.

Hawke saw how she was keeping weight off her right foot and leg. He'd have to find a way to make her stay off her feet while she helped.

When they all entered the main room with all the monitors, four heads turned their way.

"We saw the vehicle blow up. Who was it?" one of the younger men asked.

"We need that video fed to the monitor in Marty's office," Dela said, not answering the man's question.

"What are you doing back here?" Marty asked, stepping out of his office.

Dela walked by the FBI agents. "We need to talk." By continuing into the room, she forced the man back into his lair. Hawke followed with the agents behind him.

Dela explained what had happened.

"Man! I didn't see that. I went down to grab some breakfast." There was a plate with ham, eggs, and toast sitting at the console table. "What do you need?"

"We need video from the camera that watched the parking lot all night," Pierce said, as if taking control.

The younger man stared at Pierce then glanced at Dela for the go ahead.

Hawke grinned. It was obvious Dela had more authority here than the special agent.

"Please bring up the surveillance camera in the employee parking lot starting from…" She glanced at Hawke. "What time did Marks make his call?"

"About four-thirty, I think." Hawke hadn't paid that much attention to the time.

"From four on," she said.

Hawke pulled out a chair. "Have a seat. You've been up all night."

She didn't even glare at him as she sat down.

Marty pulled up the video. "There's two cameras, which one do you want to see?"

"Can you get both?" Hawke asked.

"Yeah. Hold on." Marty tapped the keyboard and two different angles of the parking lot appeared on two monitors.

Hawke pointed to Marks's vehicle. "You can speed it up until someone approaches the truck."

They didn't have long to wait. At four forty-five someone walked up to the vehicle.

Hawke knew who it was as soon as the man came into view. "That's Newcomb. He must have been up here installing the bomb before I called him and he left the Travel Center."

"Hughes had to have called him as soon as he hung up from talking to Marks." Dela leaned back in her chair. "Thank God it wasn't another employee."

Marty glanced at her. "You thought someone here put the bomb on Jerome's vehicle?"

She shrugged. "I couldn't think of anyone else who would have been close enough to do it so soon."

The head of surveillance nodded. "Now what are you going to do?"

"Keep watching for Hughes. We don't know that he isn't around here." Dela stood. "I'm going home. But if you need me for anything," she studied Hawke, "don't hesitate to call. I want to get Sherry and Meela back home."

"I will. Right now, I'm headed to have a conversation with Newcomb." Hawke pointed to the video. "Any chance you can give me a copy of that?"

"I'll have it for you in five minutes." Marty started tapping on the keyboard.

Dela left the room.

Hawke faced Pierce. "You want to help me tag team this guy?"

The Fed's face lit up. "Sounds like fun."

"Why don't you drop me off at the motel to continue the computer paper chase," Agent Tuma said.

Pierce nodded. "I'll drop her off and join you at OSP."

The two left the room. As they did, Hawke leaned down toward Marty. "See if you can capture a good photo of Agent Tuma as they leave."

"I can do that. Why? She's not exactly pinup quality."

Hawke laughed. "I think Dela has good instincts and she acts as if something is off with Agent Tuma.

Thought I'd flash her photo at the guy I'm going to question."

Marty nodded and a printer whirred behind him. "If you want, I can ask Wallace to do some digging on her. You know, unofficial."

Hawke studied the man. "It could be dangerous. If they do have her planted in the FBI, anyone checking into her would be targeted."

"Not a problem. Wallace knows how to infiltrate information bases without being detected."

"Let's wait until I see if this guy recognizes her."

Chapter Twenty-seven

Newcomb was handcuffed to his chair in the interview room.

Hawke carried in a borrowed laptop queued up to start with the man walking up to Marks's pickup. He also had a folder with Newcomb's prior arrests, and forensics from Lanie's body. OSP found a woman's scarf in Newcomb's duffel bag in the car carrier the man was driving when he was picked up. It had been sent to forensics for epithelial DNA to see if it had belonged to Lanie and could possibly be the method of strangulation. They had also sent along the man's duffel bag which would now be tested for incendiary devices to match up to the car bomb.

He'd slipped the photo of Agent Tuma into the folder before Pierce arrived.

On the way over, he'd called Dela and asked her what it was about the woman that made her study her so much. Her comment had been the woman looked familiar. Not from her military days, but recently. Which made Hawke wonder if she had been at the casino with Hughes. He'd called Marty right after talking to Dela. The savvy tech man was already looking for her in all the video they had of Hughes.

Hawke sat down across from Newcomb. The man glared at him.

Pierce took a seat to Hawke's right and started the recording device.

"Who's he?" Newcomb tipped his head toward Pierce.

"F.B.I." Pierce said, enunciating each letter.

"Why's he here?" Newcomb didn't understand they were the ones that were supposed to ask the questions, not him.

"How about we start with your name, then we'll answer your questions," Pierce said.

"Adrian Newcomb."

"And you were read your rights when you were arrested for car theft, correct?" Pierce asked.

"Yeah, but I was pulled over for speeding," Newcomb replied as if that should be noted rather than the theft.

"I have something I'd like you to look at." Hawke opened the laptop and pressed a button. Then placed it at the end of the table where all three could watch.

When Newcomb recognized himself and the vehicle, he turned his head.

"Yeah, we have you on film planting the bomb that killed Jerome Marks." Hawke closed the laptop and opened the file on Lanie. "We also found Lanie Porter's scarf in the vehicle you were driving that had stolen cars. When forensics finishes with it, I'm pretty sure they will determine it was used to strangle her."

Newcomb's brow was sweating.

"That's two murders in less than a week. From your record, you're escalating your violence. Not a good thing to do." Pierce leaned back. "You'll be in prison for a very long time. In fact, you'll die in prison."

Newcomb slammed his fists on the table as best he could with only six inches of movement. "You said if I gave you Rory you'd see that I got parole." He stared at Hawke.

"That was before you killed another person. I said I was pretty sure you were only doing what you were told."

"I was. I swear. Lanie called me, said the cops were after her and she needed a ride to Rory. I called Rory. He told me if the cops were after her, she was to be eliminated. He didn't want any connection to her." He stared at Pierce, then Hawke. "Don't you see? If I don't do what he asks, he'll have someone else kill me."

"And Marks?" Hawke asked.

"Rory called and asked me how close I was to the casino. I happened to have just pulled into the Travel Center for fuel. He told me to make sure Marks didn't talk to any more police." He shrugged. "I carry a bomb around with me in case I get caught and need to blow up the evidence. I knew what Marks drove. I hooked it up and left. Only you called and that got me thinking and I was driving too fast…"

Hawke exchanged a gaze with Pierce. The man

hadn't been pulled over because he was speeding. But let him think that.

"Are you willing to tell us about Rory and the women you helped him kidnap?" Hawke asked.

Newcomb raised his chin and clamped his mouth shut.

"You know how you are worried about being killed for talking to the police?" Hawke asked, slipping the photo of Tuma out of the folder and placing it in front of Newcomb. "That might just happen. This woman is here, in Pendleton."

"What the—?" Pierce said, getting a look at the photo.

Newcomb paled and leaned back. "No. You have to help me. I'd rather rot in prison than have her kill me."

"You know this woman?" Pierce asked, no longer being passive.

"That's who Rory usually sends to take care of his problems. I don't know her name, but I've seen her with him a couple of times. Rory likes to tell tales of what she does to people who cross him."

"Tell us how to find Rory and the women you hauled away from here this week, and we'll make sure you live a long time in prison." Hawke said, moving the photo over in front of Pierce.

"I need to make a few phone calls," Pierce said, leaving the room.

Hawke had a pretty good idea Special Agent Pierce was calling someone to arrest Agent Tuma.

"Tell me how the women were taken from this area." He leaned back as if he had all day. Which he did, until he got the information he needed.

"We hauled them in a semi-trailer. Rory reels them in, gives them a drink that knocks them out, then we get them out of whatever hotel he has them in and put them in the back of the truck. The front third has a soundproof room they are put in. I have boxes of furniture in the rest of the trailer with a path to the front." He stared at Hawke. "They have food, water, and a bucket to... you know."

"How long are some left in the truck?" Hawke didn't want to know. He was having a tough time remaining calm as his anger rose.

"Some can be in there a week before we get to Seattle." He shrugged. "I've never had one die on me."

Hawke shook his head. The man acted as if the women were cattle. "Where do you take them in Seattle?"

"To an old, abandoned hospital. The state fixed up part of it for homeless people, but Rory pays them to ignore the section he uses to keep the women until they are sold." Newcomb stared at his restrained hands.

"Can you give me the street it's on?" Hawke asked.

The man gave him the street and what road he took to turn off the freeway.

Hawke wrote it down and studied the man. "Do you think it's okay to kidnap women and sell them as sex slaves?"

"Not really, but once I started working for Rory I didn't want to die, so I kept doing it."

"Not a good excuse. Recording ended at..." Hawke recited the time, picked up his folders, and left the room.

He found Pierce in the breakroom on the phone.

The special agent ended the call and studied Hawke. "Do you know where the girls are?"

"Yeah, you need to move on it. Tuma knew we were talking to Newcomb. They could be moved already." Hawke added, "I want to go with you."

"You've earned it. I have a helicopter waiting for us. Come on."

Hawke followed the agent out of the building. He was glad he'd dropped Dog off at his mom's on his way from the casino to the OSP headquarters.

A helicopter sat in the open lot to the south of the forensic lab. They ran over to it and climbed in.

Once they were settled with headsets and taking off, Pierce told the pilot to head to Seattle. "Where are the women?" he asked Hawke.

"An abandoned hospital used by the state to house the homeless." Hawke handed the paper with the streets written down to Pierce.

The special agent read the locations and nodded. "I'll have an agent locate the piece of property and have the local law enforcement keep people from going in or out until we get there."

"What about Tuma? Is she in custody?" Hawke studied the man. He could tell he wasn't happy the agent he'd brought in to help was working for the other side.

"No. She never went back to the motel. You're probably right, they are or have, moved the women. She had to have called him as soon as she left the room, knowing we were going to have a chat with Newcomb." Pierce gave a crooked grin. "She'll have to find her own transportation to Seattle. She is persona non grata with all FBI."

Hawke nodded and watched the land below him fly by. He'd planned on taking a helicopter to Seattle, just with a different pilot. This was better. It was best to keep Dani out of the cases he got mixed up in.

His phone buzzed. Sergeant Spruel using his personal phone.

Hawke texted. *In copter with FBI headed to Seattle. Got a lead on where the women may be.*

Good news. Spruel texted back.

I hope so. FBI agent involved in the trafficking. Will tell you more later.

Copy.

He hoped the local authorities kept Hughes from moving the women. He should have asked Newcomb how long the women were kept at the abandoned hospital. Maybe they'd get lucky and Meela would be there as well.

Chapter Twenty-eight

The helicopter dropped them in the parking lot of a large derelict building.

"Is this the abandoned hospital?" Hawke asked.

"Yeah. It's the only abandoned hospital in this area."

As they climbed out of the helicopter, a vehicle pulled up. Hawke followed Pierce to the vehicle and they both got in.

"What do we know?" Pierce asked the driver.

"There has been activity in the building the last hour. We saw people moving inside through the windows, but no vehicles have arrived or left."

"I don't understand why they haven't tried to move the women," Hawke said, staring at the building as they drew closer.

"We'll move in and see what we find," Pierce said.

The vehicle stopped.

People in vests with large FBI letters, local police

officers, and two different SWAT teams all gathered near a tactical vehicle.

"Here, put this on. Do you need a firearm?" Pierce asked, pulling a tactical vest out of the back of the vehicle they'd just exited.

"I'm good," Hawke said, donning the vest and pulling his backup Glock out of his boot sheath.

"Let's go find out what they know," Pierce said, leading them over to the group of various agencies huddled around a van.

"Pierce, heard you were in charge of this dance." A lean man dressed in a SWAT uniform held out his hand.

"Dawkins, glad to have you orchestrating," Pierce said, shaking the man's hand. "What do we know?"

Hawke stood beside Pierce watching those around him and listening to the head of the SWAT team.

"As soon as your call came in two local squad cars came out here. They haven't noted anyone coming or going. Since we've arrived, spotters have seen people moving around through two upstairs windows. Male and female." He walked over to a building plan hanging from the side of the van. "This is the plan of the building in front of us. There are four other smaller buildings on the property. I've sent reconnaissance to see if there are any with people in them."

A woman wearing a SWAT uniform walked over. "All four outbuildings are vacant."

"Good to know." Dawkins continued. "We'll go in from all six doors." He pointed to the one in the front, two on the east side, one on the west side, and two in the back of the building. "Once the lower level is cleared, we'll move to the next level and so on." He faced Pierce. "What are we looking for?"

"We have reason to believe women are being held here by a trafficking ring." Pierce made eye contact with everyone within earshot.

Hawke noticed several men grimaced and the women present gave off a steely determination.

"Let's go," Pierce said. He motioned to Hawke. "Stick with me."

He nodded and waited as the others who were leading groups into the various doors were in place.

Dawkins put his hand over his ear and then motioned for the group going in the front to proceed forward.

Hawke had a feeling they were too late. The people in Hughes's organization that he'd encountered so far, wouldn't have sat inside the building waiting for the FBI to get organized. A thought came to him. He tapped Pierce on the arm.

The special agent glared at him.

Hawke held them back from the rest of the group. "When I told you last night about Newcomb, did you mention it to Tuma?"

Pierce stopped glaring and stared at him.

Hawke could see the man was running the previous night through his mind.

"Damn! I did. She knew last night that you had Newcomb in custody. We aren't going to find the women here."

"We aren't. We need a vehicle to check out the dock where the company Hughes works for has cargo waiting and any of the company's warehouses." Hawke waved a hand at the group still heading toward the building. "Want to call them off?"

Pierce let out a huge sigh. "I'm going to get reamed for this mess." He ran up to Dawkins. They had a discussion where the SWAT leader looked back at Hawke. He shook his head and Pierce nodded, jogging back to Hawke.

"Come on. They're going to go ahead and check out the people in the building and check for signs of the women having been there." Pierce strode back the way they'd come. He took off his tactical vest and held out a hand for Hawke's.

Once those were stowed, he motioned to the front of the vehicle. Pierce got behind the wheel, started the vehicle, and pressed a button.

"Seattle FBI Headquarters," answered a female voice.

"Special Agent Pierce requesting to be connected with Special Agent Taylor."

"Connecting now."

"Pierce, I thought you were plundering an abandoned hospital," a male voice said and laughed.

"We believe it's a dead end. Can you send me the addresses of all the warehouses owned by the Farris Company?"

"We have agents watching all of them. No one has reported any unusual activity," replied Taylor.

"I would still like the addresses. And has the warrant to search the cargo at the dock come through yet?" Pierce was taking an on ramp to a freeway.

"Special Agent Vernon hasn't been responding."

"Then check her GPS and find out what happened

to her." Pierce ended the conversation. When an address popped up on the screen on the dash, he pressed it and a map appeared. "Let's go see what we can find at this address," he said, pressing on the accelerator and weaving in and out of traffic.

Hawke held on. It was urgent they get to the women, but they couldn't help if they were injured or dead. "We don't have to die in the process," he said.

Pierce eased up a little and said, "Hughes had better than twelve hours notice to move the women. A lot can happen in that time."

"True, but we can't help if we are in a hospital."

As they eased up alongside another Federal vehicle near the first warehouse, Pierce's phone rang. He touched the screen on the vehicle dash.

"Pierce."

"Dawkins. No women being held hostage. There are half a dozen homeless living on the second floor. Most of them were too scared to talk, but one woman said there were eight young women being kept in a room on the first floor up until last night. She saw a small moving van back up to the building and they loaded the women up. She showed us the room. I took photos and grabbed all the evidence we could find."

"Get it to forensics. We're checking out all the warehouses. Thanks." Pierce ended the call and rolled his window down to speak to the agent watching the warehouse. "Did a moving van come in here last night?"

"Not through this gate. Check with Ron at the back gate."

"Thanks." Pierce put the vehicle in gear and headed to the back of the property.

Another Fed type vehicle sat out of sight of the building but watching the back entrance.

Pierce asked the same thing and came up negative. "Thanks."

"Were these agents sent here early enough to have caught them bringing the van in?" Hawke asked, wanting to get out and do his own search.

"The warehouses have been under surveillance since we determined Hughes worked for this company," Pierce said defensively.

"Which means Hughes knows they are being watched." Hawke leaned his head back against the seat. "We need to find a place that Hughes has that isn't connected to the company. He knows we are watching him through where he works. He would have learned that from Tuma."

Pierce pushed the button on the screen and once again asked for Special Agent Taylor.

"Have you been to all of those warehouses already?" Taylor asked.

"No. Have you dug up any property owned by Hughes that isn't owned by the company?"

"He has a condo at Pigeon Point and property on the waterfront."

"Send me both addresses," Pierce said, his index finger poised over the navigation screen in his vehicle. He entered the addresses and said, "Let Dawkins know that's where we are headed and to be ready to move if we give the word."

"Calling him now."

Pierce ended the call. "You should enjoy where we're going," he said, doing a U-turn and heading back toward the freeway.

"Oh yeah?" Hawke wasn't sure if the man was being sarcastic.

"It's the newest upscale area that is close to the waterfront. You won't see houses in your area like you'll see here pretty soon."

Hawke had never been impressed by large or fancy homes. Why people built homes with more room than they needed, he'd never know.

The freeway crossed an island. "That's Harbor Island. If we don't see sign of the women at Hughes's home, we'll go to the warehouse."

Hawke glanced at Pierce. "Why not the warehouse first? How would he explain eight women being herded to his condo? His place of residence would be on file. I'm sure you've known about it since first investigating him."

Pierce nodded.

"Has anyone looked into whether he has a business under another name? Or maybe has used Tuma as the name on record for a warehouse property?" Hawke's mind was reeling through all the possibilities. His residence would be too easy for anyone to find. He'd never hide kidnapped women there.

Pierce pulled off the freeway and stopped in a parking lot. He punched the button on the screen and asked for Special Agent Taylor, again.

"Did you find the women?" Taylor asked.

"No. Did you try running Hughes name through the business directory? Also try Raeanne Tuma."

"As in Agent Tuma?" Taylor asked. Hawke could hear keyboard keys clicking in the ensuing silence.

"Nothing on Hughes. There's a hit on a Ruben Tuma. He has a warehouse next to a container shipping business." Taylor rattled off the address.

"Send Dawkins and his team to the address. We'll meet them there." Pierce ended the conversation. "We're only about ten minutes from there." He put the vehicle in drive and zig-zagged through the streets until he slowed down.

"The building on the left. Check it out as I drive by."

Hawke peered out the window. It was a building about fifty yards wide and twice as long. An outside stairway went up the side of the building about a quarter of the way back. A man dressed in jeans and a jean jacket stood on the landing in front of the door. Hawke didn't see a weapon but that didn't mean he didn't have one close by. The man stood on alert, like he was ex-military. A giveaway that he wasn't taking a break.

"This looks promising. There's a guy on lookout on the north side of the building. Second floor staircase."

Pierce nodded and continued down two blocks. He parked around the corner and leaned over the seat, pulling out two smaller bullet proof vests. "Put this on under your shirt. It will take more than a glance to notice we're law enforcement. Wearing the vests with FBI all over it will make it harder to do surveillance."

Hawke nodded. He unclicked his seat belt, striped off his shirt, and put on the heavy life-saving vest that made it hard to move as easily. He'd preferred to go without it, but this was Pierce's expertise, not his. With his shirt back on, he stepped out of the vehicle.

"Go down the street and come up the back way or try it through the front gate?" he asked Pierce.

"Let's sneak in the back. Might be easier to see more."

They headed down the street they'd parked on and turned at the end of the long block. Hawke didn't like the mingled scents of stagnate water, oil, and exhaust that hung in the air. The street they were on, would be at the back of the building. The container business next to the warehouse took up most of the block. The sounds of heavy equipment droned in the background as various vehicles moved up and down the streets.

Activity in the container yard drew Hawke's attention. He stopped and studied the movement. It appeared they were moving containers around. But he only saw two people and one crane operator. Wouldn't the night crew be more workers?

Pierce backtracked to where Hawke watched the activities. "Never see a crane lift a container before?"

He pointed. "Doesn't that look like a small crew to be working out here?"

The Special Agent shrugged. "Could be they sent just those three back to find a specific container."

Hawke nodded. "Let's go." He still had a strange feeling the scene hadn't looked right.

They went another twenty yards and were at the corner of the warehouse property.

Pierce pulled out a small pair of binoculars and studied the area. "Looks like there is a guard at the corner of the building in the shadow. He has an AR rifle."

Hawke pointed to the other side of the building. "I'll go see if that stairway is the only way into the top floor of the building."

"We need to stick together," Pierce said.

"We need to know what we are dealing with. If this building has men with guns protecting it, I'm pretty sure this is where the women are. Call Dawkins and get his guys over here. I'll do some scouting." Hawke walked across the road and strolled along, not once peering at the warehouse across the road that he was interested in. He stopped once and acted like he was taking a leak, then moved on down the road. If anyone watching from the warehouse saw him, he wanted them to think he was harmless.

Once he passed the corner of the property, he continued a half a block beyond and slipped back across the street. Instead of walking onto the warehouse property he was interested in, he entered the gate of the property next door. This warehouse was quiet. He walked along the chain link fence between the two facilities. The side he was on had a hedge about four feet high. Before bending at the waist to keep from being seen, he glanced once over at the corner where he'd left Pierce. The agent was crouched behind the corner of the fence. Hawke couldn't tell if the special agent was on the phone or just bidding time.

He hurried along the fence, bent over, but trying to keep an eye on where he was in comparison to the building in the other lot. When he was even with the corner, he stopped and studied the shadows. There was a sentry on both corners. Continuing, he went the full length of the building. There were docks on this side of the building. A moving van was parked between two semis. That confirmed there was a strong chance the women were here.

Hawke texted Pierce. *Moving van tucked between semis. Going to get a closer look.*

His phone buzzed in his hand. *Stay put. Dawkins will be here in 15.*

He responded. *2 guards on your end. Checking front.*

The sound of a diesel engine rumbling to life drowned out the sound of the crane running in the container yard on the other side. Smoke billowed out of the stack of a truck backed up to the dock.

Hawke had to make a decision. Stay here and wonder after the truck left if it had the women in the trailer, or get over there and keep the vehicle from leaving before the SWAT team arrived.

Chapter Twenty-nine

A quick look and Hawke didn't see a driver in the truck. He glanced right and left. He didn't see anyone watching the loading dock. He used the hedge to give him a boost as he climbed the eight-foot fence and dropped down on the other side. He waited to make sure the jangling of the fence hadn't alerted anyone. No movement. No shouts. Crouching low to the ground, he hurried across the pavement and slipped under the semi.

Shoving with his feet, Hawke slid on his back toward the tail end of the semi. The bullet proof vest under his shirt kept his back from getting scraped. He reached up and cut the air brake lines. The whoosh of air had him rolling to his hands and knees and scurrying to the back of the trailer in case someone checked the lines.

Voices stopped his forward motion.

"It makes that noise when the air lines get full," a male voice said.

"You're sure? It didn't sound the same," a familiar female voice replied.

"It's fine. I don't see why we have to move them again. We just moved them last night," whined the male voice.

"Would you rather get caught by the FBI?" The female voice snapped. He'd bet all his horses it was Agent Tuma. She was here overseeing the moving of the women.

He dug in his pocket and pulled out his phone. *Tuma is here. They are getting ready to move the women. Semi on west side.*

Copy. Dawkins is here.

Hawke listened as the sound of heels clacked on the cement loading dock and disappeared. The acrid scent of a cigarette meant the driver was taking a break.

Easing toward the edge of the trailer, he crouched and walked out from under the metal container. His gaze went to the almost five-foot-high dock. The rubber bumpers for the trucks to back up to would have to help him get up there. It was that or find a set of stairs. That was too risky. Surprise would be better.

Moving to the back of the trailer, the open door kept anyone on the dock from seeing him, but it also didn't allow him to see where the person was on the dock.

He decided to go with the full element of surprise. Shoving the door hard, he grasped the rubber bumper and sprang up onto the dock. The man smoking the cigarette waited too long to draw a weapon. Hawke had an arm around his neck, choking him into silence.

Dragging the man into the warehouse, Hawke

scanned the area. He didn't see anyone else. He pulled the man behind a stack of boxes and found a roll of shrink wrap. He quickly wrapped the man's hands behind his back and his legs together. Then shoved a wad of the wrap into the man's mouth.

Hawke pulled his Glock out of his boot and studied the layout of the building. Presuming the guard on the stairway was keeping anyone from getting into the upper level, that must be where the women were being held.

The warehouse went clear to the roof on this side. He had to proceeded through the stacks of boxes to the far side of the building to find a way up to the second floor of the building. Luckily for him, the stacks of goods ran the width of the building and not the length. He continued down the aisle between two tall stacks, keeping close to one side.

As he neared the other side, he heard shots outside. The SWAT team was moving.

The sound of multiple feet ringing on metal stairs sent him that direction. He rounded the end of a stack and came face to face with Agent Tuma.

She raised her weapon. He flattened back against the side of the boxes. A round zinged by him.

"Police, everyone down!" he shouted and stepped back around the stack. He aimed at the one woman standing as she fired at him. A pain in his chest knocked him backwards. The agent fell.

Women screamed.

SWAT members surged forward, aiming their rifles at Hawke as he sat on the ground gasping for air. The vest kept the bullet from penetrating, but it knocked the air out of him.

Pierce ran up. "Not him. He's with us." The Special Agent knelt beside him. "Did you see Hughes?"

"No. Just Tuma and the guy I wrapped up by the dock. Help me up."

Pierce grabbed his hand.

Hawke winced as pain radiated through his chest. He scanned the women still on the floor. Sherry was near the back.

"Trey's waiting for your return," he said and smiled.

Sherry stood and stared at him. Recognition flashed in her eyes and she ran over, throwing her arms around his waist. "I hoped Mimi would send you looking for me."

Hawke sucked in air as her arms caused him pain. "Get everyone rounded up. The FBI is going to make sure you all get home."

Pierce stared at him. "Aren't you going to take her home?"

"No. There's still a woman missing." Hawke tapped Sherry on the shoulder. "Did you see or hear anything about Meela Skylark?"

"Is this what happened to her?" Sherry's eyes widened.

"Yes. And any idea where Rory Hughes is?"

"He was behind us coming down the stairs," Sherry said, her face paling and fear creeping into her eyes.

Six FBI agents, three female, arrived and rounded up the women.

"They'll be debriefed," Pierce said.

"Let's see what we can find up in the rooms where

they were holding the women." Hawke walked toward the metal staircase.

"Are you sure you don't need looked at?" Pierce asked when Hawke gasped for breath as they ascended the stairs.

"Having trouble breathing is all. I'd rather take this vest off." He unbuttoned the top three buttons of his shirt.

"Not until we've cleared the building and you're sitting in my vehicle. It saved your life once." Pierce sounded like his mother and Dani.

Hawke chuckled. There was a walkway across in front of what appeared to be three rooms. At least there were three doors leading off the walkway.

Four SWAT members followed them up the stairs. Pierce motioned for them to split up into twos and enter the rooms at the same time. The SWAT officers moved on down the walkway, waiting by each door. Pierce gave the sign and they all burst into the rooms.

Hawke followed the special agent into the first room. It had the door leading out the stairway on the side of the building. From the way the door wasn't closed completely, he had a notion that was how Hughes got away.

"Were any SWAT members still outside when the rest burst in here?" he asked.

"There should have been ones taking care of the sentries. Why?" Pierce glanced up from papers he was reading on a desk.

"I think Hughes left by this door. I'm going to find out where everyone was." He shoved on the door.

"I think this is the paperwork for the cargo

container the women were being transported in. I need to collect evidence." This time Pierce gave Hawke his full attention. "Be careful."

He nodded and exited the building, taking it easy going down the stairs to not jar his chest. He hoped the contact of the bullet with the vest hadn't popped a rib out. He'd had a horse accident one time that did that. The way it hurt to breathe and the pinching, he had a feeling that was what had happened.

On the ground, he found a SWAT van loading up two men with minimal injuries.

"Did you see anyone come down those stairs?" Hawke asked.

"Just you," the SWAT member said.

"It would have been maybe ten minutes ago." Hawke figured as soon as he stepped around the boxes Hughes saw him and ran. Some leader, leaving Tuma to take the fall for the women he'd kidnapped.

"Same then as now. Only saw you."

"Do you know if there were any roadblocks set up before you started your assault?" Hughes could have had a vehicle stashed on one of the side streets.

"Talk to Dawkins." The team member closed the doors on the van and walked to the driver's door.

"And he is?" Hawke asked.

"Probably where you came from. Inside." The man pointed up the stairs.

Hawke grunted. He didn't feel like climbing stairs, again. Waiting for the van to leave, he studied the fence. This side butted up against the transport containers. He walked across to the fence and studied it. Someone hastily getting away would run up to the fence, grasp it, and climb over…

He spotted a piece of cloth caught on the top. Peering through the chain link at the ground, he could see where someone had landed hard on the asphalt. Dust was displaced. Something shiny caught his eye. It looked like a metal tip from a fancy pair of cowboy boots. Hawke grinned. He pulled out his phone and called Dela.

"Hawke, what's happened? Where are you?" she answered.

"We have Sherry."

"Thank you! That's a relief. What about Meela?" Apprehension softened her voice.

"I'm still working on that. Hey, go through the videos we have of Hughes. I need a copy of a photo where he's wearing silver tipped cowboy boots."

"I'll get on that right away. Does that mean he got away?"

"Yes, but he left a silver tip behind." Hawke ended the call and punched in Pierce's number.

"Did you find him?" Pierce answered, sounding distracted. Voices in the background were asking him questions.

"No. But I need a forensic person to meet me out by the south fence by the stairway."

"I'll send someone over."

Hawke shoved his phone back in his pocket and studied the asphalt between the row of containers. It would be hard to track the man's direction. They would just have to catch up to him with the evidence of the silver tip.

<><><><><>

Hawke sat behind the curtain of an ER room waiting for his shirt to be given back to him. Pierce had insisted on an x-ray. The FBI forensic tech who had retrieved the silver tip had mentioned to Pierce that Hawke couldn't breathe without pain.

Here he was wasting time waiting for the doctor, who'd insisted on an MRI, to tell him he had a rib out. Something that would pop back in on its own.

The female doctor shoved the curtain aside and walked up to him. "You're lucky. The ribs aren't broken, but you do have costochondral separation. That's when the rib tears away from the cartilage of your breastbone. All you can do for it is take Ibuprofen, ice, and rest. And when you cough hold a pillow to your chest."

"Can I have my shirt now?" he asked.

"Are you going to rest?" The doctor was giving him the look his mom and Dani gave him when he was being stubborn.

"Yeah. Soon as I get home." He held out his hand.

"I'll send a nurse in to help you put your shirt on." She pivoted and disappeared between the curtains.

Hawke swore under his breath and pulled out his phone. He dialed Pierce.

"Hawke, didn't expect to hear from you," the special agent said.

"I need a ride to wherever you are."

"What did the doctor say?" The special agent's voice underscored the sentence.

"That there is nothing they can do for it. Just like I figured. Come on. Send someone for me. Dela should be sending me a photo of Hughes wearing boots with the silver tip. Did you get the warrant to search his place?"

"Yeah, that's where I'm headed."

"Then swing by the hospital and pick me up." Hawke didn't want to beg, but he'd only found one stolen butterfly. He needed to find Meela as well.

"Okay. Be down at the entrance in ten minutes."

Hawke ended the call and slid off the bed. He rummaged around and found his shirt stuffed in a bag attached to the foot of the bed. One arm went in the sleeve easy enough. The contortion it took to get his other arm in had his brow sweating.

"Mr. Hawke, what are you doing dressing yourself?" a middle-aged nurse asked, shoving the curtains open.

"I've been doing it since I was four. Do I need to sign anything? My ride will be here in five minutes." He buttoned his shirt as he walked through the ER.

"Yes, you need to sign these papers." She shoved a clipboard in front of him.

Hawke found the Xs and signed.

"You need your copy. It tells you how to care for your injury." She ripped a copy off the paperwork.

"I know what to do." He walked down the hall and out the door of the emergency area.

Pierce pulled up two minutes later. "Are you sure you're good to go?"

"Sitting around won't make me heal any faster. Let's go." He winced pulling the door shut and leaned back in the seat.

While Pierce navigated the traffic, Hawke pulled his badge out of his pants pocket and hung it around his neck.

"Did you find any information about the women who had been shipped?" he asked.

"The only paperwork I found dealt with the women we recovered."

Hawke's phone buzzed.

Dela sent the photo.

"We have him if we can find the pair of boots missing a silver tip."

Chapter Thirty

As they'd figured, Rory Hughes wasn't at his condo when they arrived. Pierce contacted the property manager and had the door opened. The forensic team arrived after Hawke and Pierce had made one pass through to make sure they were alone.

"What are we looking for?" the head of the forensic team asked.

"Anything that mentions women being sold and a pair of cowboy boots missing a silver tip on the toe." Pierce went back to rummaging through the papers on the desk.

Hawke pulled out a drawer in the wooden file cabinet along the wall in the office. "Has Tuma said anything?" he asked.

"You'd think working for a coward would make her tongue wag, but it isn't." Disgust tinged Pierce's words.

"Were you two close?" Hawke asked, walking his

fingers over the files, reading the names.

"This was only the second time I'd worked with her. She volunteered for the assignment." Pierce scoffed. "I should have realized it was more than a promotion she was after."

"She had the whole FBI fooled." Hawke said, his fingers stopping on a file marked Overseas Clients. He pulled it out and flipped the file open. Each line on the page had a name, country, and preference- young, blonde, brunette, slim, busty. "I found his list of clients."

Pierce walked over. Hawke handed him the list. Behind it he found a list of the names with a video number. Some numbers were circled. "I bet he sent videos of the women to the potential buyers. The circled numbers are the ones that buyer took." Hawke scanned the room. There weren't any actual videos in sight.

A computer tower sat under the desk. "Have forensics take that. I'll get a photo of Meela sent to me." A feeling that he just might find Meela had his adrenaline kicking in. He texted Dela this time.

Can you send me a photo of Meela Skylark. We're getting closer.

Good news. I told Mimi you found Sherry.

Thank you. I've been too busy.

I thought as much. Sending photo.

His phone buzzed. A photo of the first missing woman appeared in his messages.

Pierce returned to the room with a forensic tech behind him. "This needs to go to the lab. Whoever looks through the videos on it needs to text this number…" he rattled off Hawke's number, "…to look for the woman in the photo he sends and make note of the number of the video she's in."

The man nodded, bagging the tower and leaving the room.

Pierce took the file from Hawke. "See if you can find more evidence."

He nodded and continued digging through the files and drawers. In the bottom file he found logs of stolen cars and women from the last five years.

Pierce called over a forensic person to bag all of the files in the top and bottom drawers.

"This isn't getting us any closer to finding Hughes," Hawke said, leaning a shoulder against the door jamb. "That warehouse was under Ruben Tuma. Can you have someone see what other properties Ruben owns in the area?" Hawke was getting tired. The world outside the large picture window was growing darker.

"Come on, I'll put you up in a room tonight while the digging for evidence continues." Pierce motioned for Hawke to walk through the door.

"I could just stay here and see if Hughes returns…" He liked the view of the water beyond the sparkling lights.

"Not alone in your condition. He's eluded us this long; he's not going to return here tonight. Your idea of him holing up at another property owned by someone who could be his partner sounds more likely." Pierce walked through the condo to the front door. He stopped with his hand on the knob and said, "Grab everything that even remotely looks like evidence and get it back to the lab ASAP."

A woman in a forensic jumpsuit nodded.

"Come on. We have rooms down along the wharf where out of town agents stay when working in Seattle."

Hawke hurt and was tired. While he wished he could keep going, he wasn't as young as Pierce, who while saying he was ready to turn in, Hawke had a feeling he'd be back out working after dropping Hawke off.

"Any chance you carry drugs in this vehicle?" Hawke asked, easing into the passenger seat.

"Only over the counter. What do you need?"

"Ibuprofen. It's what the doc ordered." Hawke leaned his head back and closed his eyes.

"I can get you that." The back door went up and Hawke heard the agent rummaging around.

He must have dozed off because the next thing he felt a nudge on his shoulder.

"Here's a bottle. You might need more during the night." Pierce was behind the steering wheel and driving them away from the condo.

Hawke put three pills in his hand, popped them in his mouth, and swallowed.

"Want something to eat before I drop you off?"

"Just go to a drive through. I'm not picky. Better put something in my stomach with these pills." Hawke shoved the bottle in his shirt pocket.

The morning sun, filtered through fog, lightened the room. Hawke glanced at the clock by the bed. 7:30. He swung his legs over the side of the bed and sat up. His chest still hurt, but he was breathing a little better.

Sitting on the side of the bed in his underwear, he decided whether he had clean clothes or not, he needed a shower. The night before, after Pierce brought him to the room and handed him a bag with a burger and fries, Hawke ate the burger, undressed, and laid down. That was the last thing he remembered.

He'd turned off his phone because he didn't have any way to charge it. There were four texts from someone asking for the photos to match to the videos. He sent the photo and headed to the bathroom.

Banging on the door interrupted his shower. Hawke turned off the water and wrapped a towel around his lower half.

A peek out the peephole revealed a young woman dressed like an FBI agent. He left the chain on the door, opening it enough to talk to her.

"Yes?"

"Are you Trooper Hawke?" Her voice wavered as her gaze took in his bare chest.

"Who are you?" He was being careful. Hughes knew Trooper Hawke was after him. The man could have requested a hit on him.

The woman pulled what looked like a legit badge out of her pocket. "Special Agent Val Kuen. I'm here to bring you to the forensic lab. We believe we have found the woman you are looking for."

"Can you go grab me a cup of coffee while I dress? I'll meet you in the lobby."

The woman nodded and he closed the door. He texted Pierce. *Send me a photo of Special Agent Val Kuen.*

His phone rang as he pulled on his jeans. Pierce.

He accepted the call and put it on speaker.

"What are you asking me about Val for? I sent her to pick you up." Pierce said. He sounded tired.

"I'm just making sure you sent her. She addressed me as Trooper Hawke. That is how Hughes knows me." He winced and shoved one arm and then the other into the sleeves of his shirt.

"I see why you are paranoid. I just sent you a photo."

Hawke opened the message app. It was the same woman who had timidly asked who he was. "She's kind of timid for an agent."

Pierce laughed. "She's a tech person. Not usually sent out to mingle with people. But you're in good hands. She passed all the trainings top of her class."

"Thanks." Hawke ended the conversation, pulled on his socks and shoved his feet into his boots. He'd have to ask Pierce to scrounge him up rounds for his Glock. His supply was back in Pendleton in his pickup.

Making sure he wasn't leaving anything important behind, he left the room and walked down the hallway to the lobby. He hadn't had a chance to check out the view from his room. Pierce had said it was tranquil.

Special Agent Kuen stood by the door with a cup of coffee in her hand. "You didn't say if you use sugar or creamer." She held out her other hand with the items.

"Black."

She dumped the sugar and creamer in the nearest trash can and started out the door. He followed her over to a dark SUV. It beeped and he opened the passenger side while she walked around to the driver's side.

"Thanks for the front door pickup," he said.

She glanced at him as she started the vehicle. "It's protocol."

They drove for ten minutes in silence.

"Special Agent Pierce said you are usually doing tech, why are you picking me up?" Hawke tipped his cup, draining the last of the coffee.

"All the other agents are spread out looking for your suspect. Special Agent Pierce said you would want to be included in finding the woman from video number one-twenty-two." She glanced at him. "Is she a relative?"

"A cousin." He wasn't going to go into how being of the same tribe made them all brothers, sisters, and cousins.

"And you are in law enforcement?"

"Oregon State Trooper working Fish and Wildlife in Wallowa County." He loved his job. But when he returned home, even though he'd been on vacation to find Sherry and Meela, he would need sick leave to let his ribs heal. He ran a hand over his face.

"Are you two close?" she asked, obviously taking his worry over his job for worry over the woman.

"Not really."

"How did you come to be given the detail of finding her?" The woman pulled into an underground parking lot.

Hawke went on alert until he spotted a row of similar vehicles parked by a non-descript elevator door.

"It's a long story and didn't even start with her."

The agent parked and stared at him. "I don't understand."

"Maybe I'll tell you later. Or you can ask Pierce."

Hawke opened the door and stepped out.

She strode ahead of him. He followed her to the elevator. She held her card on a lanyard up to a light and the doors opened. They stepped in and she put the lanyard around her neck. She pushed two buttons. The door closed and the elevator started rising.

"Where are we?" he asked.

"FBI Forensic lab." The elevator stopped and the door opened.

The scene reminded him of the hospital the night before. Everything was white, sterile, and even smelled like chlorine.

"This way. We have all the evidence gathered together for you." She strode down the hall, nodding at people who nodded back.

She opened a door on the left of the hall and stepped in.

Hawke followed. There was a monitor straight across from him. Two boxes, several files, and a keyboard sat on the counter below the monitor.

Special Agent Kuen took off her jacket and hung it on a coat rack. She walked up to the keyboard and hit several keys. A video showed on the monitor. "Is this the woman you are looking for?"

Hawke had never seen Meela Skylark in person. Only the video of her at the casino when she entered the room with Hughes. She looked like the same woman. "Can you freeze that image?" It was a close up of her face.

The agent did and studied him. "Don't you know your cousin?"

"She's my cousin because we are of the same tribe.

But I have never met her in person. I'm going to send a photo of her to someone who does know her well." He took the photo and sent it to Dela, hoping she was awake at this time of day.

Is this Meela?

An immediate response. *Yes! You found her?*

Not quite. Just making sure this is the right person. Tell you more later.

"That's her."

"Good. I won't show you more of the video."

He studied the woman. "Why?"

She blushed. "They make her take off her clothes and show all parts of her body."

Anger boiled in Hawke's gut. He nodded. "Where is the folder with the names and video numbers?"

Special Agent Kuen turned off the monitor and picked up a file. "Here."

"You said this video was number one-twenty-two?"

"Yes."

He ran his finger down the first sheet and didn't see the number. Maybe she hadn't been sold yet. He flipped the page and there it was on the top. Uzbekistan was the country. The name was Mikhail Aslanov.

"What can you tell me about this man?" He showed the name to Agent Kuen.

She started typing on the keyboard and the monitor came to life. A photo of a man in his fifties appeared. "He owns one of the largest power companies in that region." She continued typing. "And has been known to use force to take out his competition."

"Can you look up and see if there have been any

shipments from Seattle to him in the last six months?"
Hawke didn't like how powerful the man was. It would
be hard to get a sex slave away from him without the
man knowing.

"I can't find anything."

That was hopeful. "How about from the Farris
Company to somewhere in that region. He may not
have had her shipped directly to him."

"It says he has a vacation home in Dubai."

"Check there."

"I'm on it." She continued tapping keys and
glanced his way with a smile. "He has a large home in
Dubai. And there was a crate from Farris Company
shipped to him two months ago."

"How do we get someone to Dubai to see if Meela
is there?" Hawke knew it was out of the question for
him to fly there. Or was it? He knew a pilot who had
probably flown into Dubai on several occasions.

"Special Agent Pierce will have to put in a report
and request she is contacted and then we will have to
try and persuade Aslanov to part with her." She didn't
sound confident.

"What would it take to just find out if she is there?"
Hawke asked.

"A request for someone in the area to do
surveillance." She glanced at him. "You aren't planning
on traveling there, are you?"

He shrugged. "Right now, I just want to know
when Sherry will be returned home."

The door opened and Pierce walked in. "Have you
learned anything?"

Special Agent Kuen filled Pierce in on what they

had learned.

"I'll get a request sent out as soon as I put you and Sherry on a helicopter back to Pendleton." Pierce nodded toward the door.

Hawke faced Agent Kuen. "Thank you for your help. Here's my number if you learn anything else." He put a business card in her hand and followed Pierce out of the room and down the hall.

"Is it safe to send Sherry home? Unless you have Hughes in custody?" Hawke stopped at the elevator.

"We don't have him but all seven of the other women identified him as the person who lured them into a hotel room, knocked them out with something in a drink, and they ended up in the back of a semi-trailer. He'd have to kill all of them. I don't think his kidnapping ring is that large. I have a feeling he's trying to get out of the country." Pierce held a card up to the elevator light. The doors opened.

They both stepped in.

"He's close to Canada," Hawke mused.

"I have air coverage of the border, on and off road."

The elevator stopped at the bottom.

"We'll get him eventually. In the meantime, all of the women we liberated can go home." Pierce led him to one of the identical vehicles. "Let's go pick up Sherry."

"I'm surprised you aren't driving us back," Hawke said.

Pierce glanced sideways at him as he pulled the vehicle out into traffic. "I don't have a reason to take you back to the reservation. I have a kidnapper to catch."

Hawke didn't say any more. He'd picked up Special Agent Kuen's card while she was typing on the keyboard. He pulled out his nearly battery dead phone and texted.

This is Trooper Hawke. When contact is made with Meela, I want to know everything.

K

He didn't care if she told other agents. When he knew where she was, he'd ask Pierce what was happening to bring her back. If he stalled, Hawke knew someone who would help him.

Chapter Thirty-one

Dela met them at the Pendleton Airport where the FBI helicopter landed. Hawke had texted her before they lifted off in Seattle.

She and Sherry hugged and cried a few happy tears.

"I'm so glad we were able to find you," Dela said, as she drove them back to the reservation.

"I kept hoping Mimi would call her son." Sherry had thanked him numerous times on the helicopter ride. "I knew no one else would take my disappearance seriously."

"You need to thank my mom and the people she organized to look for you. They went out kicking over rocks, looking for answers, and they got us several leads to work with," Hawke said.

"Good for them!" Sherry sat in the back of the compact car.

Hawke was having trouble breathing, folded up in

the front seat.

They pulled up to his mom's house. Mimi, Trey, and Dog stood on the porch. He waited for Sherry to get out and watched as mother and son hugged.

"Thanks for all of your help," he said to Dela. He studied her a moment and asked, "Do you have any contacts in Dubai?"

She stared at him. "Why?"

"We believe that's where Meela is."

Her eyes narrowed and her brow furrowed. "Let me make some calls. Some of my fellow MPs are still in that area of the world."

"The FBI are going to try and make contact, but they weren't positive they could do anything to get her out." He opened the door and slid out. Dog ran up to him, whining. "Good to see you too, boy." He leaned inside the car and said, "Keep in touch and keep your eyes open for Hughes. He slipped by the Feds."

Dela snorted. "They couldn't find a dog biting their ass."

He straightened and evened out his breathing before walking up to his mom. She hugged him around the middle and he held his breath.

"You did it! You brought Sherry home. Good job, Son." She led him into the house where Sherry and Trey were catching up.

"It wasn't just me. Dela, the casino security and surveillance, even the FBI all worked together to get her home."

"But no one would listen until you started looking." She waved to the kitchen. "Let's have lunch, and I'll drive you two home."

"Where's my car?" Sherry asked.

Hawke hated to tell her. "I'm pretty sure it was chopped up and sold as parts."

Mom patted her arm. "Don't worry. I've already talked to Grandfather Thunder. He has a car sitting at your place for you to use until you get the insurance money and get one of your own."

After lunch, when his mom left with Sherry and Trey, Hawke and Dog went into his room and he stretched out on the bed. He needed to contact Dani, but if she was on the mountain the only way was by radio. He took an Ibuprofen and drifted off to sleep waiting for his mom to return.

When he woke up, Hawke called Sergeant Spruel. "We found the woman I set out after."

"Good news. When are you coming back to work?"

"I'm going to use the rest of my vacation this week. I took a hit in the chest. Luckily I had body armor but I dislocated a rib." Hawke hadn't said a word to his mom.

"You do realize getting killed when on vacation while conducting an investigation would give me all kinds of paperwork headaches, don't you?" The reprimand was softened by the worry in his voice.

"Yeah. There's still one woman missing. She might not be the one I came looking for, but I feel like I need to make sure she gets home safe, too." Hawke walked down the hallway and let Dog out the back door.

"Do you know where she is?" Spruel asked.

"We believe Dubai. The FBI is looking into it." Hawke was worried. He hadn't heard from Pierce since the helicopter took off in Seattle. He hoped it was because the special agent was on Hughes's ass.

"That's quite a distance to go to retrieve her," Spruel said.

"Yeah. I'm hoping they can contact her and get her home."

"I can tell by what you're not saying, you are ready to go find her." Spruel let out a long breath. "Hawke, you aren't the FBI or the CIA. You are an Oregon State Trooper with the Fish and Wildlife Division. You can't go hopping all over the world righting wrongs. You aren't Super Tracker."

"I know. But with connections—" His phone buzzed. It was Dela. "I have to go. I'll see you in a week."

"Hey, what's up?" he asked, answering Dela's call.

"I heard back from a friend. She's headed to that area for leave on Wednesday. Send me what you know and I'll forward it."

Hawke's faith in Dela had him smiling. "I'll send you what I know." He ended the call and sent the information he'd photographed to Dela.

Next, he called Pierce.

"Are you back at the Reservation?" Pierce answered.

"Yeah."

"Then forget about this. You accomplished your mission."

"There's still a woman missing. I'm giving you a head's up. Dela has a friend in that area who is going to check up on the woman. If we find her and get her away from the person who purchased her, do you have a way to get her home?"

"Hawke. You're through with this investigation. We will bring the other woman home."

"When? In six months? A year? She deserves to be home now. If you can't help, forget I called." Hawke ended the call and ignored Pierce trying to call him back.

His mom entered the house. "Did you get some rest?"

"Yes, I did." He put an arm around her. "Does Hazel Temsee still have the HAM radio outfit of her dad's?"

"Yes. Why?"

"I need to contact Dani."

"Oh, I'm sure she wouldn't mind you doing that. I could come with you to make sure she is occupied while you talk to Dani." His mom's eyes lit up knowing he was finally actively pursuing a woman.

He'd brought Dani to meet her a couple months ago. The two had hit it off, which he'd known would happen. "Having you along to keep her from eavesdropping is a good idea." He walked to the back door and held it open for her.

"We crossing through backyards for a reason?" she asked.

"Just fewer people who know, the better."

"That you are talking to your girlfriend?" His mom studied him.

"I'm asking for her help in bringing Meela back. It's more complicated than finding Sherry." He stopped and put his hands on his mom's shoulders. "It's something we can't tell anyone. If the wrong person knew what myself and others are doing, it could harm us and Meela."

She nodded. "Nothing will slip through these lips."

"Thank you. It's important to keep people safe."

"What about you?" Mom stared into his eyes.

"What about me?" Sherry must have said something about the bullet he took.

"I understand you were shot?" Her gaze went to his chest. "Shouldn't you be resting?"

"I'm fine. I had on body armor. The bullet just knocked the wind out of me and left a bruise."

She studied him a bit longer, shaking her head before continuing up to the Temsee's back door.

Mom knocked on the screen door and called out, "Hazel, it's Mimi. Can I come in?"

The woman he remembered walked up to the screen, smiling. "Mimi, good surprise." She glanced at Hawke. "Oh, and you brought the hero. Come in."

Hawke wondered how the woman knew about Sherry's return already.

They walked into the kitchen.

"Everyone is talking about how you made the Feds look for Sherry and she is home." Hazel started setting out cups and grabbed a coffee pot.

"Hazel, do you mind if I use your HAM radio for a few minutes?" he asked, not sitting down at the table.

"Sure. It's down the hall, same as the last time you used it." She filled the cup in front of Mimi, and Hawke walked out of the kitchen and down the hall.

He'd heard the woman's father, the owner of the radio, had passed. He was surprised that she had kept it. But happy she had.

He sat down, dialed in the frequency for Charlie's Lodge, and spoke into the mic.

"Charlie's Lodge, this is Hawke, can you read me?" He repeated this several times and crackling started.

"This is Charlie's Lodge. Hawke is that really you?" Kitree asked.

"Hey, Kitree. It is. Is Dani available?"

"I can go get her. When are you going to come visit?" the child's wistful voice asked.

"Next month. I'll tell you all about what is happening now when I come visit. Could you please get Dani? I don't have much time."

"Sure."

He waited five minutes and the static was interrupted by Dani's voice.

"Hawke. What's up? Did you get the woman?"

"Yeah, she's home. But we're still missing one. We know where she is, just trying to figure out how to get her home."

"Is this why you are calling me?" Her tone inferred he needed to get to the point.

"She was bought by a man who has her in Dubai."

"I know the country well. What do you need?"

He knew she would come through. "We might need someone to fly her out of there. FBI are dragging their feet."

"I'm sure it's all government protocol. Don't want to upset the wrong people. How can I help?"

"Do you know anyone who could have a plane there ready to bring her home when we free her?"

"What do you mean we? Are you going to Dubai?"

"I don't think so, but I have contacts who are working on finding her."

"I'm going to the valley tomorrow. Let me make some phone calls. I'll get back to you tomorrow night."

He grinned. "I was hoping you'd have contacts. I'll look forward to your call."

"I look forward to your visit next month."

Hawke laughed. "Did Kitree tell you she guilted me into saying that?"

"I figured as much. Talk to you tomorrow."

"Copy." He turned off the radio and sat a moment, smiling and being thankful he had found a woman who understood his need for justice.

Out in the kitchen, he sat down and drank a cup of coffee, answering the two women's questions as best he could without telling everything about finding Sherry.

They returned to his mom's house in time for her to make dinner.

"How was your visit with Dani?" she asked.

"Good." Before he could say more his phone buzzed.

He didn't know the number. "Hawke."

"It's Marty. We had a breach of one of the exit doors. I'm following the guy with cameras. He doesn't look like the guy in the cowboy hat. But thought it was interesting he knew to come in through the fire exit."

"I'll be there in fifteen." Hawke stood. "Gotta go. I'll be back later."

"You didn't eat your dinner."

"Keep it warm." He kissed her on the head, called Dog, and strode out to his pickup.

Chapter Thirty-two

Hawke pulled up to the casino and parked as close to the front as he could get. He rolled the windows halfway down. "Stay," he told Dog and hurried into the building.

"Haven't seen you in a few days. Good job bringing Sherry home," the older valet said.

Hawke nodded.

A security guard met him. "Marty said to let you in the surveillance door."

He followed the guard to the door and waited until the door opened. Inside the room, he walked across to Marty's office.

Marty pointed to the monitor above the desk. "Here's the guy."

The monitor zoomed in and Hawke had a good look at the man.

"What's he been doing?" Hawke pulled up a chair and sat.

"Kind of the same M.O. as Cowboy Hat. He's been flirting with the young women."

"Which door did he enter through?" Hawke wondered if it was a coincidence or if the man had been trained by Hughes.

"The one by the Cineplex."

"Have a couple of security guards grab him. Let's have a talk with him." Hawke glanced around. "Who is the acting supervisor tonight?" He knew it was Dela's night off.

"Kenny Proudhorse."

"Can you have him meet me in the security office?" Hawke didn't remember meeting this man. He hoped he knew what had been happening at the casino.

Marty talked into the mic on his desk. "Kenny, Trooper Hawke who has been working with me and Dela, is here and wants to question a man that Dan and Louie will be bringing in." He listened and nodded. "He's in the office waiting for you." Marty spoke into his mic. "Dan and Louie take the guy in the green shirt sitting on carousel nine, next to Patty Scarby, to security."

They watched the man try to talk himself out of a trip with the security guards. When he tried to make a break, a third guard arrived and he was taken hold of by two security members grabbing his arms.

"He must have something to hide the way he tried to run," Marty said, sounding excited.

Hawke didn't comment. He was watching a bald man wearing a business suit ignoring what was going on while everyone else was interested in the security guards hauling the other man away.

Pointing to the monitor, Hawke said, "Zoom in on that guy. The one not paying attention to the commotion."

Marty did.

"He looks familiar." Hawke continued to study him as the guards hauled the younger man over to the security office.

Hawke caught a glimpse of a smirk on the baldheaded man. "That's the man we want," he told Marty, pointing to the bald-headed man walking toward the bar.

"Why would he come back here?" Marty asked.

"Too clean up loose ends." Hawke knew what the man planned to do. "We need to get to him before he gets to the bartender."

Hawke pointed. "Get that security guard into the Sports Bar and have him keep everyone away from Dexter."

"Dexter isn't working tonight. He comes back on shift on Wednesday." Marty faced him. "You still want him kept away from the bartender?"

"I want him picked up. If he talks to the others, he'll learn where Dexter lives. My guess is he doesn't want Dexter to give us a real description of him."

Marty spoke into his mic and two security guards charged into the sports bar. The man they wanted, disappeared out through the kitchen, the security guards on his tail.

Marty tapped on the keyboard and a kitchen came in view. The man darted by two cooks, who shouted at him, and out a door that led onto the patio seating. There he jumped the short metal fence and ran across the parking lot toward the Travel Center.

Hawke wondered if that was where the man parked or if he was just trying to find a place to hide.

"Is Dexter married?" Hawke asked.

"No. He lives with his brother," Marty said, watching the guards stop at the edge of the patio and start walking back.

"They need to stay somewhere that Hughes can't find them and I need to talk to Dexter. Call him and see if he can meet me at Dela's place in one hour."

Marty nodded. "You know where Dela lives?"

"Next to Grandfather Thunder with her mom." Hawke was sure he'd read that situation correctly.

He nodded. "Didn't know you knew that much about her." His gaze was speculative.

"I met her when I was questioning Grandfather Thunder and her mom about Sherry's disappearance."

"Make the call, I'm going to go talk to the man security is holding." Hawke texted Dela, telling her Dexter was coming over and he'd be there in an hour, as he walked over to the security offices.

A large Umatilla man in the security polo shirt, met him as he entered the office. "Kenny Proudhorse. Thank you for bringing Sherry home." He shook hands with Hawke.

"I'm happy I could help. Has Dela told you about the trafficking ring and that we're still trying to catch the head of the ring?"

"She explained it all to me before I came on duty. I can't believe what has been happening here under our noses."

"The man I had brought in here was behaving like

the man we're after. I want to find out how he knew to come in that specific door and hit on the young women." Hawke walked over to the small interview room.

"I'd like to know that as well." Kenny opened the door and they both walked in.

The man sitting in the room glanced at Hawke's badge dangling on the outside of his shirt.

"Is there a law against having a good time?" the man asked.

"No. But when you do it in the same manner as a man who kidnapped women for sale on the slave market, you will get pulled in." The man's eyes widened. "Yes, we know all about your friend, Rory Hughes's exporting women to other countries. We also know he was in the casino while you were keeping the security guards busy. Unfortunately for him, we caught him on video."

The man's face grew pale.

"Yes, you didn't play your part well enough. What do you think he's going to do to you when he realizes you were the person who blew his chance?" Hawke leaned back. "If you want to tell us why he asked you to cause a commotion and any other valuable information, we can make sure you are safe. Because at this point, you've done nothing we can lock you up for."

The man's face relaxed and he leaned back in his chair as if he now had all the cards.

"But we can make sure Hughes thinks you told us all about his operation. That would make you a target. He's killed a woman who was no longer useful and getting ready to tell us about his operation and he killed a security guard who had been helping him. Hughes gets rid of people he believes are of no use anymore." Hawke could tell by the man's rapid eye movement, he was thinking hard about what he knew and whether his boss would kill him to keep him quiet.

"I don't know anything about the man. I didn't even know his name. He approached me out in the parking lot and offered me five hundred dollars to try and pick-up women under the age of thirty. He said the best looking and builds. But I could only do it while they were playing the slots. He said I'd get another five hundred if I could get one to go up to a room with me." He glanced from Hawke, to Kenny, and back to Hawke. "Honest. I don't know the man's name. He even told me to go in the fire door."

"We'll see." Hawke stood; Kenny followed.

Out in the main office, Hawke faced the security guard. "Ask Marty if you can see this guy's conversation with the man out in the parking lot."

"I'm going to go have a chat with Dexter and Dela. Hold him until I get back."

Kenny picked up a phone. "I'll have that here when you get back."

Hawke left the security offices, crossed the casino floor, and walked up to the entrance.

"Leaving so soon?" the valet asked.

"I'll be back." He nodded toward the carousel where the altercation had happened. "The man you saw the security guards grab, had you seen him in here before?"

"Yeah. I think he came in last night. Don't remember seeing him come through the door tonight. Is he staying at the hotel?"

"I don't think so. Thanks." Hawke left the building and strode to his vehicle.

Dog wagged his tail and whined.

"Did you happen to see a man take off across here toward the Travel Center?" He scratched Dog's ears wondering if he should do a quick look over there before heading to Dela's. Deciding against it in case the man knew him by sight and followed, Hawke turned right.

There was a beat-up older Blazer in the driveway of Dela's place. Hawke suspected it belonged to Dexter. He let Dog out and walked up to the front door. He hadn't been in the house on his last visit here.

He knocked and waited.

The door opened and Dela's mother smiled at him. "Trooper Hawke, come in. They are waiting for you in the kitchen."

"Thank you, Ms. Bolden." He pulled his hat off his head and walked through the living room to the golden light of the kitchen.

Dela, Dexter, and another man, who there was no mistaking as Dexter's brother, sat at the small round table.

"What is going on?" Dela asked, placing a glass of iced tea in front of the only vacant chair at the table.

"Hughes tried to use a distraction so he could go in the bar and I think either chat up Dexter to learn his habits or to actually make sure he didn't talk." Hawke kept his gaze on the man in his twenties.

"Hughes? Are you talking about the guy in the

cowboy hat? Why would he be looking for me?" Dexter glanced at Dela and back to Hawke.

"Because I believe you saw or heard something you don't realize that could help us shut down his organization." Hawke studied the young man. "You are the only person on the whole casino staff who saw his face completely and had a few words with him." Hawke could see the man was trying to figure out what he might have learned.

Dela spoke up. "When he visited with Lanie, did you ever overhear anything they talked about?"

"Not really. They mostly sat at a table. The man would have his face toward a wall. I'd think a waitress would have heard more than I did." His wrinkled brow proved the bartender honestly didn't think he knew anything that would be helpful.

"What about Lanie? Did she ever talk to you, maybe when the cowboy hat guy wasn't around?" Dela kept mentioning Lanie.

Hawke studied her wondering what she knew.

"She was friendly with all the guys. Even that FBI agent." Dexter grinned.

"What do you mean the FBI agent?" Hawke asked.

"Right before she left the bar that last night, she leaned close to him and said something, then walked out of the bar."

Hawke knew she'd probably told Pierce she'd be right back. He would have mentioned if she'd said anything else. "And she didn't do anything else? Whispered to him and walked out?"

Dexter closed his eyes. "She left her purse. Jen picked it up later. It was sitting on the chair between her and the detective."

Hawke leaned forward placing his iced tea on the table. "Where is the purse?"

"I took it to security at the end of my shift," Dexter said.

"Then it was logged and stored in a room behind the security offices." Dela stared at Hawke.

"Evidence has been sitting in the casino the whole time." Hawke pulled out his phone. He dialed Kenny. "See if you can find a purse that was logged in the night Lanie ran from the casino."

"What do you want me to do with it?" Kenny asked.

"Hang on to it and don't let anyone near it. I'll be there in twenty to go through it with you." He ended the call and studied the brothers. "You two need to find some place to stay that isn't with relatives. And don't tell anyone but Dela where you're going. When she calls you, you can come home. It seems as though Hughes thinks you know something."

Dexter nodded. "Can we go pack?"

Hawke shook his head. "Since the guy got away, it would be best if you just take off and call Dela when you land somewhere."

They both nodded and left.

Dela stirred her tea. "My friend will let me know what she finds out as soon as she's made contact with Meela."

Hawke nodded. "I'm working on a plane to get Meela out of there. Do you think she'll go with your friend?"

She grinned. "I told my friend a couple things that

will let Meela know she is working for her freedom."

"Good. I gotta go. Keep in touch."

"Be careful. Hughes is dangerous the way he can move around."

"I hope we can get him soon. No one at the casino is safe until we do." Hawke drained his drink and stood. "Sorry to ruin your peaceful evening."

She waved her hand. "It was better than watching the shows my mom likes."

Hawke glanced around. "It's a nice house, but why do you live with your mom?"

Dela sighed. "Because I don't spend that much time here and haven't taken the time to find something else. I want to live on the reservation and there is limited housing for someone not of the tribe."

He nodded. "I'll let my mom know you are looking for something."

"Thanks. After spending so many years on my own, well, as on your own as you can be in the military, I would like a place where someone isn't constantly asking me how I am."

"Moms are that way." He walked into the living room. "Good night, Ms. Bolden."

"Good night. I hope you learned what you needed to know." She raised an eyebrow.

He had a strange feeling she was talking about his inquiring about her daughter's living situation and not the man they were trying to apprehend. "I did."

Stepping out the front door, Dog greeted him.

"Hey, what have you been doing? I hope not peeing on all Ms. Bolden's pretty flowers."

Dog gave a low woof and ran to the pickup.

Hawke shook his head and opened the door, sliding in behind Dog. He put the vehicle in drive and headed back to the casino.

Chapter Thirty-three

"You did come back," the valet said as Hawke entered the casino.

"I did. Anything interesting happen while I was gone?" Hawke asked.

"Godfrey arrived about thirty minutes after you left."

"On his day off?" That was an interesting turn of events.

"He never comes in on his days off unless Dela or Kenny call him."

"Thanks."

Hawke headed straight for the security offices. He heard voices as he opened the door. Kenny's gaze landed on him when he walked through.

The security guard nodded his direction. "Let's see what Trooper Hawke has to say."

Friday spun around. The frightened expression on his face had Hawke wondering what the man had to fear from him.

"What are you doing still running about this casino as if you are part of the security team?" Friday asked.

"There are still illegal activities going on here." Hawke tipped his head toward the interview room. "Is he still in there?"

"Yeah," Kenny said.

"Want to help me try and get more information out of the man we caught tonight? He is part of Rory Hughes's human trafficking ring." Hawke didn't miss the flick of Friday's eyes to the door and then to Kenny.

"I'm sure you can handle it just fine," Friday said. "But I want to know why all of this has been going on behind my back?"

"How do you know what's been going on behind your back?" Hawke asked.

The man's face paled and his jaw slacked. "I don't know what you're saying."

Hawke was starting to get it all put together. "You saw Charlie rigging the exit doors and told Hughes that wasn't a good way to come in. Hughes sent an innocent man in, offering him money to pretend to pick-up women. Probably telling the man how to do it, and then he walked in here to get information out of Dexter." Hawke wasn't going to mention the purse. He had a feeling that's what Friday was after. Someone had called Friday and told him about Kenny getting the purse out of the lost and found. That had to be the reason the man came here at this time of night on his day off.

Friday shook his head. His feet were shuffling, but the only way out the door was through Hawke.

"I don't understand. How could you allow that predator to take our women?"

Hawke always prided himself on not allowing his anger to show when he was interviewing suspects. However, this man, one who was the head of security, had allowed Hughes the run of the casino and hotel to bed young women and steal them to sell as sex slaves. Friday had helped the lowest of all humanity.

"He found my weakness and used it as bribery. I had no choice." Friday looked pathetic trying to make them feel bad for him.

"You did have a choice. A choice to do what was right. Not to honor evil." Hawke motioned to Kenny. "Handcuff him."

Kenny stared at Hawke, then at his boss.

"He just admitted to aiding Hughes in stealing women for trafficking." Hawke peered at Friday. "Did you have anything to do with Lanie and Jerome's deaths?"

The man shook his head. "No. Those were done before I knew what Hughes had planned."

Kenny walked over and handcuffed Friday.

Hawke said, "Put him in the room back here until someone arrives."

Once Friday was put in the small room with the man they'd questioned earlier, Hawke turned to Kenny. "Have you had a chance to look at Lanie's purse?"

"No. I barely had time to hide it when Friday walked into the office." Kenny pulled out a drawer and held up a small purse.

"Why did you hide it?" Hawke had wondered at how easy it had been to get Dela and Marty, and now

Kenny, not to include their boss in on most of the investigation.

Kenny's face reddened. "Dela and I had noticed Godfrey not doing his job lately. It was like he didn't care anymore. Then you showed up, and we learned what had been happening. All of it should have been picked up by the head of security. The rooms being used and no one mentioning it to us? That seemed off. Dela asked and the registration staff had told Godfrey."

Hawke studied the security guard. "She's known all along he could be a part of this whole thing and never said a word?" He knew loyalty to your comrades was one of the things you learned first in the military but when they were corrupt…

"She said after this investigation was over, she'd bring it up to the board. She wanted proof, not her word against his." Kenny unzipped the small purse and dumped the contents out on the desk.

Lipstick, tissues, wallet, and a small thumb drive lay on top of the paperwork.

Kenny picked up the drive and plugged it into his computer. Files flashed on the large monitor.

Financial. Women. Rory.

"Click on women. We need to know if there are more missing from this area." Hawke pulled up a chair.

Thankfully it was a short list of two. The two women they knew about.

"They must have just started to pull women from the casino." Hawke waved a hand. "Pull up what she has on Rory."

This was the best file. She had recorded conversations with him, photos of the warehouse, his condo, and the condo at Crystal Mountain. She also had information about what had happened with Jerome Marks at Crystal Mountain. The name of the so-called victim and the two men who had pretended to be police to scare Marks.

"This is everything we need to nail Hughes." Hawke stood. "Make three copies of that. We want to make sure it gets into all the right hands at the same time."

He pulled out his phone and scrolled through his contacts.

Pierce answered right away. "Why didn't you answer when I called you back?"

"I've been busy. I have a thumb drive made by Lanie Porter that will put Hughes away for a long time. I also know he is in our area. He was looking for this drive."

Pierce whistled. "You've been busy. So have I. We've confiscated all of his belongings at his condo, warehouse, and work. Tuma has kept her mouth shut but there is no refuting she was working with him. After all, she shot you while she was trying to move the merchandise."

"I have someone else on his payroll, or blackmail list, I'm not sure which. Godfrey Friday."

"No kidding? The head of security at the casino? Dela hadn't figured that out?" He sounded skeptical.

"From what I've learned from Kenny Proudhorse, she had an inkling something was off but hadn't enough to take it to HR." He glanced at Kenny who gave him a thumbs up.

"Want me to come by and pick up the evidence?"

Pierce asked.

"We'll find some place safe to keep it until you get here. I'm thinking in the morning?" Hawke really wanted to get back to his mom's and eat that dinner she was keeping warm for him.

"I'll be there at eight in the morning."

"Copy." Hawke ended the call. He stared at the door to the interview room. "Did Marty send you the video feed of the man in the other room being approached by Hughes in the parking lot?"

"Yeah, it looks like what he said." Kenny walked over to a desk, pulled out a drawer and then taped the flash drives to the back of the drawer.

"Do you think that's safer than the money vault or a safe?" Hawke asked.

Kenny grinned and tipped his head toward the interview room. "We don't know if Godfrey told anyone else the combinations to the safes I have access to. This way, only you and I know where they are."

"Good thinking." Hawke walked to the door.

"Want to cut the other guy loose?"

"Yes. And call the Tribal Police to come pick up Friday to hold until Special Agent Pierce gets here tomorrow. Then you can all hash out who gets to hold and prosecute him." Hawke knew that the tribal justice system would want to take care of one of their own. Whether or not the Federal courts would need him to testify would come out further along in the investigation.

"If you have this covered, I'm going home to eat my dinner."

"It's eleven. You sure you don't want to eat here?"

Kenny asked, walking toward the interview room.

"Nope. Mimi made me a special meal and I'm going home to eat it. See you, or whoever is here, at eight."

"It will be Dela. She's head of security with Godfrey out of the picture." Kenny opened the door, giving Hawke a glimpse of the dejected looking head of security.

That wasn't his problem. The man had made his own choices. Hawke walked out of the security offices, across the gaming floor, and out the entrance. The valet wasn't at his post.

But a fancy car pulled up to the entrance. A middle-aged couple stepped up to the vehicle and the valet slipped out of the driver's door, leaving it open for the owner, and walked around to open the door for the woman.

Hawke saluted the valet and continued to his pickup where Dog was whining.

"Let's go eat dinner."

Chapter Thirty-four

The next morning Hawke arrived at the casino at 7:30. The parking lot was nearly empty. As he stepped out of his pickup, he heard the thump of helicopter blades. Shading his eyes, he looked up and spotted an FBI helicopter heading toward the casino.

He leaned against his vehicle, watching the helicopter land on the far side of the parking lot.

Pierce and two other agents hopped out of the aircraft and headed for the casino.

Hawke set out at a long stride toward them.

Special Agent Pierce glanced his direction and slowed his pace, waiting for Hawke to catch up.

Pierce held out his hand. "Nice work."

They shook and Pierce introduced him to the other agents. "They're going to take the evidence to Spokane while I catch up with you, Dela, and the Tribal Police."

Hawke nodded. He wasn't sure he wanted to let all of the thumb drives go off with two people he didn't know, given that Agent Tuma had been in Hughes's pocket.

He followed the three into the casino, texting Dela to not give the Feds the original thumb drive.

She gave him a thumbs up emoji.

Walking into the casino, he found the two agents Pierce brought with him standing guard at the entrance.

Hawke walked by them to where Pierce and Dela stood near the statues in the middle of the casino floor. "Are you going to be on day shifts from now on?" he asked.

She shook her head. "I'm in charge until the board and HR decides if I get the job or they bring in someone else. Which means I can make my own hours. I'm here this morning to clean up this mess, and others Godfrey made, then I'll work nights on weekends and days Tuesday, Wednesday, and Thursday."

"Glad I don't have that schedule." Hawke studied the two. It appeared Dela was waiting for the agent to ask for the drives before she led him there.

Pierce finally said, "Where do you have the evidence against Hughes?"

"Kenny put it in a safe place." Dela spun around and headed toward the security office.

"Is it just me or has getting promoted made her uppity?" Pierce asked loud enough for Dela to hear.

Hawke could tell Pierce was kidding but Dela's whole body stiffened, making her limp noticeable the last five steps.

At the door, Dela stopped and studied Hawke. "Kenny said you know where he put the evidence. Do you want to get it?"

"If he told you, there is no need for me to be involved in this hand-off. I'll wait here and make sure no one comes in." Hawke stepped to the side of the door.

Pierce grinned. "Looks like we'll be alone."

Dela glared at him and they both disappeared through the door. It closed with a click.

Hawke remained on the casino floor, scanning the people milling around. Most looked as if they'd spent the night playing the slots. A thought occurred to him. He scrolled through his contacts for Kenny.

The phone rang twice and a sleepy, "Hello?"

"This is Hawke. Did you ever ask Friday how he knew to come to the casino last night?"

"No. I didn't think to ask him. The tribal police arrived about twenty minutes after you left and I handed him over."

"Would he have had enough time for someone to learn about the purse and then him show up from his home? Or would he need more time than that and Hughes called him to find the purse?"

"No, he could have made it here from the time you called and told me to look for the purse in lost and found. I had to pull up the log-in records to know where to find it. If someone was monitoring the security computer, they could have told him what I did."

"Then there is still a breach in your security. If someone on duty or working in the casino was monitoring the security computers and knew what you looked up was important to Hughes, there is someone else here besides Friday that needs caught."

"Unless Friday was monitoring what we did from

his home computer." Kenny let loose some stronger words. "If that's the case, he could have seen what I looked up, figured out it was Lanie's purse because of the night it was logged in, and came over to get it from me."

"We both should have figured it out last night when he showed up that something had been compromised. Who can check the computer to see if it was hacked?"

"That would be head of tech. Wallace Minerich. Dela has his number."

"Thanks."

Pierce and Dela stepped out of the security offices. The special agent now carried a small valise.

Pierce walked over to the two agents standing guard at the entrance and handed the valise to the younger looking of the two.

"You kept one back," Hawke whispered to Dela. She nodded.

"Another problem came up. We need to get Wallace Minerich down here to look at the computers in the security offices."

Her eyebrows raised and she did an about face back into the security office.

Before Hawke closed the door to tell her what he'd learned, Pierce stepped through the door.

"Not going with your friends?" Hawke asked.

"Not when all the answers are here it seems."

Dela picked up the phone and asked Wallace to come to the security offices. When she replaced the phone and stared at him, Hawke explained what he and Kenny had reasoned.

"You mean the computers in this room could have been hacked since Hughes started blackmailing our people to help him?" The anger and disgust on Dela's face reflected Hawke's sentiment.

"That's the only way Friday would have known Kenny looked up Lanie's purse in lock up."

Hawke's phone buzzed. Dani. Not wanting Pierce to hear this conversation, he stepped into the small interview room, flipped on the light and took a seat facing the door.

"How's your day going?" he answered.

"Well. I made contact with someone who can fly our package from Al Udeid Air Base in Saudi Arabia with two hand offs into Mountain Home, Idaho. But it needs to happen this week."

Hawke grinned. He should have known Dani would come through.

"I can meet the package in Mountain Home and drop off in Pendleton if you want," she added.

He could tell by her tone that saying no wasn't an option. "Sounds like you have it worked out. I'll ask about the pickup and get back to you ASAP."

"How's it going on your end?" she asked.

"We just about have it all cleaned up. Thank you for doing this."

"Sisters stick together," she said. "I'll be expecting your call."

"As soon as we get rid of the Fed, we'll get it worked out."

Dani chuckled and the call went silent.

He walked over to the door and was happy to see a man, who must have been Wallace, sitting at the computer and busy tapping away. Pierce leaned against the door, watching.

"Can I speak to you in private?" Hawke said when Dela made eye contact.

"Sure."

They stepped back in the interview room.

"My end can fly our package out of Saudi Arabia this week. Can you get it dropped off that soon?"

Dela studied him. "I'll see." She pulled out her phone and walked over to the corner. She spoke in a language Hawke didn't understand. He thought she was having an Army buddy in the military police make contact with Meela.

She ended the call and smiled. "I'm assuming it is Al Udeid Air Base in Saudi Arabia that my friend needs to drop the package off at."

"Yes. Let me call Dani and see how they will connect."

"Tell her the package will be returning from Dubai with Colonel Al-Amin via helicopter." Dela grinned.

"You have some high-ranking friends." Hawke said with his deepest respect.

"I saved his son from getting run over by a car while I was at the base. He told me if I ever needed a favor to let him know." Her smile disappeared. "This is the best way to have him repay the favor. A life for a life."

Hawke gave her a one-armed hug. "I hope the board, HR, or whoever is in charge of the hiring, makes you head of security."

She sighed. "Me too, but I am a disabled woman who they only gave the job to because my mom badgered them."

"You are far from disabled. You are stronger and smarter than most men. It doesn't take muscle to catch the bad guys, it takes brains and a sixth sense. You have those." He opened the door. "While I call my friend, why don't you see if you can get rid of Pierce."

"I like the way you think." She winked and stepped out of the room.

Hawke grinned and called Dani to tell her what he knew.

Chapter Thirty-five

Hawke stayed around, waiting to see if the computer tech discovered anything in the computer that would help them find Hughes.

It took Wallace about an hour to remove the hack and restore the security computer system to better than it was. "I destroyed the worm that was installed and beefed up the security. I also installed an app that will contact me if someone tries to get into the system again."

"Thank you, Wallace," Dela said. Her phone rang.

The computer technician walked out of the office as she answered her phone.

"Did you get your drives delivered?" she asked.

Hawke didn't hear the reply. However, she frowned.

"That dick did what?"

This conversation was getting interesting.

"But you got the evidence to Spokane and they

caught him?" She listened hard. "Okay. Yeah, I'll testify." She listened some more. "You can ask him. He's right here." She handed the phone to Hawke. "Pierce wants to talk to you."

"Hawke."

"I managed to get the thumb drives to Spokane. Good thing Dela thought I should use the agents in the helicopter as a decoy. Hughes tried to bring the helicopter down halfway to Spokane. We had a ground crew following the helicopter so we were able to grab him. Anyway, are you willing to testify when this all goes to court?"

"Yeah. Just let me know ahead of time so I can get time off." He glanced at Dela and grinned.

"I'll do that. We're working on getting all the women back that Hughes kidnapped. But it—."

"Will take a while. Yeah, I've heard your song and dance before."

"I promise, we'll get her back."

"Don't worry about it."

"Hawke, what are you planning?" Pierce's voice dropped to a stage whisper.

"What you don't know, won't hurt you. See you around." He ended the call.

"What kind of scheme did you talk Pierce into while you two were hidden in this room?"

"I suggested he use the valise as a way to make whoever might be watching think the flash drive went in the helicopter and for him to hang around with the real drives in his pocket then head for Spokane at a leisurely pace." Her eyes lit up. "It worked. They caught Hughes and have the best evidence against him—his own voice and face on those thumb drives."

<><><><><><>

Saturday, Hawke, Dela, Mimi, a group of MMIP advocates, and Meela's family stood at the Pendleton airport waiting for Dani to touch down. Her helicopter hovered over the tarmac for several minutes before gracefully landing.

When the blades stopped spinning, Dani dropped out of the pilot's side and Hawke hurried up to the passenger side door. He'd never met the young woman before, who looked both happy and terrified. He held out a hand to help her down. She glanced at him, then took his hand, landing on her feet on the asphalt.

He stepped aside, and her parents came rushing forward. She fell into their arms, crying.

Dani stepped up beside him and he put an arm around her waist. "This is going in my top ten memories of bringing someone back alive," she said.

Hawke hadn't asked her about her missions while she was in the Air Force, but he knew there were some dark memories.

Meela's parents drew her over to the group from the reservation who were waiting for her.

"Who is the young woman next to your mom?" Dani asked.

"Dela Alvaro. She is the one who got Meela to the Air Force base." He watched as both his mom and Dela hugged Meela.

"That's impressive. How did she manage to get a Saudi Colonel to bring that woman from Dubai?"

"He owed her a favor."

Dani stared at him. "What is she doing here, in

308

Pendleton?"

"She is the head of security at the Spotted Pony Casino."

"That's a good position for someone with that kind of *cajones*."

Hawke laughed and kissed Dani. "She would love to hear you say that. Come on, Mom has a huge pot of spaghetti ready for when we get to her house. Dela has been invited to join us."

Dani locked the doors of her helicopter and grasped his hand. "I'm anxious to meet her and visit with your mom."

"Good. Mom would be upset if you flew in and didn't stick around for dinner." Hawke led Dani over to his mom and Dela thinking he was a very lucky man.

While this book has a happy ending with both women being found and brought home, this isn't the case for most Indigenous women and children who go missing. While Native women make up only 2% of the population, they are the hardest hit with foul play. The highest margin of Native women who become causalities are those in cities. Far from home and with no one to speak up when they go missing. The MMIW/MMIP Movement is a way for their voices to be heard. It has led to the Not Invisible Act, a collaboration of law enforcement, gathered to study and come up with ways to work together on the epidemic of missing and murdered Indigenous people.

Thank you for reading Stolen Butterfly, Book 7 in the Gabriel Hawke Novels. This was a subject that I have wanted to write about for a long time. The statistics about the missing and murdered Indigenous women and children has sickened me ever since I first heard about it. Using my character, Hawke, to show what the communities face when a loved one goes missing, was a way for me to show the injustice in a justice system that should be equal for all.

I hope you enjoyed getting to know Dela Alvaro and Special Agent Quinn Peirce. They now have their own series, The Spotted Pony Casino Mysteries. If you enjoyed this book and the setting of the casino, check out the new series. The first book is titled: *Poker Face*.

Don't worry, there are more Hawke books to come. I already have the next book churning in my head. I know Badger will be in the title.

Thank you for purchasing this book. A portion of the proceeds from *Stolen Butterfly* will be donated to the MMIW effort.

Paty

Continue investigating and tracking with Hawke as his series continues. If you missed his other books they are:

Murder of Ravens
Book 1
Print ISBN 978-1-947983-82-3

Mouse Trail Ends
Book 2
Print ISBN 978-1-947983-96-0

Rattlesnake Brother
Book 3
Print ISBN 978-1-950387-06-9

Chattering Blue Jay
Book 4
Print ISBN 978-1-950387-64-9

Fox Goes Hunting
Book 5
Print ISBN 978-1-952447-07-5

Turkey's Fiery Demise
Book 6
Print ISBN 978-1-952447-48-8

Windtree
Press

Thank you for purchasing this Windtree Press publication. For other books of the heart, please visit our website at www.windtreepress.com.

For questions or more information contact us at info@windtreepress.com.

Windtree Press
www.windtreepress.com

Hillsboro, OR